FRANC
SABLE M

Francis Vivian was born Arthur Ernest Ashley in 1906 at East Retford, Nottinghamshire. He was the younger brother of noted photographer Hallam Ashley. Vivian laboured for a decade as a painter and decorator before becoming an author of popular fiction in 1932. In 1940 he married schoolteacher Dorothy Wallwork, and the couple had a daughter.

After the Second World War he became assistant editor at the Nottinghamshire Free Press and circuit lecturer on many subjects, ranging from crime to bee-keeping (the latter forming a major theme in the Inspector Knollis mystery *The Singing Masons*). A founding member of the Nottingham Writers' Club, Vivian once awarded first prize in a writing competition to a young Alan Sillitoe, the future bestselling author.

The ten Inspector Knollis mysteries were published between 1941 and 1956. In the novels, ingenious plotting and fair play are paramount. A colleague recalled that 'the reader could always arrive at a correct solution from the given data. Inspector Knollis never picked up an undisclosed clue which, it was later revealed, held the solution to the mystery all along.'

Francis Vivian died on April 2, 1979 at the age of 73.

THE INSPECTOR KNOLLIS MYSTERIES
Available from Dean Street Press

FRANCIS VIVIAN

SABLE MESSENGER

With an introduction by Curtis Evans

DEAN STREET PRESS

INTRODUCTION

SHORTLY BEFORE his death in 1951, American agriculturalist and scholar Everett Franklin Phillips, then Professor Emeritus of Apiculture (beekeeping) at Cornell University, wrote British newspaperman Arthur Ernest Ashley (1906-1979), author of detective novels under the pseudonym Francis Vivian, requesting a copy of his beekeeping mystery *The Singing Masons*, the sixth Inspector Gordon Knollis investigation, which had been published the previous year in the United Kingdom. The eminent professor wanted the book for Cornell's Everett F. Phillips Beekeeping Collection, "one of the largest and most complete apiculture libraries in the world" (currently in the process of digitization at Cornell's The Hive and the Honeybee website). Sixteen years later Ernest Ashely, or Francis Vivian as I shall henceforward name him, to an American fan requesting an autograph ("Why anyone in the United States, where I am not known," he self-deprecatingly observed, "should want my autograph I cannot imagine, but I am flattered by your request and return your card, duly signed.") declared that fulfilling Professor Phillip's donation request was his "greatest satisfaction as a writer." With ghoulish relish he added, "I believe there was some objection by the Librarian, but the good doctor insisted, and so in it went! It was probably destroyed after Dr. Phillips died. Stung to death."

After investigation I have found no indication that the August 1951 death of Professor Phillips, who was 73 years old at the time, was due to anything other than natural causes. One assumes that what would have been the painfully ironic demise of the American nation's most distinguished apiculturist from bee stings would have merited some mention in his death notices. Yet Francis Vivian's fabulistic claim otherwise provides us with a glimpse of that mordant sense of humor and storytelling relish which glint throughout the eighteen mystery novels Vivian published between 1937 and 1959.

Ten of these mysteries were tales of the ingenious sleuthing exploits of series detective Inspector Gordon Knollis, head of the Burnham C.I.D. in the first novel in the series and a Scotland Yard detective in the rest. (Knollis returns to Burnham in later novels.) The debut Inspector Knollis mystery, *The Death of Mr. Lomas*, which was published in 1941, is actually the seventh Francis Vivian detective novel. However, after the Second World War, when the author belatedly returned to his vocation of mystery writing, all of the remaining detective novels he published, with two exceptions, chronicle the criminal cases of the keen and clever Knollis. These other Inspector Knollis tales are: *Sable Messenger* (1947), *The Threefold Cord* (1947), *The Ninth Enemy* (1948), *The Laughing Dog* (1949), *The Singing Masons* (1950), *The Elusive Bowman* (1951), *The Sleeping Island* (1951), *The Ladies of Locksley* (1953) and *Darkling Death* (1956). (Inspector Knollis also is passingly mentioned in Francis Vivian's final mystery, published in 1959, *Dead Opposite the Church*.) By the late Forties and early Fifties, when Hodder & Stoughton, one of England's most important purveyors of crime and mystery fiction, was publishing the Francis Vivian novels, the Inspector Knollis mysteries had achieved wide popularity in the UK, where "according to the booksellers and librarians," the author's newspaper colleague John Hall later recalled in the *Guardian* (possibly with some exaggeration), "Francis Vivian was neck and neck with Ngaio Marsh in second place after Agatha Christie." (Hardcover sales and penny library rentals must be meant here, as with one exception--a paperback original--Francis Vivian, in great contrast with Crime Queens Marsh and Christie, both mainstays of Penguin Books in the UK, was never published in softcover.)

John Hall asserted that in Francis Vivian's native coal and iron county of Nottinghamshire, where Vivian from the 1940s through the 1960s was an assistant editor and "colour man" (writer of local color stories) on the Nottingham, or Notts, *Free Press*, the detective novelist "through a large stretch of the coalfield is reckoned the best local author after Byron and D. H. Lawrence." Hall added that "People who wouldn't know Alan

Sillitoe from George Eliot will stop Ernest in the street and tell him they solved his last detective story." Somewhat ironically, given this assertion, Vivian in his capacity as a founding member of the Nottingham Writers Club awarded first prize in a 1950 Nottingham writing competition to no other than 22-year-old local aspirant Alan Sillitoe, future "angry young man" author of *Saturday Night and Sunday Morning* (1958) and *The Loneliness of the Long Distance Runner* (1959). In his 1995 autobiography Sillitoe recollected that Vivian, "a crime novelist who earned his living by writing . . . gave [my story] first prize, telling me it was so well written and original that nothing further need be done, and that I should try to get it published." This was "The General's Dilemma," which Sillitoe later expanded into his second novel, *The General* (1960).

While never himself an angry young man (he was, rather, a "ragged-trousered" philosopher), Francis Vivian came from fairly humble origins in life and well knew how to wield both the hammer and the pen. Born on March 23, 1906, Vivian was one of two children of Arthur Ernest Ashley, Sr., a photographer and picture framer in East Retford, Nottinghamshire, and Elizabeth Hallam. His elder brother, Hallam Ashley (1900-1987), moved to Norwich and became a freelance photographer. Today he is known for his photographs, taken from the 1940s through the 1960s, chronicling rural labor in East Anglia (many of which were collected in the 2010 book *Traditional Crafts and Industries in East Anglia: The Photographs of Hallam Ashley*). For his part, Francis Vivian started working at age 15 as a gas meter emptier, then labored for 11 years as a housepainter and decorator before successfully establishing himself in 1932 as a writer of short fiction for newspapers and general magazines. In 1937, he published his first detective novel, *Death at the Salutation.* Three years later, he wed schoolteacher Dorothy Wallwork, with whom he had one daughter.

After the Second World War Francis Vivian's work with the Notts *Free Press* consumed much of his time, yet he was still able for the next half-dozen years to publish annually a detective novel (or two), as well as to give popular lectures on a plethora of intriguing subjects, including, naturally enough, crime, but also fiction writing (he published two guidebooks on that subject), psychic forces (he believed himself to be psychic), black magic, Greek civilization, drama, psychology and beekeeping. The latter occupation he himself took up as a hobby, following in the path of Sherlock Holmes. Vivian's fascination with such esoterica invariably found its way into his detective novels, much to the delight of his loyal readership.

As a detective novelist, John Hall recalled, Francis Vivian "took great pride in the fact that the reader could always arrive at a correct solution from the given data. His Inspector never picked up an undisclosed clue which, it was later revealed, held the solution to the mystery all along." Vivian died on April 2, 1979, at the respectable if not quite venerable age of 73, just like Professor Everett Franklin Phillips. To my knowledge the late mystery writer had not been stung to death by bees.

Curtis Evans

CHAPTER I
THE DEATH OF ROBERT DEXTER

TRAGEDY, ACCORDING TO ARISTOTLE, comes about as the result not of vice, but of some error or frailty in a character. It was so in this case, for if Lesley Dexter had not been a snob her husband might have lived out his three-score-and-ten years. Unfortunately, she wanted to be somebody, desperately wanted to be somebody, and if you want to be anybody in Burnham you must live in Westford Bridge, the suburb west of the river, so that when Robert Dexter was promoted to the managership of the Packing Department of the world-famous Groots Chemicals Limited she badgered him until he rented a bijou Tudor residence in River Close, and then she went ashopping at Paul & Highbury's departmental store, where the best people always went—"You simply cannot shop anywhere else, my dear!"—and bought marvellous new window hangings instead of curtains for three times more than they were worth. She next had a telephone installed, and took to calling up the butcher every morning to tell him that she wanted three chops cut in the Australian manner—"You know, cut very thin!"—or that she did not want anything at all because she would be taking lunch in town with Mrs. Courtney-Harborough.

The butcher said "Yes, ma'am," and "No, ma'am," and "Very good, ma'am," and then replaced the receiver and said "Blast the woman!" He knew her as a *petite* little woman who bleached her hair, wore her skirts too short, used too much make-up, talked in a high-pitched voice like the rest of the Westford so-and-so's, and who wanted to know if he read the Modern Poets. "She tries to look like a lamb," he said to his wife, "and I've cut up better three-year-olds for lamb before breakfast."

Mrs. Margot Rawley, next door at Alpine Villa, said she was a sweet little thing, oh dear yes. Mr. Dennis Rawley agreed with the butcher. Mrs. Mason-Tompkins at No. 37, which she preferred to be known as Colorado House, said she would be better respected by the Set if she took bridge lessons from her on Tuesday and Thursday afternoons at an extortionate fee. Mrs. Courtney-Harborough said she would make a *marvellous ingénue* for the Westford Bridge Amateur Dramatic Society, while Mr. Courtney-Harborough, who had a coarse nature, said he could find a good use for her on a week-end at Brighton.

So Lesley tripped into Himalaya Villa on quick-tapping wooden heels, nailed her flag to the mast, and settled down to break into Burnham's Four Hundred. She had a day-girl with catarrh, and a char with screws who came in on Fridays to scrub the Tudor parquet floors. She spent her mornings taking coffee at Hawton's Oriental Café in town, her afternoons toying with the latest book supplied by a society which really doubted if she could read and understand at the same time, and the rest of the time looking for opportunities to distinguish herself. She began calling her husband Robert instead of Bob, and bought twin beds because double ones had suddenly become unhygienic, and because "sleeping together is just not done these days." Bob retorted that Adam and Eve had slept together, and, oh hell, what was the use!

Eighteen months sped by, and there came an autumn night when Lesley could not sleep. She had a *feeling*, and when she achieved one of these then something was sure to happen. It usually meant that Robert got no sleep, and spent the night making cups of tea and getting into a temper. Lesley would fall asleep when it was time to get up, and stay in bed until noon, it then being understood in the Close that the delicate little Mrs. Dexter was indisposed. Robert would prepare his own breakfast in a manner peculiar to men, cut his hand with the bread-knife, scald himself with the teakettle, and stamp off to business wondering why life had suddenly gone cockeyed.

For his sanity's sake he had a hobby. He was an amateur collector of obscure Elizabethan poets—a device probably sponsored by his unconscious mind as an escape mechanism from Lesley's moderns. He was on the right side, for it was only the poets who were obscure in his case, and not their works.

And so, on this autumn night, Lesley lay in her bed and had a *feeling*. She quoted poems to induce sleep. Robert was asleep when she began the recital, but by the third verse he was lying awake, swearing silently at the ceiling.

The voice from the next bed droned on:

> ". . . the stylus of the night.
> Resting on the record
> Of Man's experience.
> The point is rusted
> And a screech ensues.
> Stirring from his sleep—"

"For God's sake go to sleep!" exclaimed Robert.

"Robert! You know that I cannot sleep! Sometimes I wish I had your bovine temperament. You can sleep anywhere and at any time!"

"I can't sleep anywhere and at any time, because I can't sleep now! Do settle down!"

"You—just—don't—understand—me!"

"I understand you all right, but I'm hanged if I can sleep with that rot being hissed and crooned in my ears. If you must lull yourself to sleep, then try Tennyson, or Wordsworth, or even laudanum. Do anything, but for Heaven's sake let me get to sleep. I have to be up at seven o'clock!"

"You will be, darling!"

"Not if that rusty stylus of yours is going to be scratching all night. And if I am it means I'll have to get my own breakfast, and you'll be idling in bed. It wouldn't be a bad thing if we moved back to Denby Street."

"No, no! I won't go back there! I couldn't go back!"

"You will if you don't let me get to sleep!"

"Ro-obert!"

"Now what?"

"I want a drink of tea . . ."

"I want a large whisky with two aspirins in it, but I'm not getting up to get either of them. You say you can't sleep! Shall I tell you why you can't sleep? Because you are idle! You slept well enough at Denby Street, when you were cleaning your own house, and preparing our meals. Sack the day-girl and that Friday woman. It's work you want—"

"Listen, Robert!"

"I don't want to listen. I want to sleep."

"But there's somebody knocking at the Rawleys' door!"

"Probably the postman. It must be morning by now."

"It's only just after midnight! Listen!"

Robert grunted, and listened.

"Did you hear that, Robert? I heard Margot say that it was next door—it must be somebody wanting us."

"Can't be," said Robert. "We don't have midnight visitors!"

There came a gentle tapping at the front door.

"Oh, Robert! It is! I wonder who it can be?"

"You've probably roused the people across the Close, and they've come to complain," said Robert, but he swung his legs out of bed, switched on the bed-lamp, and reached for his dressing-gown, meanwhile fumbling with his feet for his slippers.

"If it's a practical joker I'll knock his head off. And if it's somebody at the wrong house I'll tell him what I think about him. Who the deuce *can* it be at this time of the night? I wonder if the works is on fire?"

The knocking was resumed.

"Coming!"

Lesley sat up in bed, pulling the wrap round her body. She listened as Robert shuffled down the stairs. She heard a faint click as the hall light went on. The upper and lower bolts went back, and there came a thin squeak as he turned the knob of the latch lock. She heard him say "Oh hell!" and then he gave a grunt. There was a thud, and the sound of retreating footsteps.

"Robert! Bob! What is it?"

There was no answer.

She jumped from the bed and ran barefoot to the head of the stairs. Robert was lying across the mat, and a stream of blood was wending its way towards the door of the lounge. There came more footsteps, and Margot Rawley appeared in the doorway in her *negligée*, ghostly in the yellow light from the hall lamp.

"Margot! Oh, Margot!"

"Lesley darling! What on earth has happened?"

Lesley ran down the stairs, and fell on her knees beside her husband. "Bob! Bob!"

She tried to turn him over, then withdrew her hands and stared unbelievingly at their crimson hue. She screamed, and fell in a dead faint over her husband's body.

Margot Rawley stepped carefully round husband and wife, reached for the telephone behind the door, and called for the police. Then she stood and sobbed, and struggled for composure.

Edward Daker, Police Constable No. 98, looked at the luminous hands of his watch and cursed. Seven past twelve, and he was on ten to three. The night was a long one. Some nights were like that, and others sped along like magic; he had never solved the mystery. Since ten o'clock he had made a point with the skipper—the sergeant, tried Heaven knows how many doors to make sure that they were locked, peered up dark entries, wandered down service lanes, investigated a parked car which proved to be occupied by a very ardent and embarrassing courting couple, and now he had to wait at the corner of Wisden Avenue and River Close until a quarter past twelve in case the station sergeant had news for him or need of him. If the bell did not ring by a quarter past, then he went on his way. More patrolling, two more points with the skipper before three o'clock, and then Riley, the ugly son-of-a-gun, would relieve him hard by the Bridge Tavern.

He had noticed, shortly after reaching the kiosk, that a stream of light was striking across the road at the river end, and he had wondered about investigating, but there was really nothing unusual about a bedroom light, and· so he had waited for the expected call. The scream changed all his plans for the night. The regulation pace was ignored in the circumstances, and he went light-footed and speedily in the direction of the scream. The gate of Himalaya Villa was wide open, he noticed that even as his eyes met what appeared to be a heap of bodies lying in the doorway of the house. Then a woman in filmy white appeared and quietly announced: "I have called the police station, Constable!"

"What's happened?" asked Daker. "I heard a scream."

"Help me to lift Mrs. Dexter, and carry her into the lounge. She has fainted. I am Mrs. Rawley from next door. I will tell you all I know later."

Between them they carried Lesley to the lounge. Margot Rawley found the medicine chest and the bottle of sal volatile therein. She forced a strong dose between Lesley's lips, and then switched on the electric fire and fetched blankets from one of the beds upstairs.

Daker was meanwhile trying to do several things at once. The inquisitive residents of the Close who had been attracted by the scream were too attentive, and had to be driven away. He had to attend Robert Dexter, in case any life should yet remain within his body. He had to take careful note of the layout of the scene. And at the back of his mind he was wondering if the skipper was on the telephone up at the kiosk. But he was an intelligent man, a constable of the new order who never licked the stub of a pencil nor yet flexed his knees, and he realized that he was dealing with a body, cadaver, or corpse, and not with a living man, so he left it where it lay, and shooed the residents back to the pavement, where he mounted guard.

It was only five minutes later when the first car arrived, and from it stepped Inspector Russett, chief of the Burnham Criminal Investigation Department since Inspector Knollis's translation to the Yard. He was a stubby man with a bristling moustache and a bustling manner. He barged straight up to Daker and demanded: "What's the trouble?"

Daker saluted respectfully. He did not like the inspector, but he knew better than to irritate him by even such a minor lapse as a forgotten salute in unusual circumstances. Russett was by way of being a martinet—an idiosyncrasy, according to Daker, which tended to cover up a lot of his incompetence. And so he saluted and explained, doing both briefly.

"You haven't moved the body?" Inspector Russett demanded.

"I pulled him half over, sir. A quick glance was enough to show that he was dead, and so I left everything exactly as I found it."

Russett brushed his moustache with the back of his hand as if clearing all decks for action. Then he sailed up to the corpse.

Three more cars turned into the Close, and came to rest behind Russett's. The first decanted Sir Wilfrid Burrows, the Chief Constable. The second disgorged Dr. Patrick Whitelaw, the police surgeon. The third ejected a photographer, a "Dabs" or finger-print specialist, and his assistant. And behind them came an ambulance which nosed its way to the front of the rank and then backed up to the gate in readiness. From that moment Himalaya Villa was overrun as if by rats. Photographers took photographs, finger-print men looked for prints, Dr. Whitelaw looked for all kinds of things, and Russett and his Sergeant Rogers played at Sherlock Holmes in the approved manner.

Lesley Dexter had hysterics twice, and asked permission to go, or be taken, to her mother's house in Frogmore Street, at the other side of the city. Sir Wilfrid put his car and his driver at her service; unbeknown to her he also telephoned to the station and asked for a plain-clothes man to be detailed for guard outside her mother's house.

All through the night they worked, and at half-past eight in the morning, thrusting their way through an inquisitive throng of reporters and sightseers, a weary trio returned to Sir Wilfrid's office to drink much-needed tea and to confer. Sir Wilfrid, ruddy-cheeked and important, took the chair by virtue of his seniority. Dr. Whitelaw, pale and professional, sat and listened. Inspector Russett, his black eyebrows standing out at right-angles to his face, argued.

"We're stuck!" said Sir Wilfrid.

"We aren't," said Russett.

"We are, and you know we are," said Sir Wilfrid. "There isn't a trace of the fellow. He just came, killed, and departed."

"We're not stuck, anyway," repeated Russett.

"I'm going to ask for Yard assistance," said Sir Wilfrid.

"I hope you won't," said Russett moodily.

"I'm going to," said Sir Wilfrid stubbornly. "Make sure of the case being cleared up—and get rid of the responsibility!"

Then he broke off to swear as the telephone at his elbow jangled its summons. "Sir Wilfrid Burrows speaking."

He listened, nodding his head from time to time. Finally, he said: "Very good," and replaced the receiver.

"Chairman of the Watch Committee. I am going to call in the Yard."

Russett sat bolt upright in his chair. "For God's sake give me a chance. It's only eight hours since the man was killed, and I'm only human."

"Watch Committee, Russett. Don't blame me! They are meeting at ten o'clock this morning to authorize me."

"But you intended sending for the Yard! You can stall them if you want to! Eight hours only, and we give up!"

"Eight hours," said the Chief Constable, "and what have we got? Nothing, absolutely nothing! I'll ask for Knollis if they'll let him come. You won't object to working with him?"

"I've no objections to Knollis, or anyone else at the Yard if it comes to that, but I do think I should be allowed a chance to clear up the case. What is the city going to think about it? And do let me remind you, sir, that you let Knollis handle the Lomas affair!"

Sir Wilfrid nodded. "Quite right! I did! And I was fighting the Watch Committee all the way through, holding them off to give Knollis a chance. I won't do it again, not for the sake of my nerves. In any case, without casting any aspersions, Knollis is better qualified to handle the case. I'm sorry we had to lose him. . . ."

He stared at the ceiling reminiscently. Five years had brought many changes to the Burnham C.I.D., but the worst from his point of view was the requisitioning of Knollis by the Yard. It could not have happened at any other time, but the war had justified many unconventional happenings, so that when he fought the assistant commissioner's request for Knollis to be transferred to the metropolis he knew he was fighting a losing battle, and eventually gave in with a show of good grace. Knollis went, spent two years in the divisions, and was again transferred, this time to the Yard itself, where, if he had not as yet distinguished himself as an individual, he had proved his strength in the team.

"There is a definite reason why Knollis should not come," said Russett, breaking in on the Chief Constable's thoughts, and rationalizing his own true objections.

"Eh?" The Chief Constable blinked. "What was that?"

"He's too dangerous with witnesses. He looks too much like a detective, and witnesses dry up as soon as they look him over!"

"True enough," agreed Sir Wilfrid, "but he always gets his facts, doesn't he? Knollis has lots of tact and patience, which some people lack. It was patience that got him to the head of your department by his forty-first birthday, and five years with the Yard will have put the finishing touches to his technique. No, I'm afraid there is no point in arguing, Russett. I am asking for Yard assistance—and I'll expect you and your staff to work with him."

"Oh, we'll work all right," said Russett with a shrug. "The job is the main thing, but I still think it is a dirty trick."

He swung out of the chair and left the office, closing the door with unnecessary violence.

"Now what do you think about that?" demanded Sir Wilfrid of Dr. Whitelaw.

"Well," said the doctor slowly, "I can see both sides. I think you are right in calling in the Yard, especially as you have to do so, because it smells to me like a tricky case, and I don't think that Russett has sufficient experience to handle it successfully. On the other hand, I understand how he feels about it. He may be a wee bit dense, but the man has his pride, you know!"

Sir Wilfrid wriggled uneasily in his chair. "Oh well, it's the Watch Committee! Care for a spot of whisky? I managed to find a bottle the other day. Devilish difficult to get, eh?"

CHAPTER II

THE WIDOW OF THE DECEASED

THE DRIVER SENT to meet the Yard men as they arrived at Burnham's Victoria Station had little difficulty in recognizing them as they came through the barrier, or at any rate, little difficulty in recognizing Inspector Gordon Knollis, for Russett's assertion was justifiable; Knollis looked more like a sleuth than any creation of the imagination produced by a magazine illustrator or a film studio make-up man. He was lean, and had a long inquisitive nose especially suited for dipping into mysteries. His eyes were cold and grey, mere slits through which he suspiciously regarded the wrongdoers and suspected wrong-doers of the world. They were forbidding eyes, unsocial eyes, until one noticed the creases at the corners and realized that here was a man who could relax and smile in the right company, but it is doubtful if anyone other than his wife, his two small sons, and his few intimate friends had ever seen that smile break. Knollis at work was earnest, grimly efficient, and tenacious. The driver knew him without taking a second look, and the stocky little man at his side was a suitable companion for him, for he had a tight jaw, and there was an implication of similar tenacity in his purposeful stride.

He approached them, introduced himself and his errand, and hurried them through the city streets to the Central Police Station, where Sir Wilfrid Burrows, Russett, and Dr. Whitelaw awaited them.

Knollis looked happily at the three men across a table littered with reports, statements, and photographs provided by the laboratory. Whitelaw had always been his good friend in the old Burnham days, Sir Wilfrid had been his chief, and Russett had worked under him.

"It's good to get to Burnham again," said Knollis as he extended a hand to the Chief Constable, "but I could have wished for a different errand. And you, Whitelaw! How are you? You look tired!"

He turned to Russett. "I'm sorry to come and spoil your party, Russett, because I realize how you must feel about it."

"That's all right," murmured Russett. "It looks like being a biggish job, anyway."

"This is my companion, Sergeant Ellis, and my most invaluable aide," said Knollis. "Take a seat, Ellis, or they'll let you stand about all day. I know them!"

Sir Wilfrid blew out his cheeks, and smiled expansively.

"It's nice to see you again, Knollis, but we mustn't let pleasantries rule out the work, must we? We'll have a chat later. Anybody like a drink? It's very hush-hush, of course, and most irregular."

They then got down to the facts.

"Let us have the story," said Knollis.

Ellis made notes as it was told.

"It boils down to this," said Russett. "A man walked down River Close last night, just after midnight, and knocked on the door of Alpine Villa, which is occupied by a couple named Rawley. Mrs. Rawley, her husband being away from home, went downstairs and found a man on her doorstep. He asked for the Dexters' house, which is next door. She directed him there, and he thanked her and walked away. A few minutes later he knocked on the Dexter door. It was opened by the husband, who was heard to say 'Oh hell!'—after which he gave a grunt, and folded up with a knife wound in his chest. He died in the next minute or so without speaking. The wife scurried downstairs, and at that moment Mrs. Rawley rushed round to see what was happening. Mrs. Dexter tried to revive her husband, and then passed out. And that is all we know about it."

"Whitelaw?" murmured Knollis, glancing at the doctor.

"Carving-knife, or a similar one, Knollis. An upward thrust that entered the body below the sternum and entered the heart. I have not done the post-mortem yet, but I estimate the knife-blade at eleven inches long and about an inch and a quarter wide. The blow must have been a savage one and fetched him straight down. I arrived roughly fifteen or twenty minutes after it happened, and it looked to me as if he had crumpled at the knees, and then fallen forward on his face. The right ear and cheek are grazed, and the right side of his nose is bruised. It had also bled internally."

"No trace of the weapon?"

"No weapon, and no dabs," said Russett laconically.

"Any ideas about the assailant?"

"None," said Russett.

Knollis collected the photographs from the table and examined them. "Very clear! Now what is the age of the deceased?"

"Thirty. He's the packing manager at Groots, a fairly good job considering his age and the size of the firm. They have over nine hundred branches in the United Kingdom, and do export as well, and Dexter supervised both home and foreign packing."

"Family life?"

Russett lifted his shoulders. "Seems to be happy enough by what little I can find from the neighbours. Pretty much the same set-up as most of the families in the area—husband working hard to get somewhere, while being pushed by his wife, and the wife trying to be somebody."

"River Close?" murmured Knollis with narrowed eyes. "That is off Wisden Avenue, isn't it?"

"Runs parallel with the river, does Wisden Avenue," broke in Sir Wilfrid. "The three dead-end streets, River Close, Dene Close, and Sycamore Close run off it to the south, and meet the embankment above the towpath."

"Yes, I remember now," nodded Knollis. "Chestnut palings form the boundary between the bottom of the street and the top of the embankment. The towpath is twelve feet below. That is very interesting!" he added.

"What is?" Russett asked quickly.

"At which house was the murder committed?" asked Knollis, ignoring the question.

"Next to the last on the right-hand side. It's called Himalaya Villa for some unknown reason, although it's about as far from the Himalayas as it is from the Grand Canyon. Fully detached house, separated from its neighbours by privet hedges."

"Boundary wall or fence?"

"Neither. Just privet hedges, which are two feet six inches high. I measured them," said Russett proudly.

"What kind of paths?"

"Concrete, right round the house. All the houses in the Close are built from the same design," Russett explained. "Each is built on a concrete raft, with a concrete path leading to the rear gate, and one leading to the street."

Knollis bent over the photographs again. "Smallish porch!"

"Yes," said Russett, "it's very small. Two feet nine deep, and four feet wide, with a rounded arch. As you see there, the front door has coloured glass panels, and there is a wing on either side of it also fitted with coloured glass—the lead-light stuff."

"So that in daytime the people inside can see who is standing in the porch," Knollis murmured, more to himself than to Russett and the others.

"Why?" said Russett.

"No door-bell?"

"Not as a standard fitment," answered Russett, "although a few of the residents have them."

"Door fastenings?"

"Latch lock of Yale type, but not Yale make. Also top and bottom bolts. I took particular note of them!"

"I see that there is one step up from the porch to the hall. About five inches?"

"Yes, and there is one from the path to the porch of the same depth. I checked both those points, also."

Dr. Whitelaw leaned forward. "I think I can help you there, Knollis. It is my impression that the assailant stepped inside the hall to strike the blow, if only with one foot. Striking with a disadvantage of five inches in height would indicate a man of extraordinary stature. You see, it was a swinging underhand blow."

"I see," Knollis answered slowly. "I was wondering about that. How about the blood-stains?"

"The door-mat is in a well," Russett explained. "The majority of the blood was absorbed by the mat, but there was a small pool on the tiled floor, at the inner side of the well, which was flowing towards the door of the lounge. I take it that he would be standing there when the knife was withdrawn. Imagine him standing there with his hand on the door-knob, and you will see what I mean."

"Yes, I see . . ."

"And the pool absorbed by the mat would be the result of his fall."

"Obviously, yes. He was heard to swear, you said?"

"He said 'Oh hell!' according to his wife."

"Almost sounds as if his visitor was known to him, and also unwelcome, doesn't it?" interposed Sir Wilfrid.

"Maybe, sir," Knollis replied quietly. He then turned again to Russett. "What has been done up to now?"

Russett beamed, and consulted his notes. "Plenty, actually! Photos, and dabs; interviewed the wife of the deceased, and ditto the neighbour who was almost a witness; made various inquiries, of course—"

Knollis interrupted. "Checked his social life, acquaintances, past history, general interests?"

"Well no, not yet, that is. Although, of course, I have all those lined up." Russett wriggled uncomfortably. "There's been so little time, really!"

Sir Wilfrid smirked as he watched Russett's discomfort. There was *I told you so* written all over his full features.

"How long has Dexter been in Burnham?" Knollis asked. Nobody seemed to know.

"Any idea where he lived before he came to town—always assuming that he has not lived here all his life?"

There was no answer to that question either, and Russett ran a finger between his collar and his neck.

Knollis then turned to Dr. Whitelaw. "When do you perform the post-mortem?"

"This evening. Care to be present?"

Knollis grimaced his distaste for such operations.

"No, thank you. I'll be satisfied with the report."

"But you will want to see the body!"

"I'll have to see it," said Knollis.

"Then there's no time like the present," replied the doctor, "and I'm going to the mortuary now, so you may as well come with me."

"After which I'll go on to the hotel and have tea," Knollis said to the Chief Constable, "and then we'll really get down to work."

On reaching the door, he said: "I haven't been through the reports yet. How did Mrs. Rawley describe the man who roused her in the night?"

"I can tell you that," Russett said eagerly. "She said he was tall and thin, sallow-faced, and was wearing a very long black coat, and a black velour trilby pulled down over his face."

"How would you describe Mrs. Rawley?"

"Oh, quite the opposite build, if that is what you are thinking. She's a plump woman with blonde hair."

"Any children?"

"Er—no, I don't think so, Knollis."

"Have the Dexters any children?"

"No-o!" said Russett. "No, I'm sure of that."

Knollis knuckled his lips. "I must ask about those two points. They may be important. Thanks, Russett."

The door closed behind him, and Russett turned to the Chief Constable. "What was he getting at, sir?"

Sir Wilfrid twirled a pencil round and round on the blotter. "I haven't the faintest idea," he replied, "and knowing Knollis I don't suppose any of us will know what he is thinking until he chooses to tell us. He never jumps to conclusions."

Knollis had a long technical discussion with Whitelaw over the body, and then he and Ellis drove to Frogmore Street, which lay off the Desborough Road North.

Ellis, whose first visit to Burnham this was, peered through the windscreen at the dim-lit streets. "Any idea where we are?"

Knollis smiled at the question. "I know exactly. Five years away from the city has not blunted my knowledge of its geography. Do you realize that I pounded a beat here many years ago? No, I'm not likely to forget, Ellis. Next on the left, and then the second on the right."

"Happy days," said Ellis. "Very little responsibility, very little brainwork, and you did know when you'd finished. I sometimes wonder why I went in for this branch of the game. It doesn't give you anything you could describe as an easy life, does it?"

A short laugh came from Knollis.

Ellis asked: "What is the district like?"

"Frogmore Street, you mean?" said Knollis. "As I remember it, it is a street of semi-detached villas, all nicely kept, and with trim gardens. It's filled with decent people who have no time for suburban neuroses—mainly people who have looked after their earnings and bought their own houses through building societies. I had very little trouble in this area, and consequently have respect for it. And here's the street, Ellis, and I suppose the fellow marching about to keep warm is our plain-clothes man. You wouldn't like to go back to those stunts, would you?"

Ellis gave a grunt that was far more expressive than words.

Knollis drew up under the street lamp, and discovered that he was outside the house he was seeking. The plain-clothes man "keeping observation" walked along, recognized Knollis, and saluted. "Mrs. Dexter has not left the house, sir. They've been overrun with reporters all day, but haven't allowed any interviews."

"Good work," said Knollis.

He knocked at the front door, and it was opened by a woman a few years past middle age. She regarded him hostilely.

"Well?"

"I am Inspector Knollis, from Scotland Yard. I would like to speak to Mrs. Dexter, please."

She peered at him from the doorway.

"You are sure you are from the police? I'm sick of reporters from the newspapers!"

Knollis showed his warrant, and he and Ellis were then asked in.

The woman quickly closed and locked the door after them. "No peace with them," she commented as she took them through to the living-room. "Lesley was expecting somebody to come from the police. Want to see her alone?"

"Well, I would like to do so, if you have no objections. If it is inconvenient, of course . . ."

She sniffed. "There's nothing inconvenient if you can find the scoundrel who did Bob to death. As fine a lad as you'd find anywhere, and I regarded him as my own. No, it's no trouble. Make yourself at home, and I'll send her to you. She's upstairs just now."

Ellis looked round the room when they were alone.

"Nice pair of pot dogs on the mantelpiece, but I get a bit sick of those Crossing-Sweeper and Flower-Girl pictures; you see 'em wherever you go."

"Signs of solid respectability, Ellis, exactly as I warned you—even to the old-fashioned antimacassar over the modern easy chairs."

Ellis grinned. "Bet the old man uses hair oil!"

"Elementary, my dear Watson," murmured Knollis.

They returned to their earnest manner as Lesley Dexter entered the room. She was dressed in a light-grey costume and a white blouse. Her eyes were red-rimmed, and her hair lacked attention. She nodded dully as Knollis introduced himself.

"I'm sorry to worry you like this," he said, "but I am sure that you will realize the necessity."

She nodded silently, and seated herself by the fire.

"Perhaps you will tell me how it happened—in your own words," suggested Knollis.

"It all seems like a bad dream now," she said wearily "I can't quite believe that it ever happened, but I'll try to tell you."

Ellis took a chair and opened his notebook as Knollis began to draw the story from her.

"You were awake when this man came to the Rawleys' door?"

"Oh yes! Bob and I were having a heated debate on poetry. We often did so, and there was no ill feeling about it. You see, I am an admirer of the more modern schools, and Bob's hobby was collecting Elizabethan poets. He was keen on plays, too. There was such a contrast between our interests that we were continually chaffing each other, and last night we were carrying on the arguments."

"So that you heard the knocking?"

"Yes. I told Bob to keep quiet so that I could listen It was so unusual at that time of the night!"

"Just after midnight?"

"Four minutes past by the alarm clock, which I had set right by the wireless when I was putting the hot water bottle in bed at nine o'clock. My husband had it on for the news—"

"Did you hear the man's voice?" asked Knollis.

"No, I can't say that I did, Inspector. Margot—Mrs Rawley has a very clear sort of voice, and I heard her say: Oh dear no. It is the next door lower down the street.' I said to Bob that it was someone looking for us, and he replied that it could not be at this time of the night, and then the knock did come on our own door. He slipped out of bed, and was putting on his dressing-gown when the second knock came. He shouted that he was coming, and went downstairs. I heard him unfasten and open the door, and then he swore, and gave a horrid grunt—half a cough, it was—and then—and then—"

Knollis waited a moment, and then said: "Yes?"

"I—I got out of my bed and ran to the head of the stairs. I called him, and there was no answer. It was then I saw him . . ."

"Mrs. Rawley appeared, I believe?" said Knollis.

"Yes, just as I was starting to go down the stairs. I called to her, and she said: 'Lesley! What has happened?' I ran down the stairs and tried to turn Bob over, but . . .'"

"Yes," said Knollis. "I quite understand, Mrs. Dexter, and you need not distress yourself by telling me that, but I would like to ask one very delicate question, if I may?"

She stared up at him with round, wondering eyes.

"Was your family life happy, Mrs. Dexter?"

She buried her face in her hands. "Oh Bob! Bob!"

"Your husband held a rather important post at Groots, did he not?" Knollis asked tactfully.

Her pride thus appealed to, Lesley Dexter's eyes appeared above the square of lace she honoured in calling a handkerchief.

"He was the sole head of his department, Inspector. He supervised all the others! He was responsible for all the home and export packing for every department of Groots!"

"He had no—er—well, enemies at his place of business, as far as you know, Mrs. Dexter?"

"Bob! Bob hadn't an enemy in the world, Inspector! I can assure you that he had not!"

Knollis coughed discreetly. Dead men never had enemies, according to their families, and he could never find a relative of a murder victim who would admit the possibility—unless they wanted to incriminate someone who usually turned out to be completely innocent.

"Your husband had a large circle of friends?"

Lesley Dexter considered the question at some length. "No-o," she admitted reluctantly. "He was a home-loving man. Occasionally he would go down to the Key and Clock in the evening to play billiards, but generally he preferred to stay at home and work on his collection. It was seldom that he was away from home more than one night a week."

"Tell me, Mrs. Dexter; with regard to this collection. Did he sell as well as buy?"

"Bob? Oh dear no, Inspector. He was a true collector, and once he had bought a book he wouldn't part with it for anything. He was very proud of his books! Why do you ask?"

"No particular reason," Knollis replied lightly. "I am just trying to build a picture of him and his background. You see, Mrs. Dexter, I approach this case as a complete stranger, and most of the questions I ask you have little or no bearing on the possible identity of your husband's assailant. That background, when complete, may suggest some person whom you would never think of, and certainly never suspect. It is obvious that someone must have had a solid reason—in their own eyes—for killing him, whether you care to admit the possibility or not. And that it is no case of mistaken identity is proved by the man's inquiries of Mrs. Rawley."

Lesley Dexter looked puzzled for a moment, and then she said: "But if it was someone who knew him, then surely it must have been someone who knew where we live! And the man did go to Margot Rawley to ask which was our house!"

Knollis looked quickly across at Ellis, who grinned at his chief's temporary discomfiture.

"You see what I mean, Inspector?" Lesley Dexter persisted.

"No, not quite," Knollis admitted, "but you have certainly indicated an original line of investigation. I was told that you were an intelligent woman and, if you will permit the compliment, I shall be pleased to qualify the statement."

A little colour returned to Lesley's cheeks.

"Thank you, Inspector."

"May I ask how long you have been married?"

"Three years."

"And you have lived in the Close . . . ?"

"Eighteen months. We lived in Denby Street for the first eighteen months of our married life, and moved into the Close after Bob got his promotion."

"How long had you known your husband before you were married, Mrs. Dexter?" asked Knollis.

"Just a year. We played tennis at the same club—and he was lodging in Denby Street when he first came to Burnham."

"Denby Street? Yes, I remember it now. So that he had been in Burnham about four years?"

"Four years and nearly six months, Inspector."

"And before that?"

"With the U.C. in Birmingham. He was there for several years."

Knollis studied his finger-nails carefully as he asked the next question.

"Were Mr. Dennis Rawley and your husband good friends?"

"We-ell," Lesley replied slowly, "not exactly *friends*, but good neighbours, if you know what I mean. I'm afraid that Dennis Rawley thought himself pretty much above Bob. Still, they never had any disagreements, and they would talk gardening over the fence for hours—instead of doing the work."

"Your husband knew him before he met you?"

"Oh yes, because they were working for the same firm. Dennis Rawley had been at Groots some time when Bob went."

"And did he know Mrs. Rawley before you went to live in River Close? Can you tell me that?"

Lesley's eyes widened again. "I—I don't know, Inspector! Why should you ask that? I don't understand!"

Knollis shrugged his shoulders as he replied. "Oh, please don't read anything into my questions, Mrs. Dexter. I am still trying to feel my way round your husband's social background. Now, another question, if you don't mind. Did people ever come to the house to sell books to your husband, or to discuss them with him? Dealers, or other collectors?"

"Occasionally, yes. Two dealers from Birmingham, and one from London. They came about two or three times a year, I suppose, but Bob did most of his buying by post. The dealers would let him know when they had anything in which he might be interested. If he was interested, then they would send them on approval, and Bob would pay for them by cheque if he wanted to keep them."

"He never complained of being let down by trading in this way?" asked Knollis.

"I can answer that with certainty, Inspector, because after we were married I asked him that myself—it seemed such a risky method to me! He said he only dealt with book dealers with reputations which they valued."

"Quite logical, anyway," murmured Knollis. "Well, thank you for your help, Mrs. Dexter. We will be getting on our way. Oh, but just one more question before we leave! This again is rather a delicate one, but I would appreciate an answer. Wasn't your husband's hobby an expensive one considering his position?"

Lesley did not answer for a full minute, and Knollis watched her carefully as she thought out her answer. Then, surprisingly, she said: "Yes, it was! As a matter of fact it was the sole ground for dispute that we ever had. Bob spent far too much money on it, and I protested times without number, but he always insisted that he was investing money, and not spending it wastefully. He said that if ever we fell on hard times he would have more to fall back on than if the money was invested in shares. I couldn't see it at first, although I did grow to understand a little better."

Knollis sank down again on the arm of the chair.

"I know nothing of book collecting. Could you explain that to me, Mrs. Dexter?"

Lesley sought for words. "We-ell, you see, Inspector, it works out something like this—although I don't profess to know much about it myself; by specializing on one period he was building up what was in effect a unique collection, and the collection as a whole was worth more than all the books if sold individually."

Yes, Knollis said slowly, "I think I see the argument."

"Well, Bob was very insistent about it," said Lesley.

"Did he take any precautions to safeguard the collection?"

"None whatsoever, Inspector. I was always asking him why he didn't, but he said it was unnecessary as no thief could dispose of them because they were known to every dealer in Great Britain and America."

"He could have sold the collection almost at any time?"

"Apparently," replied Lesley, "although, as I say', I know little or nothing about them. He received several offers for the whole collection during the past year, and he turned them down. He did not want to sell, because it was getting more valuable as he added to it."

"And he had no hobbies other than his books and billiards?"

"None, Inspector—unless you can count his gardening, but that was more of a necessity than a hobby."

"Just a matter of keeping it tidy and respectable?" murmured Knollis. "Well, thank you, Mrs. Dexter, and please accept my apologies once more for having to bother you at such a time."

"That," said Ellis, as they re-entered the car, "gets us exactly nowhere!"

"I agree, but these are early days."

"Where now?" Ellis asked anxiously.

"To see Mrs. Rawley."

Ellis sank back into the cushions. "I was afraid of that. There is no rest for the wicked, and I have to suffer with them."

"Suspecting Mrs. Rawley?" asked Knollis with an amused smile.

"Well," replied Ellis, "we've got to suspect somebody!"

CHAPTER III

THE FRIEND OF THE WIDOW

KNOLLIS, on reaching River Close, found himself tempted. His avowed object in visiting the street was to interview Margot

Rawley, and on finding himself outside the house in which the murder had occurred he felt a strong urge to look round it first.

"Take me by the arm, and lead me to Mrs. Rawley's door, Ellis," he said with a faint smile. "I'm itching to get inside Himalaya Villa. We'll probably do that next, unless you have a better suggestion."

"I have," replied Ellis. "A drink, a meal, and a sleep. We haven't eaten since lunch on the train. Remember?"

"I will remember," Knollis said softly, and pushed open the gate of Alpine Villa.

Margot Rawley received them wearing a red and gold house-coat which made a colourful contrast with her green shoes. She expressed herself as pleased to see them, and ushered them into the lounge, where she switched on the electric fire.

"So you are really a Scotland Yard detective, Inspector!"

"I certainly am, Mrs. Rawley. I think you can help me in no small way, if you will."

Margot Rawley pressed a finely manicured hand to her throat and laughed insincerely. "Me? Oh dear, I really doubt it, Inspector. However, if you think I can I will do all I can to help you."

"You were almost a witness of the tragedy, Mrs. Rawley, and may be able to do a great deal towards identifying the murderer."

Margot Rawley stared over Knollis's shoulder. "You would like me to tell you what little I know, Inspector. Would you care for coffee while I am telling you? Or perhaps a drink of whisky?"

"Neither, thank you," said Knollis. "I am afraid that I am too busy. May I have your story, please?"

She sank down among the cushions of the settee and arranged herself carefully. It seemed to Knollis that the newspaper reporters would have little difficulty with her; she was revelling in the limelight that had temporarily spotted her in the public gaze.

"Last night," she began, pressing her fingers to her temple as if making a great effort to remember. "Last night now! It was just after midnight when the knock came at my door."

"I noticed that you have a bell, Mrs. Rawley," Knollis interrupted. "Isn't it working?"

"Oh yes—or is it? I'm not sure. But that is the funny part about it. The man *knocked*. So very strange, don't you think?"

"Not if the bell is out of action," replied Knollis. He signalled to Ellis, who left the room, returning a minute later to say laconically: "No joy."

"So there is nothing strange about the knock," said Knollis. "Now, Mrs. Rawley . . . !"

"I lay, and listened, and the knock came again. I got up, pulled my wrap round my shoulders, and went down to see who it could be."

"Why didn't your husband go?" asked Knollis.

"He was away, Inspector. He still is, as a matter of fact, so that there was no one else to go but myself."

"May I ask where he is?"

"In Birmingham, as a matter of fact, attending a conference. He is at Groots, you know—in charge of export sales."

"Robert Dexter worked there, did he not?"

"Oh yes, but in a different department. He was *Packing*, and my husband is *Export*—such a difference! But I was telling you, Inspector, that I came down, switched on the hall light, and opened the door."

"Risky thing to do at that time of the night, surely?"

"Well, you see, Inspector, I rather thought that it might be Dennis, my husband. He attends these conferences about once a month, and if he can get the late train back he does, although it is seldom he does so. He hates to be away from home. Very much of a home-lover! But, as I say, it was not he."

Knollis waited more or less patiently as she rearranged the housecoat over her knees. It was no good trying to push her. She would only go at her own pace.

"I opened the door," she said at last, "and I must admit that I was rather taken aback, and almost startled, because the man who was standing there did look rather sinister. He wore a long black coat that reached nearly to his ankles, and a black velour trilby hat that was pulled down over his face. I gained the impression that he was sallow-complexioned, but that may have been due to the hall lamp, which has a yellow panel in it nearest to the door.

"He asked me if this was the Smiths' house. I said that it was not. He apologized for disturbing me at that time of the night, and asked if I could direct him to the Smiths'. I told him that there was no one of the name of Smith in the Close, and then he said that this was River Close, surely. I said that it was, and he said something about it being very funny, then thanked me and walked slowly back up the path to the gate. He was standing at the gate when I closed the door."

"You then returned to bed?" asked Knollis.

She regarded the toe of her left shoe critically before replying: "No, Inspector, I did not. I switched off the light, and stood by the door, listening. I was suspicious, and if he had stayed near the house I should have rung for the police. But I heard footsteps and decided that he was going away."

"One point," Knollis interrupted. "I understand from Inspector Russett that the man asked for the Dexter house, and that you told him it was next door."

"How did he get that notion?" she asked in a surprised tone. "I'm sure I never said that!"

"It was in your original statement, Mrs. Rawley."

"Did I really say that? If I did, then it was when I was all upset, because he definitely asked for Smiths' house. I am positive on the point, Inspector. There was no mention at all of Dexters. Still, I'm sure that can be cleared up can't it?"

"It will be," Knollis assured her. "But perhaps you will continue with your story?"

"Well, the next thing I heard was the knocking at the Dexters' door, and I wondered if the fellow thought I was new to the Close and did not know all the residents. But there was a pause, and then another knocking. I slid back the latch, and opened the door an inch or so. It was pitch-dark, and I could not even distinguish the dividing hedge. Then a dim light shone on the path, presumably when Mr. Dexter switched on his hall light. I heard the bolts being shot back, and then a faint squeak as he unfastened the latch lock . . ."

"Yes, Mrs. Rawley?"

"Everything seemed to happen at once, Inspector," she said with a great sigh. "I heard Mr. Dexter say 'Oh hell!'—just like that—and then he gave an awful kind of grunt and it sounded as if he had stumbled against the door. Next he was choking, a sort of gurgling cough—a horrible sound!"

"Yes?" Knollis said gently but firmly.

"I—I think I felt a wee bit faint, Inspector, and I held on to the door for a moment. Then I heard Lesley—Mrs. Dexter—calling her husband's name. I pulled myself together, and ran out. I pushed my way through the hedge, and there he lay, face downwards on the mat, with blood streaming from under him."

"You never heard the man go away?"

"No, I can't say that I heard a sound, Inspector."

"Thank you. Please continue."

"Mrs. Dexter was standing at the head of the stairs with her hand to her mouth. As soon as she saw me she called to me. I asked what had happened, and she ran down the stairs in her bare feet and knelt beside her husband. She tried to turn him over on hi§ back, but there was an awful spurt of blood, and she screamed, and fainted. I was feeling physically sick myself, but I managed to step round them and get to the telephone behind the door, and then I rang for the police. The constable was there almost as soon as I had finished the call. I think he was at the end of the street, and had heard Lesley scream."

"And you are quite certain that you neither saw nor heard the man leave the house?"

"I never saw him after I closed my own door, Inspector. Whether he went out by the front gate, or whether he went to the rear of the house and out through the back garden, I don't know, but I am certain that I never heard or saw him."

"So that," said Knollis, "it would seem that yourself and Robert Dexter were the only two people who saw him?"

Margot Rawley looked up as if this was a new thought to her. "Yes, I suppose so, unless someone happened to be on the street."

"What kind of a man was Robert Dexter?" asked Knollis. "A quiet fellow, or a lively one, or what?"

"A very quiet, stolid man, Inspector, and I should say that he was a good husband. Lesley is one of my closest friends, and I know her well enough to say that she takes some handling. You see, she is highly strung, and very sensitive. The slightest little thing excites her, and, quite candidly, there are times when I could slap her. She works herself into an exalted state of mind, and an hour later is in the dumps. I'm afraid I have no sympathy with such temperaments."

Knollis nodded quietly. He could quite understand that. Now that Margot Rawley had finished posing he could see that she was level in both temperament and general attitude to life.

"Were there any differences of opinion between them, Mrs. Rawley?" he asked. "Differences which went further than the more or less usual domestic tiffs?"

"I hardly like answering that question, Inspector, because you may tend to exaggerate anything I say. Nevertheless, there was one point of contention. Lesley has what amounts to a passion for the modern poets, and I'm afraid that she and her husband did not see eye to eye on the subject."

"Why so?" Knollis asked as he clasped his hands round his knees and leaned forward.

"Well, you see, Inspector, Mr. Dexter also had a hobby! He collected Elizabethan poetry and plays—first editions when he could get them. Lesley was rather annoyed about the amount of money he used. She admitted that she never went short of housekeeping money, nor her clothing allowance if it comes to that, but she was worried because so little was going into the bank. Mr. Dexter's argument was that she never went short of anything, and she had no need to grumble. Of course, I gained all this information in confidence, and I feel a little mean about repeating it!"

"So that there was a certain amount of friction between them?" suggested Knollis. He leaned back in the chair and regarded her steadily.

She looked surprised by his question. "Did I say that? Oh dear me, Inspector! I thought you would misunderstand! They were really a very happy couple indeed. I mean, most married couples have minor points of dispute, don't they? You suggested that yourself. Take Dennis and myself, for instance! We are very happy, but he does not like my bridge-playing, and I certainly resent the amount of time he spends on billiards because it takes him away from home in the evenings, but we do try to see each other's point of view, and so it works out all right. I mean, I'd really hate Dennis to give up his billiards, and he'd hate me to throw up my bridge."

"So Robert Dexter collected first editions of Elizabethan poets and playwrights," Knollis murmured to himself. "That clears up one interesting point."

Margot Rawley stared wonderingly at him, but passed no comment.

Knollis turned his attention to her again. "Now tell me, Mrs. Rawley! do you think that you could identify the man if you saw him again?"

"I would know him anywhere, Inspector."

"Just a few minor points, and then I will leave you. How long have the Dexters been your neighbours? How long have they been living in the Close?"

Margot Rawley laid a finger on her cheek, and her lips moved silently as she calculated.

"See now, it will be eighteen months. It is October now, and yes they came next door on the first of May, the year that—it would be last year, wouldn't it?" she asked.

"At that rate, yes," Knollis agreed. "Perhaps you can tell me where they came from. I take it that *you* do know that, since Mrs. Dexter was such a close friend."

Margot Rawley pursed her lips. "Matters like those are generally ignored in River Close, Inspector, but I do happen to know that they lived in Denby Street before coming here. Robert Dexter got his promotion about the end of March, and they started looking round for a house in a respectable part of the city, and I believe that it was my husband who told Robert Dexter when he heard that Himalaya Villa was coming empty. They managed to get it, and moved in as soon as the old tenants moved out."

"Have they both lived in Burnham all their lives? But perhaps you have no knowledge of that, Mrs. Rawley—" Knollis smiled insinuatingly.

Margot Rawley gave him an arch smile.

"You are a terror for details, aren't you, Inspector? Should I really tell you all Lesley's secrets? Actually, she has lived in Burnham all her life. I believe she was born in Exeter Street, which, you will admit, is not the very best of neighbourhoods, is it? Her father was on the railway, and she went to Exeter Street Elementary School. Mind you, she is rather brainy in a standardized sort of way, and she got a scholarship which took her to the King Edward Grammar School although I believe her parents had to scrape together every penny they could spare to make it possible, and I don't think Lesley was quite happy there as you will understand. She was then a pupil teacher at the Far Lane School, and went on to Mill Heights as an uncertificated teacher. She was there until she married Robert Dexter."

Knollis smiled dryly. "So you don't really know much about her early days?"

"No, not really, and after all, it isn't done to poke and pry into the affairs of one's friends!"

Knollis agreed that it was not. "Robert Dexter?" he continued. "Was he a Burnhamian?"

"Oh no, his home was in Leamington, and I believe that his family was really a good one. He was well educated, too, but hadn't a great deal of push—one needs so much of it these days. Well, some men are like that, aren't they? He was with United Chemicals in Birmingham, and I know that the Groots job was offered to him, because Dennis told me so. And then, after he married Lesley, she started encouraging him."

Knollis permitted himself a secret smile at her description. He was by now building a first-rate mental picture of the Dexter *ménage*; a husband who wanted to flow easily through life, and a wife who had ideas of advancement by rush methods.

"He got the promotion after his wife started—er—encouraging him?" he prompted as Margot Rawley waited.

She perked up again, and nodded vigorously. "Oh yes, she encouraged him to study office organization, and industrial psychology, and American packing methods, and all the subjects that would help him with his job. Promotion was almost bound to follow, wasn't it?"

"Almost inevitably," Knollis agreed solemnly.

Margot Rawley twisted her fingers together and wagged her head wisely as she added: "I have no doubt that he would have gone further, much further, if this—this awful thing had not happened to him. It is terrible!"

"Tell me, Mrs. Rawley," said Knollis; "did you ever see people come to the house; dealers—I mean, connected with his hobby of book collecting?"

"Oh yes," Margot Rawley said brightly. "Quite often. Lesley used to storm about it, because they always came on Saturday afternoons or Sundays, and she said there was no privacy in the home. And her husband used to ask them to stay to meals when she wasn't prepared to cater for them. Of course, from his point of view, these were the only times when he could see them, being at work during the week!"

"Definitely a two-sided problem," said Knollis. He rose, and after thanking her, went round to Himalaya Villa.

"Well," asked Ellis quietly. "Think we've learned anything there?"

"Yes, we have," Knollis replied thoughtfully. "If you want to know the worst about a woman, ask her best friend."

As they strolled up the path to the house, a constable emerged from the shadow of the porch, and saluted.

"Evening, sir!"

"Good evening. I'm Inspector Knollis. Everything okay?"

"Yes, sir, I think so. Had to turn away a few sightseers, and the usual handful of reporters, but nothing has happened apart from that."

Knollis paused as he was about to enter the house.

"Do you happen to know the gentleman next door by sight?"

"Mr. Rawley? Yes, I think I would recognize him."

"Right! Then let me know if he returns home while we are here, will you, please? I'd like to see him."

As Knollis closed the door behind them he asked Ellis for the photographs of the crime, and he compared them carefully with the actual scene, Ellis looking over his shoulder with professional interest.

"The stairs," murmured Knollis. "Ten rises and a flat and then four rises to the left on to the landing. I take it, my Ellis, that they were using the front bedroom if Mrs. D's statement is correct. Downstairs; two doors on our left presumably lounge and dining-room. The door straight ahead will be the kitchen, and the small door under the stairs is the cubby-hole for the vacuum-cleaner and the usual domestic odds and ends. All straightforward up to now!"

Ellis tipped his hat forward and scratched the back of his head. "No possibility of an inside concealment job?"

A second later he answered his own question.

"No, there would be no point in it. He was stabbed in the chest as he opened the door. We can wash that out as an absolute impossibility. I wonder what's in here?"

He left Knollis's side and opened the door of the lounge, then switched on the light.

Knollis meanwhile turned to study the telephone that stood on a small table behind the front door.

"Study-lounge," called Ellis. "Bags of books here! Never saw so many. The man must have been a first-class bookworm all right. And he didn't wear glasses!"

"What kind of books?" asked Knollis, as he opened the front door and swung it to and fro to estimate the clearance.

"Poetical stuff," said Ellis in a laconic voice which betrayed his disgust. "Shakespeare, Marlowe, Spencer, Jonson, Sir Philip Sidney always thought he was an adventurous sort of bloke! There's a lot of names I've never even heard of. It looks as if he did some sort of writing in here as well. It's laid out like a writing-room more than a study or library! Looks a bit mixed to me."

Knollis followed him into the room and took stock of it.

A long set of bookshelves ran along the wall on his right hand, and every inch of them was packed solid. There were easy chairs in a dull green tapestry on either side of the modern fireplace, and a reproduction refectory table stood in the centre of the green and blue carpet.

Knollis gave the door a push, so that it closed behind him, and looked along the wall on his left. There was a roll-top desk against the wall that had been covered by the door, and in the bay window stood an occasional table carrying an imitation stone jar which was crammed untidily with beech twigs in full leaf. A dining chair, the only one in the room, was drawn up to the table, its back to the desk, so that the light fell on the left of whoever worked there. Before it, on the table, was a leather-bound blotting-pad, a thick-barrelled fountain-pen, and a sheaf of yellowed papers.

"I wish Russett had done a little more of the spade-work before we came down," Knollis said somewhat irritably. "Who works at this table? Dexter did, I suppose, and yet I haven't more than an idea who does what in this house." His tone suddenly changed as he took up the sheaf of papers. "This is interesting. The stuff underneath looks like black-letter English or perhaps something earlier, but he's been copying it—or perhaps I should say translating it. Listen, Ellis! How appropriate this is! *O Sable Messenger, whose errand knows no mercy!* Almost sounds like the visitor of last night!"

"What the deuce is a sable messenger?" asked Ellis.

"I'm not strong on these matters," replied Knollis, "but I seem to remember it as a euphemism for death. Old Man Death is dressed in black, you know."

"Thought sable was a fur," said Ellis bluntly.

"Well, it is," replied Knollis, "but in poetry and the language of the College of Heralds it is another name for black. It would mean black in this case."

"As you say," said Ellis, "it is appropriate in this case. Hello-o!"

Knollis looked up on hearing the tone of Ellis's exclamation. "What is it? Found something?"

Ellis was fishing amongst a pile of letters which lay on the mantelpiece, and had just taken one from its envelope.

"Read that quotation again, sir!"

Knollis blinked. "Why the excitement?"

"Just found this. An envelope addressed to Robert Dexter, Esquire. There is a scrap of paper inside it, and it just says: *O Sable Messenger, whose errand knows no mercie.* Mercy is spelt with an *i* and an *e*, in the old-fashioned manner."

Knollis was round the table in a split second, reading the note as Ellis held it out to him.

"Keep hold of it now you've handled it, Ellis, and then we won't smother any possible dabs. The same quotation, eh? Very interesting indeed! What's the date on the envelope?"

Ellis turned it over and examined the cancellation stamp. "Twenty-one, October, forty-six. Posted in Burnham."

"Park 'em both safely away, Ellis! We seem to be getting warm. I wonder why the note was sent, and where the manuscript came from?"

He returned to the table, and spent the next fifteen minutes going through Dexter's papers in the hope of finding some link between the two versions of the quotation. He eventually rose, and said a mild swear-word.

"No joy?" murmured Ellis, as he sauntered round the room looking here and there.

"No joy, Ellis. This stuff is not in my repertoire, and I don't know the first thing about it. Still, I know a fellow in town who can help me. He knows everything there is to be known about ancient manuscripts. George Friend, in Jermyn Street. We'll send this thing to him and see what he can tell us about it."

Ellis grinned at him across the room.

"We have a clue, my dear Holmes, even if we don't know what it is about, and so we should be thankful. For what detective can produce a solution unless he has a clue!"

Knollis returned his grin as he replied: "Unfortunately, Watson, we need more than one, and we have to understand the correspondences between clues before we can produce the said solution. I do, not being an intuitional detective. I wish I was one of those rarities, straight out of a detective novel! It would save such a hell of a lot of time. But for now, I think we will concentrate on the desk. I'll do that while you continue to prowl and see what you can unearth in the way of the unusual."

"Y'know," Ellis mused, "it is quite an old-established stunt to insert important documents in and between books, and so I'll wreck the shelves in hope if not in anticipation."

There was silence in the room for a considerable time, a silence broken only by the rustle of paper and the thump of books as Ellis dropped them on the carpet. By the way he was handling them they might have been telephone directories instead of rare editions.

"Damn Caxton, and Gutenburg, and the Chinese," he said at length. "And three more shelves to do!"

Half an hour more elapsed, and then Knollis commented. "That seems to be that, and all I've found, put together, won't solve a murder! Two bank books, bills, statements, invoices, receipts, and letters from book dealers from Land's End to John o' Groats. Any luck yourself, Ellis?"

Ellis flopped down on the carpet with his back against the bookshelves. "Two stiff knees. Luck never comes to me twice in one evening. I wonder if he read this damned lot. I bet his missus cussed if she had to dust them!"

"My bet is that she wasn't allowed to touch them," said Knollis. "Come on, Watson; let's have a look round the rest of the baronial mansion. Switch off as you come out."

He led the way to the dining-room, found the switch, and regarded the room studiously. It was furnished in a clean-lined modern style, with few fripperies, no ornaments, and only two pictures, both surrealist studies before which Ellis stood amazed.

"What do you make of those things?" he demanded. Knollis regarded them with an amused smile, and broke into a laugh as he caught sight of Ellis s expression.

"I don't know anything about them, but I'll make a bet that they are Mrs. Dexter's choice. They don't seem to match with the dead man's taste somehow."

"Look at this effort," said Ellis scornfully. "They call it *Morning Glory*, and it looks like a leg of pork on a messed-up meccano set. And if this other is *Dead Man's Chest*, as it says it is, then I'm Sweeney Todd sitting under a weeping willow tree!"

"And aren't you?" asked Knollis maliciously.

Ellis turned his head to give his chief a reproachful stare. "I'm beginning to wonder."

"Nothing here. Let's take a look upstairs."

"So saying," quoth Ellis, "Sexton Blake and Tinker mounted the apples and pears to take a butcher's hook."

It was very evident to Knollis that Lesley Dexter had been responsible for most of the furnishings at Himalaya Villa. The place reeked of modernity, a grotesque and yet barren modernity that had no trace of comfort, and chilled him.

"I'd hate to live here, Ellis," he muttered. "We aren't exactly Edwardian at my home, but it's more comfy than this cold hole."

"Like a factory, isn't it?" shivered Ellis.

"Got a conscience?" Knollis asked suddenly.

"Well, there's a bit of it left. Why?"

"There's a lady's handbag on the dressing-table. Think our warrant will cover it?"

Ellis nodded. "We aren't usually faddy on a murder case, are we? I don't suppose there'll be anything in it over and above the usual contents of a handbag—two bus tickets, three pencils without points, flapjack, rouge, lipstick, eyebrow stuff, an appointment with a hairdresser last year, and a piece of dog biscuit. My lady's knick-knacks!"

Knollis opened the bag and held it up to the light.

"It seems that you are right in the main, Ellis, as usual. But what's this?"

He drew out a small, crumpled and twisted piece of paper.

"Be-slim-and-healthy pills," suggested Ellis.

Knollis straightened out his find. "Wrong, Ellis! It looks interesting! A note: *B. Okay for this evening. M.* Who are *M.* and *B.*, Ellis?" he asked, and quickly added: "I don't want any remarks about a drug for pneumonia patients, either! See, Robert is also Bob. Mrs. Rawley's name is Margot. Oh-ho! Seems that we might have something here! But if this note is from Mrs. R. to Mr. D., then why should it be found in Mrs. D's. handbag? Tell me that, Ellis!"

"And what was okay for the evening?" added Ellis as he looked over Knollis's shoulder.

"Now I wonder . . ."

Knollis stared at the filament in the electric lamp for a few seconds, and then shook his head. "It won't do, Ellis! Mrs. Dexter couldn't have killed her husband, even if we had a jealousy motive. How would she account to her husband for her visit to Mrs. Rawley's door if she was trying to establish an alibi?"

"If the two women were in it together . . ."

"No, I'm afraid it is a bit too extravagant, Ellis. As far-fetched as my own conjecture. No, it's something deeper than that. I think we'll go back to the station. Collect those papers and bills I left on the table in the lounge, and you'd better put this note in your case as well."

On the way out he asked if Dennis Rawley had returned. The constable said that he had not, but he would inform the station if he did so, and would pass the message on to his relief.

"Good man," said Knollis.

Sir Wilfrid and Inspector Russett were waiting for him when he arrived at the station.

"Got anything?" the Chief Constable asked anxiously.

"Yes, I think we have," Knollis replied slowly. "Quite a lot, probably, although it is difficult to assess it as yet. It strikes me that there is a deuce of a lot of work in front of us. Now look . . ."

He spread his finds on the office table, and Sir Wilfrid and Russett bent over them eagerly, and waited for Knollis to explain.

"This anonymous note, I want it testing for prints—not that I'm in any way optimistic. The papers and the old manuscript, of which I can make little, I am sending to an expert in London. Got a sheet of writing-paper handy? Thanks."

He scribbled a note, and handed it to Russett. "Please have that put in with it. The address is at the foot. Now, for the initialled note, well, I think I'll see Lesley Dexter about it myself."

"Anything else while we're on?"

"Yes, Russett, if you don't mind. Rawley has not yet returned home. Will you contact the Birmingham people and ask them to check on his movements?"

"We don't know where he went to!" protested Russett.

"You can telephone one of Groots' executives, can't you?" Knollis suggested in an acid tone.

Russett tut-tutted, and shook his head sadly. "Never thought of that. I don't seem too bright this evening."

"Then that is about all for to-night. In the morning I'll take Ellis and we'll go to Groots. After that we'd better do the door-to-door in River Close. Somebody else must have heard the fellow! A street of that type of people doesn't retire completely before midnight, I'm sure! And then I shall want to give the towpath and the embankment a good examination. That will be enough for the present programme."

"You've certainly got plenty on your hands," said Sir Wilfrid. "Well, Knollis, they are good hands, and I have the utmost confidence in you. I haven't forgotten the Lomas case, you know!"

"Yes," said Knollis dryly, "drove the murderer into the river, didn't I."

"I examined the rear of the house, you know," Russett interrupted importantly, not liking the turn of the conversation. "There is a service lane running between River Close and Sycamore Close, with a wooden gate in the fence for each house. The Dexter rear gate was locked, which means that if our man had gone that way he would have had to climb over, and that would have resulted in deep prints where he dropped down into the soft soil on the other side. But there were none! I searched every inch of the ground. I worked it out on the spot!"

"And if he had a key to the gate?" murmured Knollis.

Dismay spread over Russett's features. He thoughtfully brushed his moustache with the back of his hand. Then he brought his fist down on the table.

"Hell! I never thought of that!"

He brightened again. "Ha! There is one factor to prove that he couldn't have gone out that way. Daker was down the service lane only a few minutes before Dexter was murdered!"

"That is interesting in itself," replied Knollis, "but it still does not prove that the fellow did not leave by the rear exit after Daker had gone back to Wisden Avenue. He had a point at the kiosk at midnight, hadn't he?"

"Yes," said Russett. "Yes, he had now you come to mention. True enough, he had!"

Sir Wilfrid shook his head. "It's all very complicated, but I've no doubt that we shall find our way through it—when I realize how Knollis and I solved our last case in Burnham. Ah, that *was* a case!"

Later that night, as he was getting into bed, Knollis was informed by telephone that Dennis Rawley had arrived home from Birmingham, looking very worried.

Knollis replaced the receiver, climbed into bed, and dropped off to sleep with a satisfied smile on his face.

CHAPTER IV
THE FRIEND OF THE DECEASED

WHEN KNOLLIS CAME DOWN to breakfast next morning, which was Saturday, he found a constable waiting with a note.

"From Inspector Russett, sir."

Knollis thanked and dismissed him. Ellis walked into the dining-room at that moment, and Knollis passed the note to him. "So Rawley engaged a room at the Granby Hotel for Thursday night, but did not take possession until half-past ten on Friday morning! I think we must see Master Rawley this morning."

So at half-past nine they were shown into the office of the managing director, and he was obviously perturbed by their presence on the premises. He nervously pushed forward the cigarette box, and bade them be seated.

"I was afraid you would be calling on us. Rather undesirable publicity, you know. Doesn't do the firm any good. I don't suppose there is any chance of muzzling the reporters? I mean, of course, as far as Dexter's connection with the firm is concerned."

"I'm afraid not," said Ellis. "To give news to the public is their job in life. If the information was prejudicial to the investigation of the case, then they would oblige, but not otherwise. But I rather fancy that you will find the publicity useful instead of otherwise. That is my experience, anyway." The managing director chewed his cigar. "I hope you are right, Inspector! And yet I would have preferred to be without this kind of publicity. Anyway, I don't suppose you have come to discuss Groots. What can I do for you?"

"Very little, actually," replied Knollis. "I'd just like you to give me permission to disturb the people in Dexter's department for a short while; there are a few questions need answering. And then I would like to see Rawley. I could have seen him at his home, but that would have meant waiting until this afternoon, and time is precious in these cases."

"I hope Rawley is not mixed up in this affair!" the managing director exclaimed in alarm.

"Good heavens, no!" said Knollis. "I understand that he and Dexter were friends to some extent, and I'm hoping that he can tell me something of Dexter's social connections."

"Oh, well that's a relief, anyway. Yes, you may go where you like, Inspector. I only wish I could help you more."

He rang for an office boy, and detailed him to take the Scotland Yard men wherever they wished to go. The boy's eyes gleamed as he replied: "Yes, *sir!*"

"Really Sco'land Yard, sir?" he inquired as he led Knollis and Ellis to the packing department.

"Yes, really Scotland Yard," Knollis smiled. "Although I used to be in Burnham, you know, and I was quite sorry to leave the old city."

"But Sco'land Yard! Gee!"

"Next time you are in London you must come to see us," said Ellis mischievously. "Just ask for Inspector Knollis." Knollis carefully trod on his heel, but it was too late; the lad's eyes were shining as he mentally arranged a trip to the metropolis.

"This is the packing department, sir."

They drew a blank here. No one seemed to know much about Robert Dexter. He came at eight in the morning, lunched in the managers' canteen, and left at five o'clock. Occasionally he absented himself during the mornings for an hour or so, and no one knew where he went or what he did on the excursions. He was a pleasant, even-tempered chief, and that was all there was to him from the employees' point of view. Discreet questioning brought denials that he had any female interests in the works, and with that meagre information they had to be satisfied.

They were next shown into Rawley's office, and here Knollis dismissed their guide, who went reluctantly—probably to tell his chums that he had been assisting the Yard.

Dennis Rawley was thirty-two years of age, tall, handsome in a quiet way, pleasing in manner, and he appeared to be anxious to help in any way he could.

"It's a damn' rotten business," he said when the introductions were over. "I wish I could lay my hands on the swine who did it! *Why* did he do it, anyway?"

"That is what we would like to know," Knollis said softly. "We are hoping that you or someone else may be able to give us a lead. You see, we know nothing whatsoever about it yet."

Rawley plastered down his hair with a shaking hand. He seemed to be ill at ease.

"I knew so little about him myself, although I have known him for a number of years. He was with me at the U.C. plant outside Birmingham, you know. I came on here two years before he did. As a matter of fact I let him know when this job became vacant, and put in a recommendation for him."

"Have you," asked Knollis, "any private ideas about who killed him, or for what reason he was killed? I'm not asking for facts, because I don't suppose for one minute that you can supply them, but even your suspicions may be useful."

Rawley swung round, and seated himself heavily on the corner of his desk, folding his arms.

"I'm hanged if I can get a clear thought on it, Inspector. I always associated murders with people who had pasts, or unsavoury private lives, but this has shaken my ideas. I can't see Bob Dexter filling either of those roles. Do you think that there was a mistake? That the fellow killed him for somebody else?"

"That is always a possibility," admitted Knollis. "Up to now I haven't found the slightest trace of a motive for the killing—and a killing without a motive is ridiculous unless you are dealing with a homicidal maniac, and this case bears all the signs of careful planning. But I have expressed myself too fully, and we are here to ask questions, and not answer them. Now your wife gave a description of the man who called at your house on Thursday night. She has doubtless repeated that description to you . . . ?"

"She most certainly has," said Rawley. "I feel that I should know him the very minute I saw him."

"Good," exclaimed Knollis. "Now, can you recall any acquaintance of Dexter's whose description coincides with your wife's description of the killer? Have you ever seen such a person in Dexter's company, or calling at the house?"

Rawley shook his head. "I'm afraid not, Inspector. You will pardon me for putting it in this way, but I don't spend my spare time peering round the front-room curtains, no matter what the rest of the Close may do!"

Knollis permitted himself a smile.

"The ladies of the Close have that tendency?"

"Tendency?" exclaimed Rawley. "It's an engrained habit. I can't get through my own front gate without seeing the curtains wave half-way up the Close."

He suddenly blinked. "Oh, I see what you mean! Yes, you may get something that way, even if it was midnight."

"So that you would regard it as a dangerous street in which to kill an enemy, Mr. Rawley?"

Rawley offered his cigarettes, which were accepted, and passed round his lighter. "Look, Inspector Knollis! I'm not given to murdering even the people I dislike, but if I did want to do anybody in, then I'd choose any street in the whole of the city of Burnham sooner than River Close. It would be positively asking for detection. Every movement is watched, believe me. It's *There goes that Rawley man again, off to the public house and the billiards!* every time I move out of the house."

"Then you don't like the Close?"

Rawley blew a column of smoke to the ceiling. "I'll be quite frank with you, Inspector; I don't. I only went there to satisfy the social ambitions of my wife. I regard the women as a set of inquisitive and lazy old buzzards—only I don't mean buzzards!"

"I'm grateful for your opinion," Knollis said smoothly. "I think you have made a point which the killer may have missed. Now for another matter; did you have a great deal to do with Bob Dexter outside business hours?"

"Well, actually, I didn't have much to do with him in business hours, Inspector. We are—were—in different departments, as you very likely know. Outside, well yes, we knocked about together to some extent. Most of our social intercourse was conducted in the Key and Clock. We had a drink together most evenings, and played billiards two or three evenings a week."

"In the same place, the Key and Clock?"

"Yes," replied Rawley. "They have a fine billiards-room with four tables. For the rest, we chatted over the fence on gardening, politics, and the weather. I liked Dexter all right, but he wasn't really a pal. Too bookish and earnest. I'm an outdoor man—ath-

letics, tennis, and fishing—or I should say that I was until this
darn job got its hooks into my soul. I have to spend a lot of valuable time these days in swotting the *Financial Times*, and stuff
like that, and keeping pace with foreign markets, but I'm still
not bookish in the way that Bob was."

"Who is likely to step into his position here?" Knollis asked
quietly.

The question seemed to surprise Rawley. "I never thought
about it! Dunno, I'm sure. I doubt if the matter was ever considered before his death, because, well, he seemed all set for a long
life, and he was a valuable man in his department. There's no
doubt about that."

"There is no natural successor in his department? Is that
what you mean, Mr. Rawley?"

Rawley rubbed his chin with his fist. "No-o! I don't see how
there can be. You see, most of the clerical staff are girls—typ-
ists and filing clerks. The packing staff are mixed, I admit, but
there's nobody amongst them qualified to take charge. As a
matter of fact, I heard only this morning that they are in a bit
of a flap down there. Dexter had all the facts and figures at his
finger-tips, and no one else seems to know much about it. Does
that answer your question, Inspector?"

"Admirably," replied Knollis. "Your wife and Mrs. Dexter
were good friends, were they not?"

"Still are, as far as I know," Rawley replied cheerfully. "Candidly, I don't see what they have in common, but then women
are better mixers than men. Don't you find it so?"

"Women are a mystery to me," Knollis stated flatly.

"M'm! Suppose they are to themselves, if it comes to that,"
replied Rawley. "Still, Margot seems quite happy with Lesley
Dexter as a friend, and so I don't ask questions!"

"By the way, Mr. Rawley, I understand that you were away
on Thursday night?"

"Yes, unfortunately," Rawley answered shortly.

"Why unfortunately?"

Rawley shuffled uneasily on the corner of the desk. He looked
up at Knollis with a fixed stare. "Don't you think the fellow might
have sheered off if a man had opened the door to him?"

"Yes, he might," said Knollis. "On the other hand he
might have knifed you! We still don't know why he did it, and
he *may* have been a maniac with a grudge against his sex."

"Good Lord!" exclaimed Rawley.

"Well," said Knollis, "no murderer has a decently balanced mind. That is an axiom."

Rawley studied the toes of his boots silently. "Birmingham, wasn't it, Mr. Rawley?"

Rawley snapped out of his trance.

"Eh? Pardon! Oh yes, Birmingham! I had a conference there, Empire Export Association. We have a monthly conference to consider the markets. Being export manager here, I act as the firm's delegate."

"Do you mind telling me at what time you left Burnham on Thursday, and at what time you returned, Mr. Rawley?" The cigarette slipped from Rawley's fingers. He took time in retrieving it and regaining his seat. "Well, Inspector—"

"You need not take exception to the question," said Knollis, "because in these cases we check on everybody. Once we have disposed of the impossibles we can concentrate on the possibles—those who had the motive if perhaps not either the intention or the opportunity."

Rawley laughed uneasily. "I'm not accustomed to police investigations, and your questions seemed to—well, you know what I mean! Anyway, I left for Birmingham on the ten-thirty yesterday morning, and I—"

"Yesterday morning?" interrupted Knollis. "This is Saturday, remember!"

Rawley smiled and shrugged the objection away. "You've got me tangled up, Inspector. I left Thursday morning, and arrived home last night sometime after eleven."

He fumbled in his pocket and produced a square of thin paper. "The hotel bill, if you are interested."

Knollis scrutinized it. "Granby Hotel. You stayed there on Thursday night?"

"Yes, I had a room there, as you see."

"But you did not use it!" Knollis stated quickly.

Rawley blinked. "I—"

"Why didn't you use it?"

"Spent the night at the Granby!" Rawley protested.

"Where did you spend the night, Mr. Rawley?"

"At the Granby, I tell you!"

"You did not," said Knollis. "The Birmingham C.I.D. checked on you at my request. You did not report to the Granby until half-past ten on Friday morning. Now I ask you again where you spent the night. Don't try to mislead me, because I can find out, you know."

Rawley pushed out his jaw. "I've a perfect right to keep my business to myself, haven't I?"

"Most certainly," Knollis agreed, "providing that you can satisfy me that you were not in River Close—or, for that matter, in Burnham. Apart from that, quite candidly, I have no interest in your movements."

"You mean it won't be made public?" Rawley asked in an astonished manner.

"Why should it be if it has no bearing on the case?"

"Yes," Rawley nodded. "I suppose that is right. But I hope my wife doesn't get interested in the same matter!"

He forced a grin. "You see, I stayed the night at another hotel with a blonde piece of business."

"And the hotel booking? And the need for the bill?"

"For my wife to find in my pocket, of course. Aren't you married, Inspector?"

"Not in the same way as yourself," Knollis replied curtly. Then he asked: "Where did you stay?"

"Oh come, Inspector!"

"I am sorry, but I must insist. It is in your own interests," said Knollis.

"Oh hell! Well, if you must know, it was the Fir Tree."

"And your companion?"

"Sorry, Inspector, but you've had that."

"That's all right," murmured Knollis. "And the conference? That was on Friday?"

"At the Albany Hall."

Knollis and Ellis then left the works, the sergeant reading his notes as they drove along.

"Doesn't seem to be much of a lead there, does there?"

Knollis turned his head and gave a wry smile. "Got any suspicions yet about the man with the black coat?"

Ellis nodded emphatically. "It has been done before, hasn't it? It's nothing new in murder cases."

"A mysterious fellow who is seen once only . . ." Knollis said dreamily.

"And is usually invented by the culprit!"

"Which would indicate Margot Rawley—and yet would seem ridiculous since we can impute no motive to her."

Ellis sniffed. "If it was her, then she got the opportunity all right while her old man was away. Couldn't have arranged it better. Pity we can't get a search warrant for her house."

"Of course," Knollis pointed out, "that initialled note may be a lead, or it may mean nothing. I think we'll spring it on Lesley Dexter, and see how she reacts."

Inspector Russett was waiting for them at the station, and his eyes were shining.

"I've got something here that will interest you, Knollis! Thought it out over breakfast, and went straight to the bank— Dexter's bank."

Knollis affected surprise. "How on earth did you think of that? It's a master-stroke!"

"Quite simply," Russett said with becoming modesty. "I was in my club for an hour last night, and Dayton, the manager of the English and Foreign Bank was trying to pump me about the case. He said he had lost a valuable client."

"Yes," murmured Knollis, while Ellis gave him a nudge.

"So I went down to see him this morning," continued Russett. "He told me that Dexter had a deposit account there, and his balance was four thousand two hundred and twenty-seven pounds."

Knollis blinked. "What! How much?"

Russett smiled complacently. "I thought that would shake you! Four thousand, two hundred and twenty-seven pounds."

Knollis whistled.

"Wrote it down for me, so that there would be no mistake," said Russett. "Here it is."

"You didn't actually see the books?"

"No, he wouldn't come clean with them as I was lacking the proper authority."

Knollis turned to Ellis. "Get Groots on the 'phone and ask the amount of Dexter's salary, please."

Three minutes later Ellis said: "Six-ten a week."

"Ask how long that had been operative."

"A level six months," Ellis eventually reported. "He was getting five-ten up to then, and that dated from his appointment as departmental manager."

"Come on," said Knollis, crossing to the door.

"Where are you going?" called Russett.

"Frogmore Street. I'll meet you in River Close in about half an hour. Meanwhile, will you get somebody working on that Sable Messenger note?"

"Have done," replied Russett. "Two prints on it, one belonging to Ellis, and one to the dead man. The sergeant is round at the post office with the envelope at this moment."

"Thanks," said Knollis, as he walked out. And to Ellis he ventured the opinion that Inspector Russett seemed to be getting into his stride at last. "Or perhaps it is our stride."

He fairly leapt from the car when he drew up before the house in Frogmore Street, and he was shown in immediately.

Lesley Dexter was showing more signs of composure, although Knollis knew from experience that the reaction was yet to come, and it might be weeks before the shock had its full effect. At any rate, she was calm now, and greeted him as a normal visitor.

"Sorry to bother you again so soon," Knollis said soothingly, "but there are one or two minor points I would like you to clear up for me."

"Anything I can do, Inspector . . ."

Knollis achieved an expression of embarrassment. "I do sincerely hope that you won't resent this question, Mrs. Dexter! Your husband's finances—perhaps you would not mind giving me some information on them."

She drew down the corners of her mouth in a deprecatory gesture. "They were not too good, Inspector. He had a paltry three hundred pounds in the Northern and Lancashire. You will find the pass-book in the desk in the lounge if you should require it. My book is there, too, with a mere hundred in the same bank."

"Then he did no business with the English and Foreign?"

She seemed to be surprised at his question, and wrinkled her finely-plucked eyebrows. "Oh dear no! Why do you ask that, Inspector Knollis?"

"Just a slight misunderstanding, Mrs. Dexter. Now would you mind telling me what insurances you and your husband had?"

"Insurances? None at all, Inspector. Robert did not believe in them. I had a tiny endowment policy, but it matured about five years ago, and I spent the money."

"That settles those points satisfactorily," said Knollis. He handled his hat as if about to leave, and then, quite casually, he said: "By the way, Mrs. Dexter, I'm afraid that you will be getting a poor opinion of detectives!"

Lesley Dexter laughed uncertainly. "Oh, and why?" Knollis coughed behind his hand, and replied: "Well, there was a lady's handbag in the front bedroom, and I'm afraid I took the liberty of examining the contents . . ." She shook her head. "That doesn't matter, Inspector! Nothing matters any more now that Robert has gone."

"But I found a rather mysterious screwed-up note."

Lesley Dexter's expression answered the question that was in Knollis's mind. "You mean that you don't know anything about it, Mrs. Dexter?"

"I certainly do not, Inspector. In fact, I don't know how it got there, because I cleaned out the bag on Thursday afternoon, and I know there was no note in it then. You don't mean a treasury note by any chance? But in any case, all my money was in my purse, and that was downstairs."

"It was a written note," explained Knollis, "addressed to someone called *B.*—the initial *B.*"

"You must be mistaken, Inspector," she replied. "I turned the bag inside out and ran the hose of the vacuum cleaner over it, because I had spilt my powder in it. There simply couldn't have been a note in it, because no one but me had been upstairs. I don't understand!"

Knollis produced the note from his wallet, and handed it to her.

"But this is Margot's writing . . . !" she exclaimed. "*B.* is surely my husband, and *M. . . .*"

"Yes," Knollis prompted gently.

"I don't understand, Inspector!"

She sank on to the edge of a chair. "You are sure you found this in *my* bag!"

"A bead bag with a zigzag design, Mrs. Dexter. It was lying on the dressing-table in your bedroom."

She nodded slowly. "Yes, that is the one. I cleaned it out on Thursday afternoon, and I am certain that this note was not in the bag when I tipped out the contents, nor did I put it in afterwards."

Knollis and Ellis exchanged glances. Lesley Dexter intercepted them.

"Inspector!"

"Yes, Mrs. Dexter?"

"There would be no point in denying it, would there? I mean, I have nothing to lose or gain by denying it if I had actually put it there?"

"I agree with you, Mrs. Dexter. You misunderstood my unspoken message to Sergeant Ellis. I was wondering who could have planted it there for you to find. It certainly is queer."

Lesley Dexter stared into the fire, and Knollis made no attempt to disturb her thoughts. At last she looked up with wide, uncomprehending eyes.

"Inspector Knollis!"

"M'm?"

"There's something more than queer about this. The note, this note, implies that Margot—Mrs. Rawley—was trying to arrange a meeting with my husband!"

"Does it, Mrs. Dexter?" Knollis murmured noncommittally.

There was a look of childlike innocence in her face as she stared at him. "My husband hated her! Hated her like poison, Inspector!"

"Now for what reason would that be, Mrs. Dexter?"

"He said she was a—a bitch!"

"He did! Now I wonder why? Can you suggest any reason? Had Mrs. Rawley ever made—shall we say *advances* to him?"

Lesley considered the point, and then looked at Knollis with a vagueness that suggested that she was puzzled about the whole of life. "I've often wondered, Inspector!"

"But come, Mrs. Dexter, I thought she was your best friend? Surely you don't suspect her!"

She shuddered. "I'm sorry if this sounds horribly hypocritical—and I know that a man couldn't bring himself to do such a thing—but I was watching her, to see if she had designs on Bob. And I hate her! I hate her! I truly do hate her!"

She buried her face in her hands.

Knollis waited, grimacing to Ellis, and all his distaste of his profession—this side of it—was in that gesture.

Lesley lowered her hands eventually, and stared dully in front of her.

"So you kept an eye on her," said Knollis, finding nothing more important or helpful to say.

"She—she pretended to be interested in Bob's collection, but she wasn't! I know she wasn't. She wanted him, and I wouldn't let her have him. She hates me as much as I hate her."

"Mrs. Dexter!" said Knollis softly.

"Ye-es?"

"Will you do something, something that may help us to find your husband's killer and bring him to justice?"

"I've told you that I will do anything!"

"So you have," Knollis murmured. "I want you to keep up your pretence of friendship for Mrs. Rawley just a little longer. You will do that?"

"And—and after?"

Knollis gave a grim smile. "After that, as far as we are concerned, you can either forgive her, or let slip the dogs of war."

There was no doubting which choice she would make as she answered: "Very well, Inspector."

"Good man," said Knollis, without realizing his incongruity.

And then an idea seemed to occur to her, for suddenly she said: "Inspector Knollis!"

"Yes, Mrs. Dexter?"

"You don't think that Margot Rawley—"

"I can't think that anybody did it, not at the moment," replied Knollis. "It is too early to frame a theory. We are only collecting facts."

"If I thought that Margot Rawley had killed Bob I would—"

"Mrs. Dexter!" said Knollis sharply.

"I'm sorry," she said wearily.

"One more point! You are still certain that Margot Rawley directed the man in the black coat to your house?"

"Well," she said flatly, "I heard her tell him that it was next door. Those were the actual words I heard: 'It is next door.'"

"And you are also satisfied that your husband swore as he opened the door!"

"He said 'Oh hell!'"

"He was in the habit of swearing?"

Lesley Dexter gave a feeble smile. "He could swear very heartily on occasion, Inspector. I used to worry in case the neighbours heard him."

"But only in moments of stress?"

"Oh yes, he was not an habitual swearer. It was just when he was annoyed, and then he used to forget himself—and my presence. Poor Bob!"

"One more question, and we will go," said Knollis. "Is there an amateur dramatic society connected with the Close? I know that there is the Burnham one, of course."

Lesley Dexter stared. "Why yes, the Westford Bridge Amateurs. They started about three years ago. Quite a few residents of the Close are members. Why do you ask?"

"Who is the secretary?"

"Mrs. Hendrick Stanley. She lives in Dene Close."

Outside in the car, Ellis said: "Well?"

And Knollis said: "Hell!"

Chapter V
THE RIVER AND THE ROPE

KNOLLIS, STANDING in the bay window of the lounge with Russett, watched Mrs. Margot Rawley sally forth on a shopping expedition. She was dressed in a fine-striped black costume, a shirt-blouse with a tie, and flat-heeled shoes.

"I don't get it," he murmured to Russett. "When I called on her last night she was trying to look as seductively feminine as she could—and now look at her, aping men!"

"Complex type," said Russett cryptically. "Shouldn't wonder if she has funny ideas."

Ellis came in from the hall. "I've rung through to the station, and asked them to get Birmingham to check Rawley's night out with the blonde at the Fir Tree."

"Good man," said Knollis absently, as he watched Margot Rawley turn the corner into Wisden Avenue. The stop for the corporation bus services was just beyond the telephone kiosk.

"So Mrs. Dexter didn't know about the large-sized bank account?" said Russett with immense satisfaction.

"Mrs. Dexter?" said Knollis, waking from his reverie. "Oh no, apparently not, Russett, and I am inclined to believe that she really didn't know anything about it."

"Double life of murdered husband—the old Sunday newspaper headline! Well, it's a change from the Waaf-found-unconscious-under-hedge one we've had for so long. What was Dexter's racket, I wonder?"

"I'm seriously beginning to wonder whether he had one."

"Oh come, Knollis!" Russett protested. "Dayton should know, shouldn't he?"

"Dayton should know about his account," corrected Knollis, "but he can hardly profess to know that Dexter had a racket! Ask him for a sample signature and a description of Dexter next time you go that way."

"You surely don't suspect an impersonation, do you?" asked Russett with uplifted eyebrows. "How would it work out, anyway?"

"Your guess is as good as mine," said Knollis. "It has been done before, you know."

He turned to the desk and found the two pass-books. "Lesley Dexter says that these contain all the cash they had in the world, a mere four hundred pounds between them. Not a great deal really for a fellow earning six-ten a week."

"Probably bought the house," suggested Russett.

"There is a rent-book in the desk," said Knollis. "Monthly tenancy at five pounds a month. No, it didn't go there. And yet I suppose it is about the average in the way of savings. It represents slightly less than a year's income. H'm!"

"What did these books cost him?" asked Russett.

Knollis fingered his ear. "You can find that out by going through the bills I took down to the office last night. As far as I can make out, he spent money on them and didn't do any selling. The man was so normal that he's a mystery—normal except for that deposit account."

He looked towards Ellis. "They have a maid next door?"

"Tricky bit of stuff," Ellis replied. "Tries to look Frenchified, and manages it until she opens her mouth, and then—oh my Gawd! Save me from it!"

"Doesn't take you long to find out those kind of things, does it?" said Knollis. "Anyway, I'd like you to go round and beg a sheet of writing-paper from her, and put it safely away. We may need it for comparison tests."

Russett was fidgeting round the room. He came to a halt and asked: "What about starting to grill the Close, Knollis?"

"Can do, replied Knollis. "Will you mind starting without me? I'd like to take a look at the towpath first, and then Ellis and I will join you. You have a side-kick?"

"Rogers will be along in a few minutes."

"Something just struck me as curious," said Knollis, glancing round the room. "I haven't seen a photograph of either Dexter or his wife in the house. Unusual, isn't it?"

"The Press managed to get one from somewhere," replied Russett. "I was talking to Dalby, of the *Courier*, on the way down, and he said he's had trouble, but finally got one taken at a works dance last autumn. He said it was a foul one that had been taken by flashlight, but it was a photograph for all his purposes were concerned."

"Oh well, I don't suppose the absence signifies," said Knollis. He turned as Ellis re-entered the room. "Made it?"

Ellis was wearing a large grin. "Didn't take long. Told her that I wanted to drop a note to my girl, and in the same breath asked her what she was doing to-night."

"And what was she doing tonight?"

"Nothing."

"And what *is* she doing tonight?"

"Still nothing," said Ellis. "I've got my reputation to think about, haven't I?"

"What reputation?" asked Knollis. Then he caught his lieutenant by the arm. "Come on, Watson; we have some Sherlocking to do, and it's turned eleven o'clock now."

As Russett and Ellis followed him outside he nodded his head towards the last house in the Close.

"Who lives there, Russett? Nobody seems to have mentioned it and its tenants up to now."

Russett waved his hand in a lordly manner. "I saw to that the morning after the do—yesterday morning. They were at a dance until half-past three."

"What dance?" Knollis asked innocently.

Russett scowled, and looked suspiciously at Knollis.

"How the hell do I know?"

"Didn't you ask them?"

Russett gave an uneasy smile. "Hell no, I didn't. Sorry, Knollis. The affair caught me bending, I'm afraid. You seem to forget that I don't get the amount of practice that you do—"

He broke off, blinked, and added: "Damned if that isn't what Bunny said, too!"

Knollis grinned at him. "You and Little Wilfrid had a few words over the calling-in of the Yard?"

"Well, how would you feel?" Russett demanded truculently.

Knollis laid a comforting hand on his shoulder. "Exactly as you do, but you still have a chance to shine, haven't you?"

"Huh? What do you mean?"

"Can't you see the newspaper reports? *Scotland Yard, with the invaluable assistance of Inspector George Russett, head of the Burnham Criminal Investigation Department . . .*"

A slow smile broke over Russett's face. "By jove, Knollis you're right! I'll show you! I'll start at the top end of the Close, and I'll get all the information we want if I have to grill 'em until they are brown on both sides!"

He hurried up the street. Ellis chuckled.

"Now what is amusing you, Watson?"

"They call it flannel these days," said Ellis, "but they used to call it soft soap when I was a lad. Cor, doesn't he suck it in!"

"Don't be vulgar," said Knollis reprovingly. "He only needs encouragement, and believe me when I say from my own experience that there isn't much of it going when you are working under Wilfrid the Bunny!"

"What was behind your remark about this last house?" Knollis's smile faded, and his eyes narrowed to their usual slit-like appearance. "I was thinking, Ellis!"

"You always are, but what was this particular batch in aid of? Got a new idea?"

"I was thinking," Knollis repeated. "If the house next door was unoccupied, and the killer knew that, then it would be quite possible for him to hide in the porch until the tumult and the shouting had died down."

"But how would he know they were out?"

"He could sound the drum in advance, surely!"

"Bit risky," said Ellis, after considering the point. "He knocked at one door as it was, and he surely didn't want the whole street to know that he was around."

"That," Knollis replied, "is the weak spot, and a justifiable argument. Trust you to find it!"

"You make 'em; I break 'em," said Ellis.

"Let's have a look at the palings, shall we?" said Knollis. "Hello, there's a gate! Very neat, too; looks like a section of the fence. Fastened by a loop of wire. Quite interesting, I must say."

He untwisted the strands of wire, and the gate swung outwards, towards the river. He slid down the twelve-feet deep embankment and regarded the scene critically.

"Quite pleasant down here," said Ellis as he joined him.

"Not at all bad," Knollis murmured. "I wouldn't mind spending a few afternoons here in the summer months. I used to patronize the lower reaches, beyond the bridge, in my Burnham days. Plenty of willows for shade. Not that they are lacking on the opposite bank from here. Seems to be a backwater, doesn't there?"

For the next few minutes he did not speak, but seemed to be watching the surface of the water. Then he dipped into his pocket and brought out a twenty-cigarette carton. "Have a smoke, Ellis?"

Ellis peered into the carton. "You've only two left. Have one of mine."

"I want to use the carton," Knollis replied with a grim smile. "I assure you that it isn't sheer generosity on my part."

"In that case," said Ellis, and took one. Knollis took the other, and they lit up.

"Watch this," said Knollis. He threw the empty carton into the river.

"Awful untidy habit," commented Ellis, and he blew a whiff of smoke down his nostrils.

"It isn't a habit, my lad. It's an experiment. Just watch it and see what happens."

"What will happen?" inquired Ellis. "If anything?"

Knollis shrugged his shoulders. "I don t quite know, but I'll be interested to see if anything does. And I think it will! Look, Ellis!"

The carton drifted lazily into midstream, moving at an oblique angle. Then it swerved, turning at right-angles to the near bank, and was quickly swept to the opposite bank, where an eddy caught it and whirled it into a small backwater sheltered by pollard willows.

"That was quick work," commented Ellis. "It must be every bit of a hundred and fifty yards across."

"I rather expected a cross-current when I noticed the sweep in the opposite bank," Knollis replied, pointing to the willows, "but certainly not such a swift journey as the carton made."

"Looks as if there is a skiff there, with its nose in the bank," said Ellis quietly.

Knollis nodded. "Slip back to the villa and ask River Station to send a launch upstream to meet us here."

Ellis was away but a few minutes, and on his return he joined Knollis in the examination of the river bank. Bending over from the towpath, he suddenly exclaimed: "There's a stake rammed into the bank here. Looks like a newish one too."

Knollis got down on his knees and leaned over.

"Newish all right," he remarked. "It's in a handy position, too. This is our first piece of luck!"

He got to his feet and stared silently at the water. One mental feat which he never attempted was jumping from a fact to a conclusion, and while he had privately conceived the idea that the murderer might have made his getaway via the river, he would have been the first to admit that it was hardly an original conception. It was merely one of a number of possibilities or alternatives, and at the moment there were no facts to support the theory other than the casual manner in which an empty cigarette packet had meandered across the main flow of the river, and the presence of a wooden stake in the river bank.

The stake might never have been noticed but for Ellis's training in observation, for the bank shelved under at this point, and there was the usual amount of herbage to be found in such places, even though it was thinning in the course of the normal autumnal change.

"How could anyone not having a legitimate use for such a stake manage to hammer it in without drawing unwanted attentions?" asked Knollis, the inevitable query mark rising in his mind.

Ellis squatted on his haunches and thought about it.

"Well," he said at last, "as I see it, there are two possibilities. One is that the killer is somebody who has a boat on the river, lives in the Close, and a legitimate right to leave a boat tied up here."

"In which case," murmured Knollis, "why should he try to get away from the Close after doing the killing?"

"Quite right, and all in order," said Ellis. "The second possibility is that if he wasn't actually interested in boating he would have to pretend to be—and well in advance of the actual commission of the crime—in order to prepare for it. How's that?"

"It boils down to the same thing, surely!"

Ellis stared ruefully at the greyish water. "M'm! I suppose it does! You got any ideas?"

Knollis started to climb the embankment to River Close, and once he had gained the street level he paid a great deal of attention to the palings, particularly where they formed a right-angle with the front fence of the last house.

"Ellis," he said slowly; "get my bag from the car."

"Tweezers and an envelope," he said when Ellis put the bag beside him.

"What have we got?"

"Hairs of rope. Look, they are caught in the raw edges of this corner rail. And here, at the foot, are more. See them in the grass? That means that a rope has been run off, or round, this rail. Judging by the amount of hairs I should say there has been considerable chafing. Now seal this lot, and mark them *Paling*. I'll collect the ones in the grass in another envelope. Now mark that one."

"Which indicates what?" asked Ellis.

"The steel inch-tape. Hang on to the end, and pass the container through the palings. I'll take it from you at the other side."

He went through the gate, walked goat-wise on the inside of the fence, and took the container. Then he allowed himself to slide down the embankment, reeling out the tape as he went. Once having gained the towpath he walked to the spot immediately above the stake, and there looked at the tape.

"Okay, Ellis. You can let go the end and come down here."

Ellis quickly followed him to the towpath. "How did it work out?"

"Twenty-seven feet six inches. Twice that is fifty-five feet, and so we'll ask the launch to drag for a sixty feet manilla rope."

"I see the idea," said Ellis, "but it was a risky proceeding, surely! I can't imagine the towpath being unfrequented all night, and there would be a danger of somebody walking into it in the darkness and creating a row—a row that might have upset the whole plan."

"And the alternative to that is—" began Knollis.

"Is what?"

"Obviously some means of keeping it flat to the bank, and then flat to the ground, which indicates a ring or bracket at the resulting angle in the rope. Let's prowl."

Twenty minutes later Knollis plunged his hand under a clump of dying nettle, and gave a quiet smile. "All right Ellis, my lad. Here it is!"

Ellis stared. "I'd have given a whoop like an Indian brave if I'd found it, and you merely smile!"

"It's a picket-ring. Looks like one of those corkscrew things you twist into the ground. Well, it's in the right spot, and it would keep a rope flat to the ground as we assume it must have been— and it means adding a few more feet to our estimate of the rope to be found. You see how it would be worked by our man?"

"Trying to insult my intelligence?" asked Ellis.

"It's impossible," replied Knollis. "Do I hear the launch in the distance?"

"You do. It's just coming under the bridge. Where do we go from here? Across to the boat under the willows?"

"Yes, but first I want you to trip back to the villa and 'phone headquarters. Ask them to send down a photographer—we may as well finish this area while we are here."

Ellis got back as the launch drew into the bank. While his crew of one tied up, the sergeant, a youngish man with a weather-beaten face, leaped to the bank and saluted.

"Sergeant Devonport, sir. River patrol."

"I've a few jobs of work for you," said Knollis. "First, I want you to take us across to the little backwater, the one with the screen of willows."

They moved smoothly across to the farther bank, and Knollis jumped ashore, Ellis following with the murder bag. For the next quarter of an hour they examined the skiff thoroughly, and Knollis went to work with his tweezers and envelopes in the stern.

"Sergeant Devonport!"

The sergeant joined him.

"You understand these craft?"

"Yes, sir, quite well. It's my hobby as well as my job."

"There is a screw-eye and a ring here in my stern-post—if that is what it is called. Is it a normal fitment?"

The sergeant shook his head decisively. "It certainly is not, sir. I can't see any need for it, either."

"I thought that would be your answer," said Knollis. He pushed his hat to the back of his head. "See the hairs of rope again, Ellis?"

"Can't miss 'em," Ellis replied shortly.

"Then you see the inference?"

"Of course."

Knollis turned to the sergeant. "All right; we'll have the skiff towed back, if you don't mind."

The photographer was waiting for them, having come by car, and Knollis proceeded to give him and the river-patrol sergeant their instructions.

"I want you to pull out about ten yards from the bank, and get a shot which includes the towpath and the embankment, the picket-ring affair, and that paling at the extreme left from here. That done, I want close-ups of the stake, the picket-ring, and that paling. Then photograph the stern of the boat, both from inside and outside, and after that about six shots of the backwater from different angles."

"I've got that, sir," said the photographer.

"Then I have another job for you to do now if you have a suitable lens, and I am staying to watch because it is purely an experiment. I want you to set up your camera—but wait a minute, and I'll demonstrate. Give me your cigarette packet, Ellis."

Ellis tipped his cigarettes into his pocket and handed over the carton, which Knollis dropped into the river.

"Now watch," he said, "and see what happens."

The five men silently watched it as it zigzagged its way to the opposite bank.

"Queer current there," muttered the sergeant. "You expect the boat to take the same course, sir?"

"My theory is sunk if it doesn't," Knollis said quietly.

"And you want me to photograph it?" asked the photographer.

"Yes, at two-minute intervals, and each from the same position. Got enough plates?"

"Plenty, sir."

In due course, when the photographer gave the word the skiff was untied. It followed the same track as the cartons, coming to rest nose first in the reeded banks of the backwater.

"Nifty!" commented the sergeant.

"Right," said Knollis. "Now fetch it back and get the other photos for me. When you have finished I want you to remove the screw-eye and the ring from the boat; also the stake, picket-ring, and the paling, and have them sent to headquarters."

"And the boat, sir?"

"Take that down to River Station for the time being."

"Very good, sir."

"Now," said Knollis, as he and Ellis returned to the street level, "do you see how the thing was worked?"

"Ye-es, I think so."

"One end of the rope is passed through the ring in the stern. Both ends are then brought together, passed through the picket-ring, and taken up the embankment. They are then tied to the chestnut paling. To release the boat without going through the gate and down the embankment, all you do is untie the rope and pull one end until the other has passed through the ring in the stern."

"But that wouldn't assist a getaway," protested Ellis.

Knollis smiled. "I know it wouldn't!"

"Then what on earth . . . ?"

"It might make a sharp-eyed but careless detective think that somebody *had* made a getaway by drifting across the river. We weren't supposed to find either the hairs of rope or the ring in the towpath, nor, if it comes to that, the screw-eye in the stern of the boat."

"Pretty clever," Ellis nodded. "What does it indicate to you?"

"Isn't it obvious, my Ellis? That somebody who lives in the Close killed Robert Dexter, and tried to make it look as if it was somebody who did not live in the Close! It was a clever red herring—or would have been if we had fallen for it."

Ellis scratched his ear. "But look! If it was somebody who lives in the Close, then surely Mrs. Rawley would have recognized him!"

"There's an answer to that," said Knollis. "Mind you, this is only conjecture, and wild conjecture at that, but if our man was made up so that his general appearance was altered, then he might have got away with it."

"Damned risky!" was Ellis's only comment.

"Not really. Remember that the only light was from the yellowish hall lamp, and that she only saw him for a few brief seconds—probably no more than a minute. His collar was up and his hat was down. How much would she see of him? His clothes, too, were unusual ones for him. Listen, Ellis. Here is an extreme example. Suppose that our killer is normally seen as a fresh-complexioned fellow who wears a bowler hat and a herring-bone tweed coat. Then suppose that he changes into this long black coat and trilby, and wipes his face over with—well, even his wife's face powder, which would temporarily eradicate any wrinkles. See what I mean? In the short time in which she sees him, she is going to get an impression, one that will befuddle her if she has to attend an identification parade."

"M'm!" Ellis grunted doubtfully. "I suppose it is possible, and it has been done before. That Roxby case at Liverpool is a case in point. All that he needs is a decent alibi, provided by perjury, and he is comparatively safe. Yes, it could be done."

Then he grimaced. "What about the knife?"

"How far is it from the gate of the villa to the river?"

Ellis considered the front gardens of the two villas.

"Well, we'll say each house had a forty-foot frontage. That makes eighty feet, plus the width of the embankment and the towpath. About a hundred and ten feet."

"Think you could throw a carving-knife forty yards?"

"Yes, certainly. Whirl it like a boomerang, and it would go a hell of a distance."

"Then slip down to the towpath and ask the sergeant to organize dragging operations for the rope and the carving-knife. They should find the rope if nothing more."

"Sixty to seventy feet, eh?"

"That's it, Ellis. I'm not particular to a few feet."

On Ellis's return they went into the villa, and Knollis looked thoughtfully round the lounge.

"I wonder where he hid the English and Foreign pass-book?"

"I don't see that it can be in the house," said Ellis, "because we've turned the place upside-down already."

"I think we must pay a visit to Inspector Russett's, Mr. Dayton," said Knollis. "I'd like to know who signed all the cheques that he must have paid in. Oh, damn Russett! He never finishes a job properly."

He stared at the bookshelves. "I wish I knew something about books. The key to the case must lie amongst them somewhere. I think I'll telephone George Friend this evening. Those papers and the manuscript were sent to him?"

Ellis nodded. "They went by rail, to be picked up by messenger at the other end. Russett had them photographed before he let them go."

"Well, that's one mark in his favour, but, Ellis, *Inspector* Russett, if you please!"

"Inspector Russett it is," said Ellis with mock gravity. He then added: "That's the worst of only being a sergeant!"

"What is?" Knollis murmured absently.

"Why, never eating when a case is on the books. According to my watch it's now one o'clock."

"Just nicely in time for lunch. All right, my hungry friend, we'll go back to the hotel and eat. Now you mention it, I'm beginning to feel a wee bit peckish myself. Good Lord, I've just remembered! Russett is still grilling the Close!"

"Inspector Russett?" Ellis asked innocently.

Knollis gave him a look, and then grinned.

They met Russett outside, also on the trail of lunch.

"How's the game?" asked Knollis.

Russett laid a hand across his forehead. "Don't ask me! All the talkative ones know nothing, and I can't make out whether the oysters know anything or not. I shall relish your help this afternoon. How have you done this morning?"

"Get in the car," said Knollis. "The sergeants can take the other, and I'll tell you on the way back."

Russett listened eagerly as Knollis detailed his discoveries without revealing his ideas.

"I know who owns the boat!" exclaimed Russett.

"Who?"

"George Courtney-Harborough at number thirty-five, although his wife insists that it is Sandringham House—they don't like numbers in the Close! Anyway, he potters in it on Saturday afternoons and Sundays. Leaves it tied to the bank, and keeps the oars in the garage at the side of the house."

"I must have a talk with Mr. Courtney-Harborough," said Knollis.

CHAPTER VI
THE RESIDENTS OF THE CLOSE

MR. GEORGE COURTNEY-HARBOROUGH had not intended spending his afternoon on the river, but he had hoped for an afternoon's golf on the Sandy Moor course. In some ways he regretted the loss of it, but on the other hand it was not every afternoon in the year that one was consulted by a Scotland Yard detective, and an inspector to boot. So he swallowed his disappointment and washed it down with two fingers of whisky, which, together with cigarettes, he also offered to Knollis and Sergeant Ellis.

"Beastly sort of job," he commented as he measured the whisky into each of three glasses. "I rather liked Dexter. Not quite out of the top drawer, perhaps—and I do hope that doesn't sound snobbish—but nevertheless I liked him. Quiet, truthful sort of a bloke. Wouldn't be an earthly bit of use as a golfer or angler, because he couldn't tell a whopper if he tried, not even for the fun of it. Decent sort, was Dexter. Pity he had to go this way."

"You seem to have taken to him," Knollis said dryly.

Mr. Courtney-Harborough nodded thoughtfully. "Yes, yes! Quite liked him. When one reaches the mature age of fifty-five one can see a little deeper into people, you know! One's hair doesn't whiten as a result of not using the brain! Yes, a decent bloke."

"And his wife?"

Knollis looked the picture of earnest attention as he asked the question.

Mr. Courtney-Harborough chafed in his seat. "Bah! I'd like to take her over my knee!"

"Which way up?" interposed Ellis, and was immediately silenced by a glance from Knollis.

"Face down, with a hair-brush in my hand," replied Mr. Courtney-Harborough. "She's a little fool! Quite a nice kid she was when they first came down the Close, and then she caught it like the rest of them. Tried to live up to a standard she knew nothing about, and like the rest of 'em she just made a mess of it. My wife was always pretty decent—tried to make her feel at ease, y'know."

He pulled at his ear, and smiled wryly.

"Now I come to think about it I dunno that she was ever anything else but at her ease. Must have a tough hide! Just carried on as if she had lived in our set all her life—as if she was bred and born in it, y'know. Never realized when she made a *faux pas*, or if she did she just sailed gracefully on as if it didn't matter. But you know the type well enough, getting around as you do!"

Knollis heaved a patient sigh. "Yes, but it was about your boat that I came to see you."

"My skiff? It's down on the river, just below here."

"I'm afraid it isn't," Knollis murmured gently. "I've had to commandeer it for the time being. It is down at River Station."

Mr. Courtney-Harborough sat bolt upright, and stared. "Good Lord, you haven't!" he exclaimed, and had to recourse to the decanter. "What on earth for?" he asked when the two fingers had disappeared.

"All I can tell you, without going into details, is that use was made of it by Dexter's killer," replied Knollis.

"Good Lord! It wasn't!"

"I'm afraid it was," said Knollis.

Mr. Courtney-Harborough shook his head sadly. "Well, I'll be damned! Just shows, y'know! Never know from one minute to the next, do you? I'd have had it taken to the club boathouse if I'd suspected anything like that. Well!"

"How long have you had it, sir?" queried Knollis.

"Oh-h, about six months. Yes, I took delivery of her in time for Easter—fancied the idea of a pull up the river during the holidays, y'know."

"How did you tie-up to the bank?"

"Obvious," said Mr. Courtney-Harborough. "Knocked in a stake. Two of them, as a matter of fact. Some fool got playing about with the first one I put in, and the whole thing drifted down-river—skiff, painter, and stake."

"And you had to fetch it from below the bridge, I suppose?" Knollis asked innocently.

Mr. Courtney-Harborough frowned. "As a matter of fact, no! It worked its way across the current to a backwater. Very queer that, and most intriguing."

Knollis gave a sigh of relief.

"Can you explain that?" he asked.

"I made inquiries about it," said Mr. Courtney-Harborough. "I have a friend who is a geologist. It seems that there is a sort of deep cleft in the bed—split-strata or something he called it—and it causes a fairish cross-current. Damn' queer, all the same. Anyway, I had to walk round and fetch it back. After that I hammered a six-foot stake into the bank—and I'll warrant they don't pull that out!"

"You never used a corkscrew picket?" Knollis asked.

Mr. Courtney-Harborough stared his surprise at the question. "What is it? Never heard of 'em. I used a single wooden stake. Nothing more is necessary, y'know!"

Knollis stubbed his cigarette in the tray, and looked across at his host. "Tell me, sir; what was the first thing you knew or heard about Dexter's death?"

"Well now, let me see. . . . I heard Mrs. D. scream—and who didn't! But before that I think I heard someone knocking on a door. I can't say whether it was Dexter's or not, because I was trying to get to sleep, y'see, and I didn't know a murder was booked for the night, or I'd have been out like a jiffy. But then, as I say, you never know from one minute to the next, do you?"

"So that you never heard the killer talking to Mrs. Rawley a few minutes before Dexter was killed?" asked Knollis.

Courtney-Harborough shook his head, and refilled his own glass. "Not a blessed sound of it. Pity he didn't swipe her instead of poor Dexter."

"You don't like Mrs. Rawley?" Knollis ventured.

"Well, I've nothing against her, really, y'know! It's just that I don't like masculine women—and she's a better man than a good many fellows I know. No, I can't say that I've anything against her, except that I think Rawley is far too good for her. But then that's no exception in this Close! Most of the women are bloody fools, and they get under my skin. I like a natural woman, a feminine woman, and most of 'em round here are poseuses. Bah!"

Knollis excused himself. He had got what he wanted in the way of information, and it was evident that he was not likely to get more. He and Ellis made their departure, and waited in the Close until Russett emerged from his latest interview.

"Where haven't you worked, Russett?"

"Top twelve houses on the right side going up. Thank God that you are lending a hand, because I'm sick of this game. Nobody knows anything, and they all try to interview me, instead of answering my questions."

"The human race is notoriously and proverbially curious, Russett. You just have to keep a tight hold on the reins and make them go your way," said Knollis.

Russett nodded despondently. "Now tell me something I don't know. You aren't a bit original, Knollis! Oh well, let's get going again."

"Wait a minute," said Knollis. "What does Courtney-Harborough do for a living, if any? Is he independent?"

"Must be," answered Russett. "Spends all his time on the golf course, or in the Oak Room at the Green Man. He's a member of the city's two posh clubs, and he and his wife are leading lights in the Westford Bridge Amateur Dramatic Society. Taking it all round, I don't think he has too bad a time of it! Wish I was in his shoes, anyway."

Russett turned away, but Knollis caught his arm, and then hurriedly sought his notebook and consulted it. "Mrs. Hendrick Stanley? What can you tell me about her?"

"Secretary of the A.D.S.," Russett said wearily. "Lives in Dene Close, but I don't know the number. How did you get to know about her, and why are you interested? Haven't we enough to do as it is?"

"I asked Mrs. Dexter if there was such a society," replied Knollis. "It seemed likely."

"And why should you be interested in them?"

"I'm sure I can't tell you," said Knollis, and with that ambiguous reply Russett had to be satisfied.

Knollis waited until Russett and his assistant had vanished through another doorway, and then touched Ellis on the elbow.

"Let's go and have a chat with Mrs. Stanley."

Mrs. Hendrick Stanley proved to be a lady of forty, brusque in manner and practical in outlook. Knollis found her refreshing even when she returned leading questions instead of answers. Her eyes were evidently wide open to the whims and foibles of the members of the society.

She opened the door to them herself. "My girl's day off," she explained without preamble. "Can I do anything for you? You are, of course, the detectives from New Scotland Yard. I've read a lot about it, and regard it as a most efficient institution—and I do so admire efficiency."

"Inspector Knollis, ma'am, and my assistant, Sergeant Ellis. Whether you can help us or not remains to be seen, but I would like a chat with you if you can spare the time."

She stood aside. "Come in, by all means. I don't see how I can help you, but there's no harm in trying, is there? You won't mind sitting in the kitchen, will you? As I said, it is the girl's day off, and I haven't put a fire in the lounge or the dining-room because I don't like to face her with a load of work when she comes back. Now then, take the chairs, and then let me know what I can do for you!"

Knollis plaited his fingers, and leaned forward. "Can you give me a list of the members of the Westford Bridge Amateur Dramatic Society, Mrs. Stanley?"

"Of course! But why on earth do you want it?"

Knollis shook his head. "Sorry! I can't tell you that. You will doubtless get to know in due course."

She folded her arms and huffed her shoulders. "Oh well, if you can't, then you can't, can you? If you will excuse me for a minute I will get the subscription book for you. You can borrow it for a few days in case you wish to copy it."

When she returned, Knollis asked: "Where do you—er—perform?"

"In the Westford Hall, Inspector. You'll find it just a few yards beyond the bridge."

Knollis nodded vigorously. "I remember it now. So that is where you work?"

"Play," she corrected sharply. "We play when we are working, and rest when we are not."

"Thank you," Knollis said gravely. "You must excuse my ignorance; I know so little about theatrical matters. Now your—er—props. That is the right name? Are they kept there, or have you some other store-place?"

"Such as we have, we keep there, Inspector. We generally hire from the costumiers, although we keep a stock of what you might call general props—stuff suitable for curtain raisers. They are in wicker baskets in an ante-room at the rear of the building."

"Dances are held in the same building, Mrs. Stanley?"

"Dances, whist drives, political meetings, lectures, and art exhibitions," she replied, ticking them off on her fingers.

"It has not altered since I was working in Burnham," commented Knollis. "Would it be possible for anyone attending any of these functions to get at the props, do you think?"

"They could get at the prop baskets, but no further, because I have the key—the only key."

Mrs. Stanley paused, her finger on her lip. She suddenly pointed it straight at Knollis. "You think that someone used our props on Thursday night!"

"I assure you that I think nothing of the kind," Knollis replied with a smile, "but I am interested in the possibilities, which do exist!"

"There are no such possibilities," she protested vigorously. "It would not be possible! I assure you that it would not. There isn't a chance."

"Anything is possible to a desperate man, Mrs. Stanley!"

She thought over his statement, and then nodded her head as energetically as she had shaken it a minute before. "Yes, perhaps you are right, Inspector. The padlocks on the baskets are only cheap ones when all is said and done, and a man who really wanted to open them could do so. Inspector! What are you *really* looking for?"

"A long black coat and a black velour hat."

She closed her eyes for a moment, and then opened them again. "We never had them. I'm quite sure of that."

"Your scenery, Mrs. Stanley?" asked Knollis.

"What about it, Inspector?"

"Do you hire that?"

"Oh yes, except for a permanent backdrop which hides the rear wall, which is a brick one and not particularly beautiful."

"Ropes, pulleys, and tackle generally?"

"We have all that kind of thing," said Mrs. Stanley. "We share them with the manager of the hall. He gets other smaller clubs putting on children's pantomimes, plays, and also cantatas."

"Mrs. Stanley," said Knollis, "can you tell me exactly what equipment you have at the moment?"

"In just two minutes," she replied. She disappeared again and came back with a two-penny exercise-book. "My stock-book. You may care for the loan of it."

"Thank you very much. You have helped enormously." She eyed him suspiciously. "You are not going to drag the society into this, are you, Inspector?"

"I wouldn't dream of doing so, Mrs. Stanley. And I see no reason for it, I assure you."

"Oh well, I rather liked Mr. Dexter, you know. We were hoping to have him as an active member. Both Mr. Rawley and his wife were trying to persuade him to join us."

"Mr. Rawley is a member?" Knollis asked.

"Not a member; no. He comes along to see our productions, but I rather fancy that his appearances are more due to domestic pressure than to interest. He is so obviously bored that I wish he would stay away. He is bad publicity as far as we are concerned, and upsets the people around him. He's always so ill at ease that his mood spreads."

"But Mrs. Rawley is a very keen member?"

Mrs. Stanley laughed.

"Oh yes, she's very keen, but she's a very bad actress. Still, in societies like ours you always do get the two types of member."

"Two types?" Knollis prompted, with a puzzled frown.

"Yes, the genuine ones, and the lunatic fringe—you know, the people who like to be in at it so that they can tell their neighbours that *I am, of course, a member of the Westford Amateurs!* or *As I was saying to Mrs. Stanley at the Amateurs' rehearsal last night . . .*"

"Quite so. Quite so," Knollis murmured uncertainly.

"But, mind you, Inspector, they come in useful—if one knows how to employ them to advantage."

"Do they indeed?" muttered Knollis. He kept his eyes rigidly away from Ellis, for he could sense a grin working up on his face.

"The subscriptions. They help the ones who can act. And they are useful for arranging the stage and the auditorium."

Mrs. Stanley lowered her voice almost a full octave.

"Strictly speaking, we can't manage without them!"

"Interesting! Very interesting!"

"Mrs. Rawley is one of this type," Mrs. Stanley went on confidentially. "She'd be furious if she knew how I use her, but I always give her the job of clearing out the props baskets, and sorting the tickets, and chores of that nature—you know! I mean, you have to use people according to their abilities, don't you?"

"To each according to his needs . . ." murmured Knollis.

"What did you say, Inspector?" inquired Mrs. Stanley.

"Nothing! Nothing at all!" said Knollis blandly.

"Anyway, if there is anything else I can do for you, just let me know. Any time, you know. Now you will be wanting to go, won't you? I mustn't detain such busy men. I am pleased to have made your acquaintance."

Before Knollis and Ellis were quite sure what had happened, they found themselves on the pavement with their hats in their hands, watching the front door close.

"Well," said Knollis. "What a woman!"

"Certainly knows how to clear the house," grinned Ellis.

Then he glanced round and gave a groan.

"Watch out! Here's trouble!" he said out of the corner of his mouth. "Inspector Russett on the trail. Coming round the corner like a bat out of hell. Wonder what's gone wrong, because that's the only thing that would make him fetch you."

Russett came chasing up, and laid his hand on Knollis's arm, standing so until he had recovered his breath. "Phew! Got something, old man! Really got some news this time!"

"Such as what?" Knollis asked quietly. He was getting accustomed to Russett, even if Mrs. Stanley had bowled him out.

"An actual witness! Saw everything! Daren't come forward in case the killer came back and slit her throat. Had a deuce of a job getting the story out of her. Young woman with a new baby. Up warming milk and all that, heard the rumpus at Rawley's place, and peered round the blind. Saw everything. Thought I'd better get you straight away. Phew!"

"Lead me to it," said Knollis.

"Seventh house on the left, facing the river, that is," panted Russett. "As soon as I got the first word out of her I left Rogers to keep her warm and chased round for you. I guessed where you would be, because I realized that you had some sort of bee in your bonnet about the dramatic crowd. We're almost there now. Seventh house. Name of Newnham. Husband works in an outfitters' place in the city—branch manager. Decent bloke. This is it."

Knollis knocked on the door and walked in. A thin-faced man came forward to meet him, an anxious expression wrapped right round his features.

"Inspector Knollis? I'm Newnham, Fred Newnham. Look, Inspector, you'll be gentle with the wife, won't you? It's only four months since she had the baby—you know what I mean, don't you?"

Knollis spared him one of his rare smiles. "I haven't come to torture her, Mr. Newnham. I only want to ask a few very simple questions."

"Thanks, Inspector!" said Newnham. "That's good. But you know how it is? Police in the house for the first time in our lives. Bound to be upsetting, isn't it?"

Knollis patted him on the shoulder. "Your wife will quite probably be more thrilled than upset, and will have something to talk about for months. Don't you worry!"

Newnham pushed Knollis through into the dining-room.

"Elsie, this is the inspector from Scotland Yard. My wife, Inspector."

"How do you do, Mrs. Newnham! Inspector Russett tells me that you may be able to help us a wee bit. All these little portions of information come in useful."

Elsie Newnham, a pale young woman of about twenty-eight years, leaned forward confidentially, meanwhile lacing her fingers and trying to screw them off.

"Thursday night it was, Inspector. I'd set the alarm so that I could get baby's milk warmed. Fred does it at two o'clock, and four o'clock, and six o'clock—"

"Elsie!" said Newnham reproachfully.

"Embarrassed he is," said Elsie Newnham. "Doesn't like people to think that he helps in the house—but he does! Washes up and cleans, and helps me no end, as well as helping with baby's milk—"

"Elsie! Inspector Knollis doesn't want to know the ins and out of all our domestic arrangements. He—wants—to—know—what—you—saw—on—Thursday—night!"

Elsie giggled. "I was coming to that. Sorry, I'm sure, Inspector! As I was saying, I'd set the alarm, and as soon as it went off I got out of bed and put my dressing-gown on, and then my slippers. Jimmy—that's the baby—was lying in his cot looking so innocent, and I bent over to look at him, and just at that minute I heard a noise in the street, so I peeped round the edge of the blind. I couldn't see anything because of the reflection from the bedroom light, so I switched it off, and then had another look. I couldn't say whether it was a man or a woman, but whichever it was seemed to be pushing between the privets in the hedge dividing Rawleys and Dexters."

Knollis's eyebrows went up, and he cast a glance at Ellis.

"Going which way, Mrs. Newnham?"

"To Mrs. Dexter's house, and from Mrs. Rawley's."

"And then?"

"Well," continued Mrs. Newnham, "I could see better after a minute or so because my eyes were getting used to the dark. Then a light went on in Mrs. Dexter's front bedroom, so that it sort of lit up the front of the house, or gave a dim glow. I heard more knocking, and it seemed to be at Mrs. Dexter's door. The hall lamp came on next, and I could see the person standing on the step of the porch. All at once there was a funny noise—and I heard it quite plainly because we keep the top two lights open at night, believing in having plenty of air in the bedroom."

"What kind of a noise was it, Mrs. Newnham?" Knollis asked keenly.

"A sort of a loud grunt. I can't quite explain."

"And then what happened?"

Elsie Newnham shook her head vaguely. "I'm not sure. I came over faint, and when I next looked out I saw Mrs. Rawley in her night things standing full in the light from the hall, and there was a loud scream from inside."

Knollis said "Damn!" under his breath.

Aloud he said: "You did not recognize the first person you saw? It was no one you knew?"

"I couldn't say, Inspector. It was just a dark figure."

"Well," said Russett, full of self-satisfaction. "That is what you wanted to know!"

Knollis gravely thanked Mrs. Newnham, warned her that he may have to call on her again, and ushered his company from the house and down the street to Himalaya Villa.

Russett flung himself into the Dexter settee, put his hands behind his head, stretched his legs across the carpet, and repeated: "That is what you wanted to know!"

"My dear Russett," Knollis said patiently, "she told us no more than we knew already from the statements of Mrs. Dexter and Mrs. Rawley!"

"But Mrs. Rawley said that the fellow went back up the path to the street!"

"Yes," said Knollis, "and she also told us that she then closed the door, and the next item on her programme was when he was knocking at this front door. There was nothing to prevent the fellow walking back down the path and pushing through the hedge—although why he should do so is beyond my imagination."

"Well," said Russett surlily, "I suppose you may be right, but I think you're ungrateful, Knollis—and me working like billy-o."

"I am grateful," Knollis replied absently. "I wouldn't have missed the woman's story for anything, but it does not give us a new lead, and that is what is wanted."

Russett curled himself into an ungainly heap on the settee, and glowered foully at Knollis.

"I still think the fellow made a mistake and killed the wrong person, which is why we are making no headway."

"In which case we can expect another killing?" suggested Knollis.

"Well, look at it for yourself. Mrs. Rawley insists that he asked for the Smith house. Then what more natural for him to think, when she told him that there was no Smith in the street, that she was scared of him, and lied to get him out of the street? So then what happens?"

"You tell me, Russett. I'm interested," said Knollis.

"Well, he thinks he has been bluffed, and has got the wrong house. He is satisfied that the next one must be it, and so he goes to the next house, knocks up Dexter, and lets drive as he opens the door. And didn't realize he had made a mistake until it was too late."

He shuffled round on the settee and glared defiantly at Knollis and the two sergeants. "It's as good a theory as we've got up to now."

"I haven't got a theory yet, my dear Russett," said Knollis slowly. "Look, I'll show you something! It is getting dark, and if it was darker I could demonstrate still more efficiently. Come outside with me. Now, Ellis, I'm going to knock on the door, and I want you and Rogers to toss up as to which of you answers it. Oh, and I want the hall light switching on before you open up. Come on, Russett!"

Outside, he waited a minute, and then knocked. The hall light came on, and a figure approached the door.

"Which of them is it?" he asked Russett.

"Ellis, of course. I can tell his shape."

"Exactly! And that is the whole of my argument against your theory of a mistaken killing! As soon as the light was switched on the killer would be able to see who was about to open the door to him. In other words, he would know whether it was Dexter or this mythical Smith, and he was not likely to make a mistake. No, Russett, our man wanted Dexter, and he got him. Why he wanted him, well, I'm damned if I know, because there doesn't seem to be the slightest of motives."

"I think I see your point," Russett admitted grudgingly. "Still, it doesn't rule out my theory altogether!"

"Another point which may fan a spark in your mind," went on Knollis. "You have seen both Mrs. Rawley and Mrs. Dexter?"

"Of course. Why ask that?"

"Would you say that they resembled each other in any way?"

"No-o!" Russett said thoughtfully. "Mrs. Rawley is plump and masculine, and Mrs. D. is sketchy, almost boyish."

"So that, if you were Dexter's killer, and you knocked at a door and saw Mrs. Rawley coming to open it—as you would if she had switched on the light—then you would be satisfied in your own mind that it was not Mrs. Dexter?"

"Oh yes, decidedly," said Russett.

"Exactly," said Knollis, more patiently. "And you would have plenty of time in which to withdraw in the darkness before she opened the door and saw you?"

"I should say so. Yes."

"And you wouldn't stay at the door if you did not want to be recognized?"

"Er—no!"

"Then what do you infer from that, Russett, my friend?"

Russett produced all the symptoms of a bout of intense thought, and finally murmured: "I'd rather like to hear your ideas on the subject, Knollis!" He added: "I have my own notions, of course."

CHAPTER VII
THE EXAMINATION OF THE DETAILS

SIR WILFRID BURROWS' office was, that evening, the scene of the second conference. Russett was absent from the early stages for reasons of his own. Sir Wilfrid, as self-important as ever, blew out his cheeks and looked thoughtfully from Knollis to Whitelaw, and casually to Ellis and Rogers.

"Suppose Russett will turn up some time or other," he commented caustically. "However, I have the report of the inquest here—but you were present, Whitelaw, so perhaps you will tell Knollis anything that may interest him?"

Dr. Whitelaw uncrossed his legs and rehitched his trousers, and then answered. "There was nothing of importance. The coroner directed the jury to bring in a verdict of 'Murder by a Person Unknown,' and that was all there was to it. The usual identification of the deceased by the widow, and Mrs. Rawley's evidence about the fellow who knocked at her door, and then her evidence about the finding of the body. Nothing new, of course."

"No questions from the jury?" asked Knollis.

"None," said the doctor with a dry smile. "I think the foreman would have had a good time if he had been given the chance, but he wasn't given an earthly."

"Why the use of the singular in the verdict?" asked Knollis. "A bit unusual, and a bit cramping if it comes to that."

Dr. Whitelaw shrugged. "Blame old Barlow, the coroner. He directed the jury that way. Said it was obvious from the evidence of the two women that only one person was concerned, and that it was senseless to complicate the affair by imagining a second person into existence."

Knollis grimaced. "It's all right on the face of it, but it will make matters darned awkward if there was an accessory before or after the fact. Still, Barlow can sort that out for himself if it does happen. Any other useful information?"

"Not from the inquest," said the doctor.

Sir Wilfrid leaned forward. "Here are the photographs, taken down on the river by your order. Think you got anything important this morning, Knollis?"

"I'm sure I did," Knollis answered. "At the moment I'd hate to say which way it will lead. The killer drew some fine herrings across the track, and I wouldn't like to say that I've finished with them yet."

"I could do with a good plate of herrings," murmured the Chief Constable.

"I am grateful to them in a way," Knollis continued. "They seem to show that the murderer didn't feel too confident of his plan, and his lack of confidence may prove to be his downfall."

"The dope on Rawley is through, you know," said Sir Wilfrid. "Came through about ten minutes before you arrived. They wired it in code, and confirmation comes later. Rawley spent the night at the Fir Tree Hotel with a lady called Nancy Locke, known locally as Goldie. Rather good, that, eh? Goldie Locke? Damn' good! Anyway, she says she isn't keen on the police, but is prepared to admit where she was and who she was with if Rawley gets into trouble. All facts duly checked at the hotel, and so that seems to put him out of the file!"

"I suppose so," said Knollis. He nursed the photographs carefully. "Any report on the dragging operations?"

"Not unless Russett has it. I'll get him, if I can find him. You know, Russett would dearly like to pull this case out of the bag by himself!"

He pressed a switch and spoke into the blower. "Please try to find Inspector Russett for me, and ask him to come to my office."

As he looked up again, he asked: "What have you got on your list for attention, Knollis?"

Knollis consulted his notebook, and ticked off various items with a pencil. "Rawley's whereabouts on Thursday night, which can be wiped off now. Source of Dexter's account with the English and Foreign. Courtney-Harborough's boat—also settled satisfactorily. Mrs. Hendrick Stanley—I interviewed her, but still have to visit the Westford Hall. George Friend; to be 'phoned this evening. Trace source of rope, if and when found. I take it you read my report, Sir Wilfrid?"

Sir Wilfrid answered with a nod.

"Then," continued Knollis, "I want Russett to check the book purchases. I don't suppose he will object to a trip to Birmingham. We'll get the Yard to do the London dealers. Then I have a note reminding me to decide whether the killer asked for the

Smith house or the Dexter house, and a final query regarding Dexter's last words."

"I don't see any point in those last two items," remarked Sir Wilfrid, as he made longhand notes. "I mean, surely Mrs. Dexter should be sure of what she heard?"

"Yes, I suppose so," said Knollis. He tried to hurry on to his next point, but Sir Wilfrid had his teeth into the matter and would not let go.

"Now the booksellers," began Knollis.

The Chief Constable waved a chubby hand. "Never mind the booksellers for now, Knollis. Let's get this last-words business settled. Either he said 'Oh hell!' or he did not. Isn't that the point?"

"Yes," Knollis replied warily. "And he did. There is no doubt about that."

"Then what the devil are you quibbling about? Cross it from your notes, or it will confuse you. The point about whether the fellow asked for Dexter or Smith? What is worrying you about that?"

"Surely it is obvious?"

Knollis tried to make his tone respectful, but it did not quite realize his intention, and Sir Wilfrid blinked.

"Herrum! Well, Knollis, surely Mrs. Rawley should know!"

"I agree that she should," said Knollis, "but in the statement Mrs. Dexter made to Russett we find that she and her husband were lying in their respective beds talking about poetry—implying that she was wide awake and capable of understanding whatever she heard. But wait a minute; you have the statements there?"

Sir Wilfrid pulled a file from a drawer in the table.

"Here is the Dexter woman's statement. I'll find the other for you in just one minute."

Knollis took it and read from it.

"Here we are! I heard Mrs. Rawley say it was next door, and I asked my husband if he had heard that. He said that he had not, and that I must he mistaken, for who would want to call on us at this time of the night."

Knollis looked across the table at Sir Wilfrid.

"Now look at the Rawley statement, sir."

Sir Wilfrid read:

"The man asked my pardon and could I direct him to Smith's. I told him there was no Smith in the street, and hadn't

he made a mistake? He shook his head, apologized for bother-
ing me, and walked back up the path to the street."

"Well?" demanded Knollis.

Sir Wilfrid waved the statement wildly. "The woman, face to face with the fellow, could hardly mistake the name Dexter for Smith, or vice versa, now could she, Knollis?"

"And," Knollis retorted, "if Lesley Dexter heard Mrs. Rawley say that the house he wanted was next door, then surely she could not be mistaken either. I am satisfied that Mrs. Rawley is lying, although I can't imagine why she should do so."

Dr. Whitelaw leaned forward.

"Excuse me butting in, but have you taken into account the effects of shock on a witness? You know from your own experiences that witnesses never do agree on details."

"I agree with you in principle," said Knollis, "but there is such a divergence . . ."

He glared at the statement in his hand. "Hey, but wait a minute! Who lives next door to the Rawleys?"

Sir Wilfrid cocked his head. "What on earth are you getting at, Knollis? The Dexters, of course."

Dr. Whitelaw smiled and silently nodded his head.

Said Knollis: "But they have neighbours on the other side as well!"

Sir Wilfrid flopped back in his chair. "Oh Lord, yes!"

Ellis entered the conversation for the first time. "Surely, if the woman was directing the fellow to either one house or the other she would indicate the direction by a movement of her head, or a wave of the hand? I mean, even we frigid English don't exactly stand to attention to help an inquirer, do we?"

"That is right enough," said Knollis. "And yet, for curiosity's sake, who does live on the opposite side?"

Russett entered the room, all smiles, and Knollis swung round to face him. "Just the man we want! Who lives in the next house to the Rawleys, Russett?"

Russett's smile faded. He blinked. "The Dexters, of course. Where's the joke, if there is one?"

"That's just it," explained Knollis. "We have all fallen for the same idea—that Rawleys had only one set of neighbours. Now who is the neighbour on the other side?"

"Oh!" exclaimed Russett. "I see what you mean now. Crafty point that! I have it in my pocket-book. Here we are—Mr. and Mrs. Henry Sampson."

"Not Smith, anyway!" commented Knollis. "What is he by profession?"

"Solicitor! Came to town about four years ago, and went into partnership with Dibland. Tall, thin, miserable-looking bloke. Looks as if he's never had a decent meal in his life, or else puts it into a bad skin. Haggard and starved he looks. Makes you feel sorry for him as soon as you see him."

"Sounds a lot too much like Mrs. Rawley's description of the killer," Ellis said suspiciously.

Knollis nodded to him, and gave a rueful smile.

"Go on, Russett, tell me that he wears a long black coat and a velour!"

"By God and he does!" exclaimed Russett. "How did you guess that?"

"Did it need any guessing!" said Knollis. "It is just one more of our pound of red herrings. You'll have to check on the poor fellow, but he'll be as innocent as a new-born babe."

"Damn' these red herrings!" exploded Russett.

"No, I wouldn't say that, Russett," said Knollis. "I rather welcome them. Red herrings are of two kinds. One kind tends—or intends—to lead us to the wrong person. The other merely intends leading us away from the right one. We are dealing with the second type here, and I don't mind them at all, inasmuch as they help me to define the mentality of the killer. What, by the way, did you learn from the Sampsons?"

Russett examined his notes. "In bed, and fast asleep. Never heard a thing until the ambulance drove away. That disturbed them, and they both got up, inquired what was wrong, and made a nice cup of tea to revive their fainting spirits."

He rubbed his forehead reminiscently. "There was something else. Oh yes! River Station rang up just before I left my office. They found the rope, but no knife as yet. Seventy five feet of manilla rope, as prophesied by you—and I still don't know how you do it! They are sending it along, and will continue dragging for the knife to-morrow morning."

Knollis's lean face broke into a smile. "Highly satisfactory. Now we have something concrete to work on!"

Russett grimaced. "I suppose I get the job!"

"No, Ellis and I will do that. I'd like you to spend a day or so in Birmingham, checking on Dexter's purchases. We have to find the source of that four thousand pounds. Look, I wonder—"

He was interrupted by the entrance of a constable.

"A gentleman to see Inspector Knollis. Name of Friend."

Knollis jumped up. "Now what brings him down here? Show him in, please!"

A grey-haired, intellectual-looking man entered the room, and grasped Knollis's outstretched hand. "I had to come, Knollis. As soon as I saw the manuscript—oh, I beg your pardon!"

Knollis introduced him to Sir Wilfrid and his colleagues, and then pushed him into a chair. "Now work it off your chest, for the love of Heaven!"

Friend opened his case, and laid the document on the table, together with Dexter's scribblings.

"I examined it, as you asked me to do, and I can't see anything fishy, as you termed it. The manuscript isn't an Elizabethan play as you suggested."

"I was only guessing," Knollis explained. "I know nothing about such things."

"Well, even your guess was wrong," Friend continued. "It is a much earlier manuscript, a morality play to be exact, and this is a copy—probably itself done in the time of Edward the Second—of a very early morality play, by an unknown author or authors. It is quite genuine, and if the owner cares to sell this *Sable Messenger*, then I am prepared to pay a very good price for it."

"But the pages in Dexter's writing—Dexter being the late owner, of course—what about them?" asked Knollis.

Friend's lips twitched as he replied: "I'm only guessing, but it looks to me as if your man was trying to translate it and adapt it for the modern stage—and making a shocking job of it. Dear me, yes!"

"Look," said Knollis; "what could he do with it when he had finished? Sell it, or what?"

"Very little, actually," Friend answered. "He could, of course, attempt to publish it in the hope of gaining a modicum of kudos, but scholars would only laugh at such a puerile attempt. The man was illiterate. Oh, I don't mean in the general sense of the word, but as far as this business is concerned. It is a very clumsy job, Knollis!"

Knollis h'm'd, and tapped his pencil on the table thoughtfully. "How much is the original manuscript worth?"

"I'll give the owner seven hundred pounds for it—and I hope to get to her before anyone else does so," said Friend.

Knollis scribbled on Sir Wilfrid's pad, tore off the sheet, and handed it to Friend. "There is the lady's present address. In case you don't know, we are investigating the murder of her husband. I think she will sell. Meanwhile it must remain in our custody."

"Thank you, Knollis," said the dignified Mr. Friend. "And if she will sell . . . ?"

"Unless there is anything criminal in the way he obtained it, then you can claim it from us on written authority from Mrs. Dexter."

Friend rose, and chewed his lower lip. "You know, Knollis, I'd like to know where he did get it from, because I've never even heard of it before, and neither has anyone else."

"And yet you are satisfied that it is genuine?"

"I'll stake my reputation on it," said Friend.

"That is good enough for me," remarked Knollis. "And thanks very much for coming along to help us."

Friend smiled. "I'm afraid I came along to help myself. Good night all! Good night."

"Well," said Sir Wilfrid, when the door closed, "how does that help us?"

Knollis shrugged his shoulders. Instead of answering, he passed round his cigarettes, and sat regarding the smoke as he blew it down his nostrils.

A constable entered with a sandbag and an envelope. The latter he handed to Sir Wilfrid, and laid the bag on the floor.

"From River Station, sir."

"H'm," said Sir Wilfrid a minute later. "Found sixteen yards from the bank, lying in twelve feet of water. Position, a few yards east of River Close. Sent to us exactly as found."

Knollis bent, and shook the rope from the bag. It was roughly coiled, and one end was looped in a simple hitch to retain it as a coil.

"Any ideas as to its probable source?" he asked the company at large.

There were no replies, and so he slipped the rope back in the bag.

"I think I'll borrow that manuscript again, sir," he said to Sir Wilfrid. "I'm going along to have another chat with Mrs. Dexter."

"Anything you say, Knollis. Do anything you like if you think it will help to clear up this infernal case."

"That's what I say," murmured Russett. "Let me get back to breakings and enterings, and stolen bikes. There's too much hard work about an affair like this."

"Well, isn't that exactly what I told you?" said Sir Wilfrid tactlessly. "It needs experience to handle a murder case. Remember when you and I solved the Lomas case, Knollis?" he added, and beamed complacently.

"I'll never forget it, sir," said Knollis. He winked discreetly at Russett, and beckoned Ellis to follow him from the office. "See you again in the morning, sir. Something may turn up by then."

Ellis closed the door, and heaved a sigh as they marched along the corridor.

"Am I glad that's over. Having to sit like a kid at Sunday school, mouth closed like an oyster, and not expected to interrupt the deliberations of the Great I Am! He's got the brain of a child of five. And yet," he added as an afterthought, "why should I insult a child of five?"

"Ellis! Ellis!" Knollis chided gently.

Ellis crammed his hat on his head. "It's all right for you to suppress me, but you are as bored with them both as I am, only you won't admit it. Dr. Whitelaw is the only intelligent man of the three—and he keeps his mouth shut and just smiles to himself."

"An example for you," said Knollis. "And yes, Whitelaw is a good chap. Keen amateur criminologist, too. It's a pity he isn't a sleuth instead of a sawbones. However, let's regard them as our cross which we have to bear, and meanwhile go and chat with Lesley. You drive, Ellis; you know the way by now."

They crossed the pavement, and Ellis went round the front of the car and slid under the steering-wheel.

"What do you think about the rope?" he asked as he turned out of the Square, and on to the Desborough Road.

"I dimly remember the Westford Hall," murmured Knollis reminiscently. "It has a small stage, probably thirty feet across, and eighteen deep. The height must be eighteen to twenty feet."

"And you think the rope was swiped from there?"

"It's an unusual length, Ellis," said Knollis. "Too long for a scaffolding rope, and not strong enough for, say, one of the barges which ply up and down the river. The Westford Hall stage—I wonder if it did come from there? If so, then I can almost guarantee that the trail will lead back to River Close."

"And Mrs. Margot Rawley?"

Knollis nodded lightly. "And Margot Rawley, yes. But where is the motive? She had the opportunity, and there is no doubt about that, but the motive!"

"That note in Lesley's handbag?" suggested Ellis. "That any guide?"

"Another of our red herrings, Ellis, and I don't set much store by it. Unless I am very much mistaken, Margot Rawley put it there after Dexter was killed. And that is another stunt that has been pulled countless times before, isn't it?"

"Draw attention to one's self in order to get safely in the clear! Yes, it has been done before, and too often."

"You know, Ellis," Knollis said in a confidential tone, "that cuss-word of Dexter's is intriguing me. It has soaked through to the back of my mind, and I feel that there is some significance attached to it which is still escaping me. I suppose it will come when it feels like it. One of the mysteries of the subconscious mind!"

"Tell me when to turn," said Ellis. "I'm not quite sure of my way."

"Next turn on the left, and then first right and left," directed Knollis. "I wish I could reconcile those two statements, too! Rather puzzling. I mean, Ellis, that if Margot Rawley is responsible and wants to keep herself in the clear, then why the heck didn't she follow Lesley's lead and make it look as if the alleged man in the black coat was really after Dexter? Either the killer has slipped up badly, or we have missed a point somewhere. Pull under the lamp."

A plain-clothes man sauntered towards them as they approached the door of number twenty-nine, but wandered away as he recognized them.

"Any news for me?" Lesley Dexter asked wanly as she took them through to the living-room.

"Not yet, I'm afraid," said Knollis. "I am still searching for information, and perhaps you can supply some of it. I have brought along a manuscript which I found on the table in the lounge at your home. Your husband had apparently been working on it. Can you tell me anything about it, please?"

Lesley took it from him and examined it. "Oh yes, I recognize it, of course. He came by it in rather a curious way."

"Yes?" asked Knollis, striving to conceal his eagerness.

"Robert has a cousin who is in the antique furniture trade. He has no shop or showroom, but furnishes his own house with the pieces he buys, and then invites possible purchasers to visit his home, the idea being that the antiques look better in a furnished home than in a shop, if you see what I mean?" she asked ingenuously.

"Yes, I think I see the point," Knollis replied mildly.

"Well, Richard—his cousin—travels round the country districts, picking up a piece here and a piece there, in country cottages, inns, and such places. Some time ago he bought an old chest from some place or other, and when his man started to clean it he found it had a false bottom—nothing exciting, but just a loose board that fitted in somehow or other, and under it was—"

"This manuscript?"

"Exactly, Inspector. He brought it along to Robert because he knew that he was interested in such things, and asked him how much it was worth. Robert said he didn't know, but he could find out, and so Richard left it with him. Robert was terribly excited about it after Richard left, and said it was worth no end of money, and would be a real investment if he could persuade his cousin to part with it."

"And did he part with it?" asked Knollis.

"I—I don't know, Inspector," Lesley stammered. "I know that he saw Robert twice afterwards, but as I was not in the lounge when they were discussing it, well, I don't really know. Actually, I don't suppose I should have known as little about it as I do but for the romantic way in which it was found."

"Ah!" said Knollis, "that reminds me, Mrs. Dexter! I passed it on to an acquaintance who is an expert in such matters, and he is coming along to see if you are prepared to sell it to him. He values it at seven hundred pounds." Lesley's eyebrows arched. "As much as that!"

"He is a reliable judge, Mrs. Dexter. His name is George Friend, and I think he will call on you in the morning."

"But I don't think I can sell it!" Lesley protested. "I don't even know whether Robert paid for it or not!"

"We'll find out for you in due course, Mrs. Dexter. We shall have to interview this cousin—oh, and perhaps you will give me his name and address?"

"Richard Dexter. He lives in Hawthorn Grove. I don't know the number, or the name of the house. I suppose you can get that from the telephone directory?"

"Thank you very much," said Knollis. "By the way, I don t suppose you can tell me why your husband was translating it into modern idiom, can you?"

Lesley blinked. "Was he? I didn't know that, Inspector. I took so little interest in his hobby—and I think now that it would have been better for me to have done so. But I'm afraid I can't help you."

Knollis re-collected the manuscript, and he and Ellis left the house.

"Interesting," remarked Knollis, as Ellis drove away. "I really think we are getting warm at last. But I'd like to ring Russett's neck—and his Mr. Dayton's!"

"Why that?" asked Ellis, frowning.

"Isn't it obvious?" queried Knollis.

"No," Ellis replied flatly.

"Carry on to the office to pick up the rope and drop the manuscript. Then on to the Westford Hall. A bill in Frogmore Street announces a dance there to-night, which means that the manager should be in attendance."

Arriving at the hall, Knollis invaded the manager's office, which somewhat startled the gentleman.

"Scotland Yard!" he exclaimed. "No trouble, is there?"

"I only want your advice," said Knollis, whereat the manager preened his feathers, as Knollis had intended he should do.

"Proud, I'm sure."

Knollis threw the rope on the table. "Ever seen that before?"

"I've seen some like it. I'll get Charlie."

He swept round the table and through the doorway, returning two minutes later with a weedy little man who was mainly remarkable for a vivid red tie which glared from a background of blue shirt.

"That rope, Charlie! The inspector wants to know if you've seen it afore."

The weedy little man examined it. "Seen it afore! I should say I ruddy well 'ave. Where did you get it, Guv'nor?"

"You're certain you've seen it before?"

The little man looked at him for a moment. "Come with me!"

He led them down a corridor, and took them backstage. "See these ruddy drops? What do you think I pull 'em up and lower 'em with, eh? And some ruddy idiot ties up my back drop with a length of wire and half-inches me rope. Six weeks ago since I missed it. I'd know it anywhere. Had a dozen from Goodwoods— see, the ends is bound for fraying. That good enough, Guv'nor?"

"Goodwoods on Friar Street?" asked Knollis.

"Right an' all. An' me name's Sam Sharp. I lives in Canal Lane, although you can mostly find me 'ere."

"I may need you to go into court and swear to this rope!" Knollis warned him.

"Swear? I'll swear with every oath I know!"

"You won't have to go as far as that," grinned Knollis.

Chapter VIII
THE COUSIN OF THE DECEASED

SUNDAY IN BURNHAM never was an exciting day, and this one was no exception. The City Fathers are members of the Old Brigade, and take their religion sadly, so that apart from the mournful tolling of church bells, and the still more dismal chiming of Old John—the clock over the exchange—the city was silent, and even the steel-tyred tramcars seemed to achieve rubber wheels for their Sabbath peregrinations.

In the lounge of the Green Man, Knollis and Ellis had managed to monopolize the two chairs nearest to the fire and were working on their notes and reports. The only other occupants were three of the residents, the "regulars," two middle-aged ladies living on their investments, and a middle-aged Burnham doctor who had travelled the world and then fled screaming to the security of the quietest cage he could find.

All three were discreetly interested in the detectives, and from time to time the two ladies looked over their knitting, and the doctor over the top of his respectable and lethargic Sunday paper, and glances of mutual understanding were exchanged; there would be a slight bow of the head, and everything was as before.

Knollis was unaware of all this, being absorbed in his work, and at the same time enjoying the brief respite from the physical side of the chase, which he was inclined to find exhausting. He was busy with the pieces of the Dexter jigsaw puzzle, trying to find two which, when in proximity, would produce a continuity of line and shade. The pieces refused to oblige, juggle them as he would.

Knollis was not impatient. He realized that but two full days had passed since the commission of the murder, and that, considering the short time, quite a lot of ground had been covered. He always found himself at a disadvantage with this kind of puzzle, one he never experienced when sitting at home before the fire with an actual jig-saw puzzle spread out on his wife's tea-trolley. Then, if the going was difficult, he would watch his wife to make sure that she was not looking, and snatch a crafty glance at the picture on the box—and his wife would invariably look up and in a reproachful voice say: "Gordon!"

And now, well, there was no box bearing a miniature re-production of the complete picture. He was ready for a break, but the bar in the Oak Room would not be open yet, not until eleven o'clock, in another half-hour's time. He fingered his left ear, and then doodled with the pencil in his right hand. He glanced across the hearth at Ellis. Ellis was passing on the time between glancing at the clock, glancing over his shoulder towards the door of the Oak Room, and drawing geometrical patterns on a sheet of paper.

They sat in this way until three minutes to eleven, and then Ellis rose, slipped notebook and pencil into the capacious pocket of his jacket, and stretched himself. "How about a snifter, sir?"

Knollis looked up with an air of complete surprise.

"Good heavens! Is it that time already? Well, yes, I think we will have a drink."

With a deep sigh of relief he stowed away his notes and accompanied Ellis to the bar. The doctor shuffled for a few seconds, and then suddenly folded his paper and followed them. He caught them up as they reached the bar.

"Care to have a drink with me, Inspector Knollis? And you, Sergeant?"

Knollis accepted for them both. "And mild beer for me, please."

The doctor glanced at Ellis.

"Bitter, please."

"Sure you won't have whisky? I believe he has a bottle tucked away somewhere. You won't? Well, I will. Every man to his choice, Inspector!"

He propped an elbow on the edge of the bar. "I remember you when you were in Burnham."

Knollis smiled. "I remember you, too, although I'm afraid that your name escapes me for the moment."

"Latham. I was in practice here until a few years ago. My wife died, my daughter married a surgeon at Barts, and I—well, I sold my practice and my home, went round the world, and then settled in here the year before the war. I am probably going to get myself snubbed now, Inspector, but I'm very interested in this case you are working on—hello, here are the drinks. Well, your very good health, and success with the case!"

Knollis and Ellis returned the wishes, and winked at each other over their glasses.

"Yes," continued the doctor, "I envy Whitelaw. I would have liked police work, and I don't know why I never went in for it. Sordid and all that, but interesting. I've always been interested in criminal psychology. The criminal mind is interesting. The homicidal mind is, of course, a different matter from the mind of the habitual criminal! What would you say is behind the average murder, Inspector?"

Knollis sipped his beer and smiled at the doctor.

"You should know the answer to that as well as I do, Dr. Latham. There are a variety of reasons for murder. Revenge and vengeance—which are not the same thing by any manner of means; fear of exposure, jealousy, quick acquisition of wealth, and, of course, you have the passionate killing in hot blood."

The doctor pursed his lips and said: "Hum! Er—I don't suppose you've decided to which class this belongs?"

Knollis shook his head and took refuge in his beer. He was not to be drawn, and at the same time he did not wish to snub the doctor, who seemed a decent fellow and badly in need of someone to talk to.

"I knew the girl—Mrs. Dexter—quite well at one time. She was one of my patients. Working-class family, eminently respectable—but then the working class always are more moral than the middle class and the so-called upper class. Her parents were good, solid, stolid folk. Wanted her to get on, and not be stuck in the same rut as themselves. They did not realize exactly how lucky they were! However, the girl worked like the devil, got a scholarship, and finally had to be satisfied as an uncertificated teacher. The family income would not stretch to meet college expenses, and, well, the girl's brain was not quite good enough to take her any farther without help. Tragic, but commonplace!"

The doctor emptied his glass, and Knollis signalled to the barman.

"That," continued the doctor, "is where the science of psychology would have stood her in good stead if she had possessed any knowledge of it. You know what happens to a man when he is bowling along in a car at forty miles an hour, and suddenly rams on the brakes? He goes through the windscreen. It is, of course, the old problem of inertia. Letitia Drake, as she was then, had developed ideas about speed and progress—individual progress. She worked from a standstill to bottom gear, into second, and into third. She thought she was going into a fourth gear, into top, and as she progressed in her scholastic career, so she went ahead with her social ambitions which were to match them. The two sides of her were going forward together. You see what I am driving at?"

Knollis expressed his interest by a silent gesture.

"She learned that college was out of the question, and that she would have to go out into the world as a wage-earner, but not as a fully-competent wage-earner. The brake was on, and she banged her head on the windscreen, but she didn't go through it. Instead of a break-up, or what is known as a breakdown, she merely got a temporary headache, and then she began looking around for a compensatory device. She didn't have to look far, for her social aspirations were still alive, and she added to them the energy she had reserved for her further progress in the scholastic sphere."

He lifted his glass to Knollis, and then took a drink.

"That was when she became Lesley Drake, and conveniently forgot the Letitia. She tried to get out of her class. No blame to her for that! But she lost her balance. Then Dexter came on the scene. I met him during the war at various meetings, and liked him. I saw him with Lesley, and my professional habits encouraged me to watch them. Oh, I knew what was going to happen! I could see poor Dexter being pushed along like an express train. It was a transference of intention. She had been brought to a dead stop herself, but she was going to make her husband-to-be achieve success for both. Well, she married him, and she pushed him into River Close, and from time to time I would see her name in the local papers as being 'among those present' at various functions, and if I heaved a sigh—well, who shall blame an old man's regrets at seeing good material ruined?"

"This is all very interesting," murmured Knollis. "You seem to know a lot about the Dexters."

The doctor looked sideways at Knollis. "She almost didn't marry him, you know!"

"Oh?" said Knollis. "Why was that?"

"His cousin was after her as well. You see, she joined a tennis club, and the cousin was a member. He it was who introduced Bob Dexter to the club, and it was there that he and Lesley met. I know all this because it is my old club, and although my playing days are over I remain on the committee. A man like myself, Inspector, bereaved, and with no occupation, gets a certain amount of pleasure—and consolation!—in watching the younger generation's early and fumbling attempts to build. Sometimes in the spring, I go out into the country with a pair of binoculars and sit on a gate watching the rooks building. They act in pretty much the same way as humans—or should I say that humans act in much the same way as the rooks?"

He regarded his glass dismally. "Have another?"

"Thanks, no," Knollis replied. "We really must be going now, for we have work to do. Thank you for an enlightening half-hour. I hope to see more of you before leaving Burnham."

They returned to Knollis's sitting-room. Ellis perched himself on the arm of a chair, saying: "Well, if you don't know anything about Lesley by now, you should!"

"All very interesting, Ellis," said Knollis thoughtfully.

He walked to the window and watched the pigeons circling round the dome of the exchange. Seen carelessly, they appeared to have no plan of life, no objective, and yet, when regarded with the full mind in action it was seen that while all conformed to what might be called a pigeon-pattern, each had also his own purpose, a purpose based on the unconscious urge to live and to thrive. They snatched crumbs and titbits from under each other's beaks; they pushed, jostled, and thieved.

"I wonder if they murder each other?" Knollis murmured.

"What did you say?" asked Ellis.

"Oh, nothing," said Knollis, turning from the window. "Get into your outdoor clothes. We'll have a chat with this cousin of Dexter's before lunch. He sounds promising."

Hawthorn Grove was—and still is—on the north side of the city, a solidly respectable area populated by the professions of the city, an old tree-lined street of mellow, deep-red-brick houses, each with its three stone steps and porched doorway. Inquiry of a boy who was delivering *Observers* and *Sunday Times* took them to No. 43, where they left the car and rang the front door bell.

A neat maid took Knollis's private card, and soon showed them into a study. On the way, Knollis absorbed detail as a cormorant absorbs fish, almost without realizing the action, and he stored away an impression of a well-furnished house. There were clashes of period and style, but in some way there was no incongruity. He had time to notice no more, for the opening of a door at the far side of the study brought the owner face to face with them.

"Mr. Knollis and Mr. Ellis? Yes, I know you both by sight. I patronize the bar at the Green Man! I am Richard Dexter. In what way can I assist you?"

He was a man of forty, thick-set, but not clumsily so. His face was square, decorated with a military moustache, and his head was amply supplied with dark-brown hair. He had the manner of a man of the world, and it would have been difficult to imagine any possible situation in which he would not have felt fully at his ease. He was a good mixer in every sense of the word.

All this Knollis observed and noted as he replied: "I am not at all sure that you can help me, Mr. Dexter. I am merely hoping that you can, and that in a very minor matter. While examining your cousin's effects I came upon an old manuscript entitled *Sable Messenger*. Mrs. Dexter informs me that you were its original owner, and for reasons of my own I am anxious to learn something of its history."

Richard Dexter brushed back his hair, unnecessarily.

"That damned manuscript is becoming my King Charles's Head. It's cropped up again, has it! Take seats, won't you? And a cigarette while I am telling you the story. I have my lighter here . . ."

He seated himself, clasped his hands, and watched the smoke playing round his fingers as he went on: "I'm blessed if I see how it ties up with Bob's death, but here is the yarn. If you have seen Lesley, then you know all about me. I deal in antique furniture, and I buy from farms, cottages, and anywhere else where I can pick up genuine stuff. I pay fair prices, and I can lay my hand on my heart and say that I have never twisted anyone I have bought from. It has paid me, too, for I am trusted in the country districts, and old customers recommend me to their friends.

"It was such a recommendation that took me to a rectory in the Peak district. An old parson who was on the rocks wanted to dispose of a few pieces, and that old chest in the corner there was one of them. I bought that from him, together with four chairs and a monk's bench. At the back of this house I have a workroom, and employ a man and a boy to tidy my purchases. Old Tompkins, my man, found that the chest had a false bottom . . ."

He went to the corner and dragged the chest into the middle of the room, opening the lid.

"You will notice the knot-hole in the bottom. Well, by slipping a finger through it and pulling, up comes the bottom and you have another two inches of room. It is, as you see, no more than a shelf resting on two bearers. And that is where we found the manuscript. It looked rather ancient, and so I took it along to Bob, knowing he was interested in such matters, and asked him how much it was worth. He did an Indian dance round it, speaking figuratively, and said he would make inquiries for me. That was about a year ago, and I have been unable to get it back."

"Then he did not buy it from you?" asked Knollis.

"No; he just hung on and would not let go."

"So that it remains your property?"

Dexter shook his head, and flicked his ash into the chest. "No! I maintain that it belongs to the old boy. I bought the chest, Inspector, and, whether he knew about the manuscript or not, it remains his property."

"I have had it valued," Knollis said quietly.

"You have! What is it worth?"

"Seven hundred pounds. It is described as a previously unknown morality play."

Dexter whistled softly. "That will just about put the old boy on his feet. I know he's hard up for cash, for I got a hint last week to the effect that he wanted to sell more furniture—and God knows that the place was beginning to look empty when I was last there. Seven hundred! It will be manna from heaven to him!"

"I admire your altruism, Mr. Dexter. Does the rector know about the manuscript?"

"Yes," said Dexter, "I told him. He's applied for its return several times since then. That is why I got so annoyed with Bob. He told me that he gave it to a fellow in London to be valued, and that it had not been returned. I suspected that, knowing the magpie propensities of collectors. I'm glad that I am a dealer and not a collector. Collecting deadens the soul, Inspector. *What I have, I hold*, is the motto of such people—and Bob was no exception."

"Will you give me the name and address of the rector?"

"Certainly," said Dexter. "The Reverend William Saunders, Windlow Rectory, near Tideswell."

Knollis nodded. "I remember the village, although not the rectory or the rector. And now I must thank you for a very clear statement of the situation, and leave you. Now I wonder . . ."

"Yes, Inspector?" said Dexter.

"Well," said Knollis, with an excellent show of hesitation, "I was wondering if I dare venture a really personal question?"

Dexter stared for a moment, and then gave a short laugh. "I don't see why you shouldn't try. There is nothing in my life that I am anxious to hide from the police."

"It is about Mrs. Dexter," said Knollis. "Am I correct in believing that you were once Robert Dexter's rival?"

Dexter laughed loudly. "Good Lord, yes! The whole city knew about it, Inspector! Bob only won by a short head."

"There was no bad blood between you?"

"Of course there was—at the time. But these things wear thin, and I'm not so sure now that it wasn't a lucky break for me."

"Oh!" said Knollis. "In what way?"

"Lesley drove him too fast as she gained a hold on him, and after they were married—phew! Now I don't like being driven. Life should flow, easily and naturally. You never get anything by pushing. Isn't it the Chinese who say that water is the greatest force in the world because it achieves its goal by flowing through, and round, and over all opposition? Well, that is my philosophy. If I want something badly, and there is opposition, then I sit back, go on with something else, and wait. This confounded manuscript is an example. I could have got it back by fighting Bob for it in court, but by sitting and waiting I've got it without it costing me a penny."

"There is a lot in what you say," said Knollis. "I may take it then that you bore your cousin no grudge?"

"Good heavens, no!"

"Can you give me any hint as to what purpose your cousin had in mind in translating the manuscript?"

Dexter stared in bewilderment. "Translating it? Bob? I can hardly believe it. In fact, I didn't think he could read that old script, anyway. Probably trying to take his mind off things."

Knollis blinked, and quickly recovered himself. "Take his mind off things . . . ?"

"Yes—Lesley and Dennis Rawley, of course."

Then Dexter opened his mouth, closed it again, and finally said: "Lord, have I said something?"

"You certainly have," Knollis agreed. "Either too much or too little. Don't you think you should qualify your statement?"

Dexter fumbled for his cigarettes, lit one, and threw the packet on the table.

"I thought you would know, or I wouldn't have let that slip. Lesley and Rawley were on the verge of an *affaire*. I don't know much about it, mind you, but there was some kind of an inter-neighbour mix-up, and Bob was worried about it. The last time I called to see him about the manuscript he was very fidgety and nervous, and when I asked him what was wrong he said that all women were the devil, and why couldn't they be satisfied with one husband."

"So you concluded . . ." suggested Knollis.

"Well," replied Dexter, "what the hell else could I conclude? Bob wasn't the type to go wandering and philandering."

"You were surprised by his remark?"

"I was, because although Bob is such a quiet type, I've always regarded Lesley as a one-man dog. Shook me a bit. I mean, a man values his judgment of women, dogs, and horses."

"Quite so," commented Knollis. "You know Rawley?"

"Used to meet him in the Key and Clock occasionally. I've made up a four-hand at snooker or billiards on odd evenings. Quiet sort of fellow who looks at you from under his eyelids, if you know what I mean. You catch him looking at you, and he lowers his eyes as if he's guilty of something or other. I put it down to excessive shyness. He's quite all right for an evening's billiards, mind you, but I wouldn't do business with him if I could avoid it. I just don't like his type."

"Mrs. Dexter did say that Mrs. Rawley hated her," Knollis said under his breath.

Dexter looked quizzically at him, but passed no remark.

Then Knollis asked: "Are Robert Dexter's people alive?"

Dexter smiled ruefully. "My uncle, Joseph, is. That's Bob's father, of course. His mother died a good many years ago. Usual story of the old man marrying again, and stepmother trouble for Bob. He cleared out to work his own passage without interference, and I don't think that he and the old man even corresponded after Bob left home. They live in Leamington if you want to get in touch with them. The old chap was in business there, but I believe he's retired now."

"M'm! Nothing useful there," said Knollis.

"Any idea who did Bob in?" Dexter asked quietly.

"None whatsoever," Knollis replied, and watched his man closely. There was no visible reaction.

"I'm surprised that you did not visit River Close when you heard of your cousin's death," Knollis remarked.

Dexter looked slightly uncomfortable.

"We-ell, I suppose I should have done so, really, but I didn't for a variety of reasons. I saw the report in the Friday morning's *Courier*, and I wondered if I ought to roll round, but I thought it would look as if I was merely after the manuscript, or as if I was morbidly curious. Then again, I had seen Rawley on the Thursday afternoon, and he hinted that relations were not as friendly as they might be, and I—well, I don't know, but I hate strained atmospheres."

Ellis nudged Knollis's elbow, but he need not have bothered. Knollis had not missed a word. He leaned forward.

"You say you were talking to Rawley on Thursday afternoon, Mr. Dexter?"

Dexter stared wonderingly. "Why yes! Wasn't he supposed to be in town? Am I blabbing again?"

"Where did you see him?" demanded Knollis.

"Well," said Dexter, heaving a deep sigh, "I suppose I'd better go the whole hog again—and I do hope I'm not putting Rawley into any trouble. I was down at Little Watney, looking over some stuff, and on my way back I saw Rawley coming out of the pub there—what's its name? The Angel, isn't it? I pulled up and asked him what the deuce he was doing in such a one-eyed hole, and he gave me a broad wink and told me to forget that I'd seen him. A nod is as good as a wink to a blind horse, and I really had forgotten until a minute ago."

"You are sure that it was Thursday, and not either Wednesday or Saturday?"

Dexter took out his diary from his pocket and flicked over the pages.

"Thursday. Tall-boy and grandfather clock bought from Isaac Turton, Green's Row, Little Watney. I haven't fetched them yet, but I paid the old boy twenty quid in notes."

Knollis stared at the opposite wall.

"I feel a bit sick over this business, you know," Dexter stammered. "I've apparently told you things that I should not have mentioned."

"That's all right," said Knollis absently. "We aren't asleep, you know!"

He removed his gaze from the wall and transferred it to Dexter's eyes. "I suppose you could account for all your movements on Thursday night, if it was necessary?"

"Ye-es, I think so. I was in bed when Bob was killed."

"Could you prove that?"

"Why no, I don't suppose I could if it came to the pinch. The maid does not sleep on the premises, and the cook had taken the day off. No, I couldn't *prove* it."

"That's the trouble with alibis," Knollis said smoothly. "They need such a stack of corroborative evidence to hold them up. Ah well, thanks for everything!"

Within the privacy of the car Ellis broke his silence of an hour and a quarter. "Dirty sort of rat, isn't he? He's so openly honest that everybody trusts him. Of course, he didn't really want to give Rawley away twice—oh dear no! All he wants is—"

"Lesley Dexter," said Knollis. "And I'm afraid he will get her, which is a pity, for her."

CHAPTER IX
THE SMALL CHANGE

AFTER LUNCH, Knollis and Ellis once more entered the car, and Knollis steered it through the almost deserted city streets and out into open country.

"Watney?" said Ellis.

"A peaceful little village eight miles out," replied Knollis; "the sort of place you and I dream of retiring to when the pension becomes due."

"And the parson," asked Ellis; "does he live out the same way?"

"Thirty miles in the opposite direction. If you'll notice the sun you'll see that we are going eastwards now. We may see the rector to-day, and if we do, then you'd better turn up your coat collar, because Derbyshire is bleak in October."

"This is a hell of a case," Ellis soliloquized as they sped along the country road. "At the moment it looks horribly complicated, and I know that it will shuffle itself round while we aren't looking and be there, all at once, in one straight line, and we'll wonder why we didn't see it at first."

"There are so many factors to consider," said Knollis. "Lesley has accused Margot Rawley of immorality. Well, she may be immoral. On the other hand it may be nothing but a catty remark, or unconscious spite because Margot was between herself and Dennis Rawley. Then again, regarding the conflicting statements of the two women over the inquiry of the man in the black coat; they may be in conflict merely because whichever of them is wrong refuses to back down and give the other woman superiority. We also have the insinuations of Dexter's cousin; on the face of them they indicate possible guile in previously unsuspected quarters, but who can attempt to judge without facts to substantiate them? Oh, it will clear, but I fancy it is going to be a long case."

"Have you any private ideas about the culprit?" Ellis asked curiously.

Knollis cast him a quick glance, hesitated, and then gave an almost imperceptible nod. "Yes, but I don't believe in uttering them until the whole thing is clear in my mind. Ever studied your own mind, Ellis?"

"Who hasn't?" Ellis retorted.

"Oh, probably ninety per cent of the population!"

"Well, I have—and without much success."

"I don't suppose anybody achieves a great measure of success in dealing with their own mind, but a study of it can have benefits. I find that if I put all the facts down inside, and leave them alone, then in time they achieve a pattern; you hear a click, and the whole thing is before you as plain as a pikestaff. At the moment, for instance, I could put all the facts of this case on paper, but I couldn't do the same with my thoughts and opinions, mainly because they are not yet mature—they are stewing *down there*, wherever that is. Mixing my metaphors, I've let the facts ramble about to their hearts' content, and while I may have suspicions I don't allow them to rise to the surface. That click will come in due course, and then somebody will take one of those famous nine o'clock walks, and Teddy Jessop will earn another tenner."

He grimaced.

"That is the part I don't enjoy. I relish the chase, and the intellectual exercise, but I'm never comfortable in my own mind when I think of the hanging of some person I've hounded down—and this is my fourth murder case. Some years ago I was present at a hanging. It was the execution of Holroyd, the Lincolnshire murderer. I went willingly enough, although God knows why! I came away physically sick. No, I don't like capital punishment, Ellis. I think it fails as a deterrent. You often hear a fellow say he would swing for So-and-so—but would he talk like that if he knew he was booked for life imprisonment if caught? I wonder! Oh well, we don't make the laws, do we?"

"You didn't get a hanging with your other Burnham case, did you? Didn't the fellow commit suicide?"

"True enough," answered Knollis. "Lomas drove his car into the river, just a few miles from here. It was a nice tidy end to the case from my point of view; a short inquest, and it was all over. There was only one snag to it."

"What was that?"

"I was suspected of negligence or collusion, because I've never made any secret of my dislike of capital punishment. I hope nothing of the kind happens in this case, or I'll find myself in trouble!"

They finished the journey in silence, and it took no more than half an hour to confirm Richard Dexter's statement that he had been in Little Watney on the Thursday afternoon. Another hour produced a witness who had seen him pull up to chat with a stranger who had just left the Angel, and the landlord of the inn picked out Rawley's photograph from a handful he was asked to examine. Rawley had arrived shortly before noon, taken lunch, and stayed until three o'clock, when the inn closed. The landlord had seen nothing more of him, and as far as he could remember he had never seen him before.

Knollis turned the car's nose westward, and in a little under two hours he drew up before the iron gates of Windlow Rectory.

The rector, a thin and stringy man of between fifty and sixty years, was scared by their appearance, and of what he was scared Knollis was not sure. He played for safety, hoping that reason would emerge.

"We must apologize for disturbing you, especially on Sunday," he began, "but we are seeking your advice. You possibly read of the murder in Burnham on Thursday night?"

"Oh, I did! I did, Inspector! A terrible affair!"

"Well," continued Knollis, "while going through the dead man's effects we found an old manuscript. We traced it back to Richard Dexter, the dead man's cousin, and he tells me that it is your property. Perhaps you can verify that for us?"

The rector's head came out of his collar like a turtle's head from its carapace. *"S-s-sable Messenger!"*

"Yes, sir, that is the one."

The rector was dithering from head to foot, and Knollis longed to take him by the shoulders and shake him into coherence. But the rector managed to control himself to some extent, and he answered:

"It is mine, Inspector. Oh dear yes. I sold an old chest to Mr. Richard Dexter, you see, and he wrote to say that he had found the manuscript in it. He was having it valued for me, and would then return it. Very honest he was! And he—he said it might be worth a great deal."

Knollis decided on shock tactics.

"I've had it valued, Mr. Saunders. It is worth seven hundred pounds."

The reverend gentleman's Adam's apple went up and down like a celluloid ball in a shooting-gallery. "Seven hundred pounds! That would make all the difference in the world. Who— who would give that for it?" he pleaded.

"A friend of mine who is an expert," replied Knollis.

"But Mr. Dexter told me possibly a hundred," complained the rector.

"Mr. Dexter was only guessing, sir. It had not been valued then."

The rector hastened to reassure him.

"Quite so! Oh, quite so, Inspector. I would not suspect Mr. Dexter of trying to deceive me. A most honest man, Inspector, and most liberal in business!"

"You attempted to get the manuscript back?" asked Knollis.

"Several times, Inspector, but apparently the cousin was experiencing difficulty with the valuers."

Knollis had been taking stock of the room, and he nodded towards the table at which the rector had been writing.

"Busy with your sermons, sir?" he asked in a casual tone.

The rector nodded. "Yes, yes, and it is so difficult to make them sound different. I never was a good writer of sermons. Never very good, I'm afraid."

Knollis twisted his head to study the written sheets.

"Your handwriting seems to be remarkably neat, if I may say so, sir!"

Something approaching a gleam of life came into the rector's watery eyes. His thin lips smiled.

"I am rather proud of my calligraphy. I used to win prizes for it at school, and later I studied the subject to some extent. Perhaps you would care to see my ordinary, everyday writing, which I pride myself is more readable than most? Here, you will appreciate it better now. It was upside-down to you while on the table."

Knollis took the sheet of notepaper. With a dry smile, he said: "You know, sir, you really should not have sent that anonymous note to Robert Dexter! Your writing is too distinctive!"

The rector's finger-tips went to his mouth.

"Oh! I—I knew I would be caught! I meant no harm, Inspector! I was trying to frighten him into sending back my manuscript to his cousin. I thought it out late one night, and then I wrote the two lines from *Sable Messenger* on a sheet of paper and sealed it in an envelope. I found the address in the telephone directory, and I posted it after I had called on Mr. Richard Dexter and learned that his cousin was still withholding my manuscript. I was pressed for money, Inspector. I needed it badly—I still do! You see, I borrowed a hundred and fifty pounds from a gentleman who wrote to me—"

"A moneylender?" Knollis asked gently.

"I am afraid so," the rector answered sorrowfully. "I cannot meet the terms . . ."

"Moneylenders are not of the old Victorian order these days, Mr. Saunders," said Knollis. "I advise you to see a solicitor. I will ask my friend to get in touch with you, although this is complete-ly outside my province. We may be able to free the manuscript within a few days. Having proved ownership, I see no reason why you should not negotiate for its sale if you care to do so."

"Thank you, Inspector," said the rector. "And—and the note! What will happen to me about that?"

Knollis smiled. "The late Mr. Dexter made no complaint to the police, and it does not seem to have had any bearing on his death, so I think it can be forgotten."

The rector was almost in tears as he showed them to the door. "I will never forget your kindness, Inspector. It seems that I still have friends . . ."

Knollis was pleased with life as he drove back over the Der-byshire moors.

"That is another small point well and truly cleared up. We are getting rid of the undergrowth, and shall soon be able to see the real shape of the wood. But the old boy does seem to have got himself in a mess, doesn't he! I must get hold of George Friend, if he doesn't find me first, and see what he can do about the rector's financial state."

"What are we going to do about Rawley?" asked Ellis.

"Play softly for a time, I think. I don't want to alarm him. It is only too evident that he wasn't in Brum on Thursday, neither at the Granby nor the Fir Tree. That means that Goldilocks is in the game—shielding him. I'll get Russett to bring her back. Oh, and there's a job for you! Find a photograph of Richard Dexter for our collection. An idea is buzzing in my head . . ."

Back in Burnham, Knollis went to Sir Wilfrid's office, and carried on with the routine reports for the Yard. He stated that he had hopes of clearing up the case within a week or ten days. There was a good deal of spade-work yet to be done, but he re-mained hopeful of a successful conclusion, together with a suffi-ciency of facts for placing before the public prosecutor.

On entering the office he had first telephoned to Birming-ham, asking for Russett to call him when he could be found. The call came through in an hour's time, and Russett anxiously asked why he was wanted.

"Goldilocks," Knollis said grimly. "Invite her to return with you, but get her here if you have to abduct her. And don't tell her why we want to interview her!"

"How can I," complained Russett, "when I don't know myself? What has happened at your end?"

"All I'll tell you on the wires is that Rawley was in Little Watney a few hours before the job was done. That suggest anything to you?"

"Perjury," Russett said quickly.

"How right you are!" returned Knollis. "By the way, I've cleared up the ownership of the manuscript, and the origin of the *Sable Messenger* note, which latter means nothing at all. The case is narrowing, Russett. When do you think you will be through there?"

"Tomorrow evening," Russett replied. "I had a stroke of luck. One of the bookshops was open this afternoon. Saw it on the way from the station, so I went straight round after I'd parked my bags. All Dexter's business there was strictly on the up and up. Nothing suspicious at all."

"Good work," said Knollis. "By the way, you can promise Goldilocks the usual expenses, although I suppose I'll have to pay them out of my pocket, the system being what it is. That's all for now. Good hunting and good night!"

He rang off, and looked up to see Ellis standing before him, holding out a photograph.

"Luvly picture of Dicky Dexter. Got it from the *Echo* office. They photographed a dinner at which he was present. Anything else before tea?"

Knollis consulted his watch, and then grinned.

"Too late for tea, my friend. I suggest that you find a convenient constable and ask him to rustle up a pot of tea. Then I want you to slip along to Frogmore Street and diplomatically ask Lesley if she would mind coming along to help me with one or two points. The term is euphemistic. I want to tackle her about the relations existing between the two villas prior to her hubby's death, and I'm not at my best in her mother's home. The atmosphere is all against me."

"I know," said Ellis. "A man's a king on his own midden!"

"And tomorrow, Russett and Rogers being away, you'll have to go on your lonesome and see Goodwoods about the rope. *And* I want positive identification, Ellis!"

"I know," Ellis retorted. "Do I ever come home with anything but the truth, the whole truth, and nothing but the truth? Am I Inspector Russett?"

A smile faded into Knollis's features.

"Go and see about that tea—and a few sandwiches or pastries wouldn't go down badly."

"You seem to forget that we are in the midst of a peace," Ellis retorted as he wandered out.

Lesley Dexter arrived a few minutes before six o'clock, and Knollis went to a certain amount of trouble to make her comfortable and set her at her ease.

"The matter on which I wish to consult you is rather a delicate one," he said smoothly. "You have known the Rawleys for a little over eighteen months, haven't you?"

"More than that, Inspector," she replied. "They were both members of the tennis club when I joined, and it was Mrs. Rawley who suggested that we should live down River Close. Mr. Rawley let Bob know when he found out that Himalaya Villa was coming empty, so that he was able to negotiate for it before the other tenants left."

"I see," said Knollis, drawing cats on the blotter. "Then the Rawleys were married when you first knew them?"

"Oh yes! They had been married quite a few years."

"Now, Mrs. Dexter," said Knollis, settling himself in his chair; "has Dennis Rawley at any time shown attentions to you?"

Lesley Dexter seemed surprised. "Good gracious, Inspector! Why should you ever think of such a thing? He certainly has not! I am surprised that you should suggest it."

"I did not suggest it," Knollis replied quietly. "I was merely asking. I am seeking a motive for your husband's death, and must consequently explore every possibility, no matter how far-fetched it may be. You don't seem able to suggest any motive, nor yet any possible person who could be guilty."

Lesley dabbed at her eyes with a handkerchief. "I wish I could, Inspector. It—it's awful, and I'm afraid!"

"Afraid of what, Mrs. Dexter?"

"I—I don't know!"

"Am I correct in assuming that your husband's cousin was his rival at the time he was courting you, Mrs. Dexter?"

Her eyes appeared over the top of the handkerchief, wide eyes that stared. "Ye-yes!"

"Would you say that there was any bad blood between them?"

Lesley considered that. "I hate all this!" she said at length.

"So do I," said Knollis, "but I would remind you again that I am investigating the circumstances surrounding your husband's death!"

"Have I got to answer your questions?" Lesley asked timorously.

"You don't *have* to answer them," Knollis replied firmly, "but I prefer to learn the real state of affairs from you rather than from common gossip and spiteful acquaintances."

"Oh!" Lesley said limply. She added: "Richard did take it rather badly at the time."

"And your husband? How did he react to his cousin's attitude, Mrs. Dexter?"

She squared her shoulders, and her chin took on a more jaunty angle as she replied: "He was violently protective—said he would thrash Richard if he persisted in trying to persuade me to marry him!"

Knollis nodded, and made a note.

"And after you were married, Mrs. Dexter? Have you seen much of Richard Dexter? Has he attempted to pay court to you? I'm really sorry about these questions," Knollis aided.

"No-o," she replied; "he hasn't pursued me, but I always think that he would have me if he could get the chance—although that may be vanity! But he wasn't bad, Inspector! He was—well, very much in love with me."

"And you have seen him occasionally?"

"Well, yes," she admitted reluctantly. "I've run into him in Hawton's sometimes when I've called for morning coffee—purely accidental meetings, of course!"

Knollis added to his notes, and then looked up and asked: "So that I take it you see him most weeks?"

"Well, yes!"

"You visit Hawton's Café most mornings, I believe—up to the time of your husband's death, that is!"

"Yes," she said in a small voice.

"And so does Richard Dexter!" stated Knollis.

"Not—not every morning, Inspector. Oh, why must you ask all these awful questions? You strip every shred of privacy from me!"

"Somebody," Knollis replied dryly, "stripped your husband of his life! I am only interested in him, and whatever it was that brought about his death."

Lesley lowered her eyes, and was silent.

"I am now going to suggest, Mrs. Dexter," Knollis went on, "that you have flirted to some extent with your husband's cousin during these—er—accidental meetings?"

"Inspector Knollis!" she exclaimed in a shocked tone.

"I would like an answer," said Knollis.

"Well, I may have done, mildly. There was no harm in it! I've known him for a very long time—and he *was* Bob's cousin, you know!"

"Quite candidly, Mrs. Dexter, I don't care whether he was cousin or brother to your husband. I am not in any way interested in the ethics of your behaviour, being only concerned with facts. Now, in a previous interview you hinted that Mrs. Rawley was interested in your husband?"

"Did I?" Lesley asked in the most innocent of voices.

"You most certainly did, Mrs. Dexter. Do you wish that accusation to remain in your statement?"

"Well, it was true!" she replied.

"Mere suspicion, Mrs. Dexter? Or perhaps you have definite proof that she was interested in him!"

"She set her cap at him in no uncertain way!" Lesley snapped back. She was growing belligerent, and Knollis watched her through his narrow eyes.

"On what occasions?" he asked briefly.

"She dragged him off to one of the Amateurs' meetings, a rehearsal it was, and then she started calling round to see him during the evenings. She was calling to see him, and not me! I know what she was doing, all right! She tried to treat me like a child in front of Bob, and talk to him as if they were both of an age. And she made a pretence of being interested in his collecting. She tried to get him to write for the Amateurs, and that is what he was doing with that old manuscript, if you want to know!" she added defiantly.

Knollis sighed his relief. Lesley's tongue was loosened, and he had no intention of breaking the train of thought she had released.

"Robert, of course," she went on, "was too blind to see her game. He was flattered, and resented my lack of interest all the more. And then, about six weeks ago—well, I don't really know what happened, but he had been round to see her while Dennis Rawley was out, and he came back in a roaring temper. He said she was a foul bitch, and—oh, a lot of things I never knew he was capable of saying. He wanted to know if one husband wasn't enough for her, and that she could go to the devil as far as he was concerned. I managed to calm him down, and he gave me a sheepish grin and said he was glad that I wasn't like that. To tell the truth, I felt a wee bit mean about the way I'd flirted with Richard, and I made up my mind to put a stop to it. . . ."

"Yes," Knollis murmured gently.

"A few days later I was walking to the bus stop, and she came out of the gate and joined me, and I couldn't avoid her without being openly rude. We walked to the end of Wisden Avenue together, and she was making insinuations all the way about Bob being an incompetent husband, and how sorry she was for me, and—oh, I couldn't tell anybody!"

"There is no need to do so, Mrs. Dexter."

"Then the threatening letter came. It was unsigned, but we knew it was from her."

"Threatening letter?" asked Knollis.

"It was a quotation from the manuscript that Robert was working on, and it couldn't be taken any other way but as a threat!"

"That was the note we found on the mantel in the lounge? The one about the *Sable Messenger*?"

"Yes, that is the one," Lesley agreed.

Knollis considered the matter, and decided not to enlighten her as to its real source. So long as she was incensed against Margot Rawley, just so long would she drain her mind.

"How did your husband react to the note, Mrs. Dexter?"

"He was very annoyed," said Lesley. "He said it was obvious where it came from, for nobody but himself and Margot Rawley had seen the manuscript. Richard had not bothered to read it, and I was not even interested, and so it must be Margot. He said he would do nothing about it unless it was followed by another, and then he would come along to the police."

"So the translation—and adaptation—was for the Amateurs?"

"Yes, even after his row with Margot Rawley he carried on with it, because he thought that Mrs. Stanley would see about it being put into production. He was hurrying with it because Richard was pressing for the return of the original," she said.

"Did Richard Dexter call at the house at all?"

"Three times, Inspector. I was out on the third occasion, but Robert told me when I got home that he had called."

"Richard Dexter was wanting it back," murmured Knollis. "Have you any idea why, Mrs. Dexter?"

"Oh yes," she said frankly. "He said it represented money, and that he wasn't in business for the good of his health. I'm afraid that Robert told him that it was still in London! Still," she added naively, "it was a harmless deceit, wasn't it? I mean, he was trying to give something to the world! I *do* wish now that I'd shown more interest in his work, because he would have been so much happier . . ."

"Do you think that Dennis Rawley had any idea about his wife's interest in your husband?"

Lesley hesitated. "I don't know, but I think he did. After the row that Robert had with Margot he—Dennis—seemed much kinder in his manner towards me. I can't explain, but it was as if he was sorry for me! But then, I don't really know whether he knew anything about it or not, do I?"

"True enough, Mrs. Dexter," Knollis agreed. He went on: "Dennis Rawley's attitude towards your husband?"

"Well, I didn't see them together very often, but I do think that Dennis was watching him—just as if Margot had accused Robert of making suggestions to her!"

Knollis rose and went round the table.

"Thank you for coming along, Mrs. Dexter. You have made the situation crystal-clear to me. I am grateful for your kindness."

Lesley looked shyly at him. "I've said some awful things, haven't I, Inspector?"

Knollis gave a slight bow. "I am a very discreet man, Mrs. Dexter. In my line of work one has to listen and not repeat. Now let me show you out . . ."

He later remarked to Ellis: "That is all the small change duly collected. We can now count it and see what it makes in shillings."

CHAPTER X

THE STORY OF GOLDILOCKS

KNOLLIS RECEIVED a message from Birmingham early on the Monday morning. Russett, eager to shine, had already seen Nancy Locke, and in her devotion to Dennis Rawley she had promised to return to Burnham with him, and had turned down the offer of expenses.

Knollis read the dictated message with a cryptic smile, and went out to interview Margot Rawley. He went early, before she had time to get properly awakened, for he suspected her of having a far shrewder mind than appeared from her expression.

She received him gracefully enough, even though there was a large question-mark written on her forehead.

"I'm sorry to disturb you so early in the day," said Knollis, pushing forward his favourite pawn. "I was hoping to catch your husband before he went to business."

Margot Rawley's eyes turned with surprise to the clock, the hands of which showed half-past nine. "My husband has been at the works a full hour, Inspector Knollis."

"Perhaps, in that case, you can help me yourself, Mrs. Rawley," said Knollis, quite unabashed. "There are so many details in a case of this nature that one never gets them all cleared up straight away."

"Well, if there *is* anything else . . ." she said in a doubtful voice, and she eyed him warily.

"My question is mainly about Robert Dexter," said Knollis, "which is why I was hoping to see your husband, as being more in touch with him. It appears that Dexter was interested in old manuscripts—plays and the like. I wonder if you happen to know anything about the one he was rewriting for the Amateur Dramatic Society?"

"I did know that he was doing something of that nature," Margot Rawley said cautiously, "because Mrs. Hendrick Stanley mentioned it to me. He came along to meetings and rehearsals on several occasions to get ideas on production, but I'm afraid I can tell you nothing about it!"

"Yet you were interested in his hobby, Mrs. Rawley!" Knollis pointed out. He made it a definite statement of fact, and no question.

"Oh? Was I?" she retorted defiantly. "I didn't know!"

"Your good friend, Mrs. Dexter, told me so. She said that you were very helpful to her husband on more than one occasion while he was working on the manuscript!"

Margot Rawley was instantly all sweetness and cream.

"Ah, dear Lesley! Such a child, Inspector! And so lacking in understanding of her husband! Instead of taking an interest in his little hobby-horse she merely ridiculed it, and I do think that there is nothing worse than a wife lacking in understanding!"

"I'm sure you do, Mrs. Rawley," said Knollis briefly. "Tell me; were you helping him right up to the time of his death?"

"Do I have to tell you *everything*?" she asked with a fair imitation of arch supplication.

"You don't have to, but I hope you will!"

"But the convention, Inspector! You know—*De mortuis nil nisi bonum!*"

"He's dead," said Knollis dryly. "I don't think you can do him much harm, and I happen to be interested in the whys and wherefores that brought him to his death. I am searching for a killer, and conventions cannot be allowed to stand in the way."

"Then I suppose I must," said Margot Rawley with a deep and regretful sigh. "Of course, Inspector, you must realize that I did not cause any trouble over it. When a man is *so* neglected by his wife, and in such *vital* ways, he is inclined to do things and say things which are normally completely foreign to his nature."

"You are trying to say that Dexter made improper suggestions to you, Mrs. Rawley?"

She lowered her eyes, and stared at her shoes.

"Yes," she said in a small voice.

"Dear me!" murmured Knollis diplomatically. "And, of course, you reported this to your husband!"

"I had to, of course," she said, looking up. "I had quite a job with him, too! I cannot blame him, but he wanted to go round and thrash poor Mr. Dexter. I persuaded him not to do so, if only for poor Lesley's sake. He saw my point after a long argument, and it was *only* for her sake that he promised to let the whole matter drop. It would have caused such a scandal in town!"

"Your husband respected Mrs. Dexter?" asked Knollis. "Am I to infer that from your statements?"

"Yes! He was sorry for her because—how I hate saying it!— Bob Dexter was such an awful boor. He could talk about nothing but his books and his work, and, after all, he was only in *Packing*, which seems to me to be such a very dull subject!"

Knollis tapped his toe on the carpet. "I see your point, Mrs. Rawley. Now perhaps you could clear up one other angle for me. Did you by any chance happen to know Dexter's cousin, Richard Dexter?"

"Well, I have met him," she replied. "Occasionally I would drop into Hawton's for morning coffee, and I would see him there with Lesley."

"They met there? Is that what you are suggesting?" She gave a short laugh. "I wouldn't say that, Inspector, but as they both frequent the same café, and the same table!"

"I see," Knollis replied shortly. "By the way, do you happen to know Richard Dexter's address?"

"As a matter of fact I do, because I once called round with Lesley. She was wanting a few pieces for the house, and she wondered if he had anything that was likely to be suitable. He is an antique dealer, you know!"

"Really!" murmured Knollis. He felt round his pockets. "Perhaps you could jot down the address for me? I appear to have left my notebook in the car—a very foolish thing to do, and unusual for me."

Margot Rawley went to an escritoire in the window, and returned with a scrap of paper on which she had scrawled the address. Knollis gave it one short glance, and a fleeting expression of satisfaction passed over his lean features.

"I don't suppose that any correspondence ever passed between yourself and Mr. Dexter?"

Margot Rawley exhibited all the signs of being shocked.

"Correspondence indeed! Of course not, Inspector!"

"Then perhaps you can explain the existence of a note, in this handwriting, and initialled by yourself, which we found in the Dexter house?"

Margot Rawley poised a finger on her chin. "Ah! Now wait a minute! I did push a small note under the door one evening when he was going along to the Amateurs! But I would hardly term it correspondence, Inspector!"

"Perhaps not," admitted Knollis; "but you do agree that it was written by you?"

"I admit the writing of one note, but whether it is the one you mention—I can hardly say that until I have seen it, now can I?"

"Quite a fair conclusion, Mrs. Rawley. You shall certainly have the chance of identifying it. Good morning!"

He went back to his car, and as he slammed the door he saw Margot Rawley's figure close to the coloured lights in the wing of the porch. She was busy on the telephone. Knollis screwed his lips into an expression of utter distaste, and drove back to the city centre.

He parked his car, and walked along the street to Hawton's Oriental Restaurant and Café. He entered, found himself a convenient table which was partly hidden by a circular coat-stand, and ordered coffee and biscuits. Then, having sidled in without being recognized by Burnham's Smart Set, whose rendezvous this was, he settled down to listen to the conversations.

"Nothing more in the morning papers about the Dexter man, I see!"

"Oh, they may as well close the case and forget it. You know what the police are like, my dear! And, after all, in spite of the fuss they make about Scotland Yard, they aren't so clever after all. I mean, look at those Brighton trunk murders! There must be simply dozens of murderers who get away with it every year."

"These detectives are so troublesome when they are around. I believe poor dear Lesley has been simply swamped with them since Thursday night! I was talking to Mrs. Stanley yesterday evening, and she tells me that they have even been round there to see if anyone could have borrowed a disguise from her props! Ridiculous, isn't it?"

"I haven't seen the other Dexter fellow around since it happened. Still, it would look rather bad for him to be seen around with Lesley just now, wouldn't it? He's so awfully keen on her, isn't he? And poor Lesley's so slow—I wish he would try to seduce me . . ."

"Your hubby would be annoyed, dear, surely!"

"Oh well, we'd have to murder him, wouldn't we? Thank heavens he isn't as dull as Lesley's husband. Never went to parties, or got drunk, or anything, and I believe that he only took her to the theatre once a year, on her birthday. I sometimes wonder whether it's better to have a husband who makes too much love, or the other way round. And not being allowed to have more than one official husband—you do see what I mean?"

Knollis decided that there was nothing to be learned that he did not already know, and so he went to the Key and Clock, and engaged the barman in conversation.

"Mr. Robert Dexter used to patronize this house, didn't he?" he asked, leaning on the bar and giving an order.

The barman scowled belligerently across the counter.

"Who the 'ell are you?"

"Inspector Knollis, New Scotland Yard."

"Oh! Sorry, sir, but we've had too many unofficial detectives and nosy-parkers round here for my liking. It's the same every time I serve a drink. But answering your question, sir; yes, I knew him well. Used to come in two or three evenings a week. Sometimes he'd go in the billiards-room for an hour, and another time he'd have two sharp and then leave. Very nice gentleman was Mr. Dexter," he said reminiscently. "Pity he got knocked off!"

"You'll know his cousin?" asked Knollis.

"Mr. Richard Dexter? Yes, I knew him."

The barman swept a duster over the counter, and added: "If I ain't treading on any corns, well, I didn't like him half as well."

"His neighbour, Mr. Rawley? You knew him?"

"Him and Mr. Richard is pretty thick. Spend a lot of time with their heads together, they do."

Knollis suddenly became interested.

"They do, eh? Found something in common just recently?" The barman tacked away from Knollis.

"Well, I can't really say that, sir. There's a lot of gents comes in here, and I don't have time to watch em, even if I wanted to, but things have been a bit quiet this last week or two, and it seemed to me that the two gents you mention had found something in common—and not that you'd expect 'em to either, 'cos they don't seem that way."

"They never talked against the bar?" asked Knollis. "I mean, there was no chance of you overhearing their conversation?"

"No, sir. Usually stood over there by the door what leads into the yard, but I haven't seen anything of either of 'em for a few nights. By the way, sir, it never struck me till just now. I 'ope neither of them is in trouble!"

Knollis laughed. "You needn't worry."

He returned to the station, to find Ellis waiting for him with a smile.

"The rope trick's finished. Goodwoods recognized it as their stuff, and as supplied to the Amateurs."

Knollis shook his head doubtfully.

"That's all right in its way, Ellis, but I sincerely hope that I don't have to bring it into court as a vital piece of evidence. A good defence would soon produce a dozen like it from various parts of the country, and then ask Goodwoods to identify their own—and that wouldn't help us one little bit! It's quite interesting, and quite satisfactory from our point of view, but I'm hoping it will only be needed as a lead to more valuable evidence."

He paused.

"I suppose you know that Goldilocks has volunteered to come back with Russett to clear Rawley?"

"M'm!" said Ellis. "I saw the message on the desk before I went out this morning. It should be an interesting interview. She'll have to be a good liar to get away with it."

Knollis shook his head at Ellis. "I'll be surprised if she has to lie at all. In fact, I think you will be surprised at the way things will turn out."

"What have you got up your sleeve this time?" Ellis asked with a suspicious glance at his chief.

"Just wait," Knollis replied impishly. "Let me have a chance to turn on the drama for once in a while. Most of this business is so prosaic that I sometimes wonder if I am going flat-headed."

Ellis stood on tiptoe, and sank down again.

"There's still a fairish dome on top. I wouldn't worry if I were you."

"We'll away to lunch, Watson, and then we must beard Dayton in his own den. I'd like a confidential chat with that gentleman. Considering his responsible position he is either singularly obtuse, or singularly careless, and I am not quite sure which!"

"What on earth have you got hold of now?" Ellis queried.

Knollis stared at his assistant. "What is wrong with you? Good Lord, I know it's Black Monday, but surely you have seen through Dayton! It hits your eye as you walk past."

Ellis puckered his brows for a minute, and then shook his head. "Sorry, sir, but I don't get it."

But he saw Knollis's suspicion, and saw it proved as truth a few minutes after they were seated in the bank manager's office.

"I am Inspector Knollis. A few days ago you informed Inspector Russett that the late Robert Dexter was one of your clients . . ."

The manager stayed him with a raised hand.

"I know! I know! I made a horrible mistake—a gaffe! I only saw the headlines of the paper, and it was not until the photographs appeared in the *Echo* and the *Courier* that I realized my error. I am truly sorry, Inspector, and especially as I revealed details of a client's account. It is unpardonable, and I only hope the client, Mr. Richard Dexter, will not hear of it. I can only offer my apologies and hope that it has not caused you any great inconvenience."

"It has," Knollis replied gravely. "We have spent two full days trying to discover the source of Robert Dexter's income—about which his wife naturally enough knew nothing. It was not until I learned of Richard Dexter's existence that I realized the mistake you had made, and was able to call off my men from the job."

Ellis pursed his lips and nodded his understanding.

"If there is anything I can do . . . ?" the manager muttered.

"There is," Knollis said firmly, "and you will probably object to the idea. I would like to know if money has passed between the two Dexters, or between Richard Dexter and a Mr. Dennis Rawley."

"Well," said the manager hesitantly, "I do not like providing the information, but I am under a great obligation to you, and if you care to wait a few minutes I will examine the books. Excuse me, please."

Ellis chuckled when they were alone. "I never thought of that. He jumped to conclusions, eh? I hope he doesn't sleep o' nights for all the trouble he has caused us."

"I don't suppose he will for a few nights," replied Knollis. "He has been extremely indiscreet for a man in his position. He can't do much for us by way of return, and I quite expect his answer to be in the negative."

Knollis was proved right once more, and after receiving further apologies they returned to the station and the routine business of writing up reports.

Russett returned from Birmingham that night, and shortly after eight o'clock he telephoned to Knollis's hotel and asked him to go round to the station. "I've got little Goldilocks with me, and, oh boy, wait until you see her!"

Miss Nancy Locke was willing, eager, and almost anxious to help. She was also very blonde, very curvacious, very blue-eyed, and very well dressed, surprisingly, in a quiet style. Knollis discreetly eyed her up and down and decided that she was not as black—or red—as she had been painted.

"So you are Miss Locke?" he murmured as he placed a chair for her in such a position that the light from the hanging bowl shone fully on her face.

"Nancy Locke, and no monkey business," she retorted.

"And no monkey business," Knollis replied. "I see that you don't trust the police!"

"Who does?" came the quick answer.

"Oh, thousands of people! Probably hundreds of thousands. We aren't really bad, you know, and we haven't hanged many innocent people."

"Perhaps not," she replied surlily, "but you won't let honest people alone!"

"Honest people?" Knollis asked in surprise. "Such as—"

"Well, Denny Rawley for one. You've evidently got a bee in your bonnet about him, and I'm here to take it out. I want to help him—and I wouldn't do it if I didn't know that he was as straight as they make them! Not Nancy Locke!"

"Good enough," Knollis said cheerfully. "If you can clear Dennis Rawley of whatever it is you think we have on him, all for the best! We're here to prove people innocent as well as guilty, you know. All I want to know is how long you have known him."

Nancy Locke hitched her skirt upward for half an inch, and contrived to show an extra inch and a half of leg—a feat of sleight of hand which no man could achieve in a lifetime of practice.

"A year; that's how long I've known him."

Knollis looked puzzled. "A year!"

"A solid year of twelve months, or three hundred and sixty-five days as it isn't leap year," replied Nancy Locke.

"Quite!" murmured Knollis. "I appreciate the general knowledge supplied at no extra cost, but I was surprised to hear that you had known him so long. Do you mind telling me where you first met him?"

Miss Locke shook her golden curls from side to side as she answered pertly: "Not at all."

Knollis suppressed an exclamation of impatience.

"Then where did you meet him?"

"In the Granby Hotel smoke-room. Well, it isn't exactly the smoke-room, because that is the men's room. Call it the saloon bar, and you'll be right."

Knollis leaned forward. "How long have you known him as Dennis Rawley?"

Nancy Locke's head jerked sharply, and a hint of admiration came into her eyes. "You're different to most of the coppers, aren't you? Got a head on your shoulders! You're a clever one. But how did you know that he gave me a wrong name at first?"

"A conjurer doesn't give away his tricks," replied Knollis. "But it's quite a regular thing, isn't it?" he asked in a tantalizing manner.

"Right. They do. Denny told me that his name was—"

"John Smith?" suggested Knollis.

She met the suggestion with scorn. "You lose a mark there! You aren't as clever as I thought. It wasn't John Smith. It was Ralph Denham."

Knollis smiled. It was the old trick of sticking to the original initials.

"When did he tell you that his real name was—er—Dennis Rawley?"

Goldilocks tossed her head. "Oh, only a few weeks ago. I played hell with him for keeping me in the dark, but he said he was a careful sort of chap, and hadn't wanted to tell me until he had made up his mind to stick to me. Here, that is his proper name, isn't it?"

"Why shouldn't it be?" demanded Knollis, extending his hands.

Nancy Locke rested her chin on her knuckled hands and pondered for a time.

"I'm not sure," she answered eventually. "You see, I noticed the initials inside his hat—in gold letters, you know! *R.D.* they was, and when I asked him why they were wrong way round he said it was a habit he'd picked up in the army—he was a captain, you know!"

"I didn't know," said Knollis.

"Anyway, he said they always had the surname first on all army papers. Is that right?" she asked anxiously.

"Quite correct," Knollis replied disarmingly.

She relaxed with a deep sigh. "It didn't seem right to me, but if you say so, then goody-goody says me. I *knew* he was on the level. *R.D.* does stand for Rawley—Dennis, doesn't it?"

"It could do, Miss Locke!"

She smiled at Knollis. "You're different to most of the mob I've met. You're polite! Back in Brum, when they've tried to fasten something on me—you know!—they call me *Blondie*, and *You there*, and *Oi!* You call me *Miss Locke*, and it sounds good, coming from a copper. You're a gentleman!"

"Thank you," said Knollis. "And yet, perhaps I am just tricking you, trying to keep you in a good mood while I get the information I need. I wouldn't trust the coppers, Miss Locke!"

She shook her head vigorously, so that her curls danced again. "No, I don't think that. You are different—like Denny. I say, Inspector . . ."

"Well, Miss Locke?"

"You haven't really got anything on Denny, have you?"

"Shall I be frank with you, Miss Locke? Rawley's neighbour was murdered, as you already know if you read the papers. We had to check on everybody in the neighbourhood—you know that routine well enough, don't you?"

"Don't I!" she exclaimed expressively.

"Rawley said he was at the Granby Hotel that night. We checked on his statement, and found that he had booked a room there for that night and the next day, but that he didn't claim it until half-past ten on the next morning. Since you also know how suspicious we policemen are, you will realize that we wanted to know where he really was, and he refused to say."

"That's Denny!" she said excitedly. "Protect a woman! Good old Denny!"

"And so," Knollis went on, "we checked further, and learned that he had spent the night at the Fir Tree Hotel with a lady. Now you see why we were interested in you! If Rawley was in Birmingham with you, then he could not have been in Burnham, could he? And, to finish the story, we found an oldest inhabitant in a nearby village who said he had seen him that day, Thursday. So we just had to invite you along to clear him."

"Well, that's fair enough and straight enough," said Nancy Locke. "I'll tell you what I wouldn't tell another soul on earth! He really was at the Fir Tree, and we spent the night together, and if you want that putting on paper and signing, I'll do it."

She traced the pattern on the carpet with her eyes.

"Denny's been real good to me since I knew him, and there's nobody else for me but him. He got me fixed up in a little place all on my own, and when he comes over we go out to an hotel so that nobody won't notice nothing. He's straight with me—he says he is!"

"How much has he told you about himself?" asked Knollis.

"Not much, really, because I haven't asked him. Things like that don't matter when you like somebody. But I've been to theatres and places since I've known him—places I hadn't been to before. And the things he knows! He's been all over the world, and he's promised that one day—when they start again—he'll take me on one of those cruises."

She tipped her head thoughtfully.

"You know, Inspector, I think I could get him to marry me if I tried hard!"

"Then why don't you?"

She shrugged her shoulders. "Oh, I don't know. It doesn't seem fair to tie him down. He's too decent for that."

"That must be your own affair," said Knollis. "For myself, I thank you for coming along. Will you do one more thing for me? Will you go straight back to Birmingham without trying to see him, and promise not to see him for a full week?"

She hesitated, and then said: "Okay, Inspector! But I don't know where he lives, in any case. He always telephones me when he is coming over. I was going to try to find him, but I won't since you ask me. Is there a train back to-night?"

"We'll find out for you. In the meantime you must have a meal, and then we'll take you to the station by car. Ellis! You will see to Miss Locke."

Ellis folded his notebook.

As Nancy Locke was following him from the office, Knollis took a handful of photographs from the drawer of the desk.

"As a final identification, will you please sort out Rawley's photograph from these?"

She shuffled them, and smilingly separated one, which she handed to him. "That's Denny!"

"Thank you," Knollis said solemnly. "Good night, Miss Locke."

He lowered an eyelid. "Look after her, Ellis!"

They ran into Sir Wilfrid Burrows and Russett in the doorway, and passed through as they stood aside.

"Well," asked Russett, "what did you get from her?" Knollis indicated the photograph lying on the table.

"She identified Dennis Rawley for me. As I suspected, it is Richard Dexter's photograph!"

CHAPTER XI
THE LEAD-IN

DESPITE BOTH Sir Wilfrid's and Russett's earnest advice to rush out and arrest somebody, Knollis slept on Nancy Locke's information, and slept soundly. With the morning he saw the case in a new light, and he knew that the rushing-around stages were over. From now on it was to be patient, plodding work which would consist of tracing here, checking there, and slowly building a mountain of definitive fact that would justify the public prosecutor in taking the case before a jury.

Knollis had three suspects on his list now: Margot Rawley, Dennis Rawley, and Richard Dexter. He was inclined to dismiss Margot Rawley, for on the face of such evidence as he possessed it seemed that she had been completely ignorant of her husband's intentions, and, presumably, of any murderous intentions he might have conceived and put into commission against Bob Dexter.

And yet there was another angle. If the husband was the killer of Bob Dexter, then she had either not recognized him when he knocked on his own door—which seemed preposterous, or else she was an accessory both before and after the fact.

And if she was an accessory, then why should husband and wife go to the trouble to create a story about a man in a black coat and hat calling at the wrong house? Again, why should Margot Rawley stick to her story that he had asked for the house of the Smiths?

If Margot Rawley was innocent of collusion and conspiracy, then could it be possible that she had not recognized her husband? It would need a clever disguise to stand such a test, and Dennis Rawley, so far as the evidence went, was not even a novice in such matters. And why should it be necessary? If Rawley wanted to kill Dexter, then what was to prevent him going straight to the Dexter door and killing Dexter? He had an alibi in Birmingham, and quite a good one it was—or would have been if Richard Dexter had taken Nancy Locke completely into his confidence; for it was fair to assume that she would have played squarely with him.

Was Margot Rawley's story a fabricated one? Had she recognized her husband as he went to the Dexter door, or as he came away? Had she invented the story *after* Dexter's death in order to cover her husband's activities? And did Rawley know that his wife had both seen and recognized him?

Knollis was quite satisfied that the story of the man-in-black was an invention—but with what end in view? Again, he was faced with the undeniable evidence that Lesley Dexter had overheard the conversation. If the story was, as he believed, a fiction, then it surely indicated that Lesley Dexter was a party to the conspiracy, and that in its turn suggested that three people had conspired to kill one man whose death apparently benefited no one.

Now cut out both Lesley and Margot as possible conspirators. That left Richard Dexter and Dennis Rawley. What purpose could they hope to achieve by killing Bob Dexter?

No! The theories were all fanciful and conjectural. What, Knollis asked himself, had he in the way of actual fact? He seated himself at the table in his bed-sitting-room, and began to make a list of his suspects:

LESLEY DEXTER: widow of the deceased. She had been the cause of a rivalry between the two cousins, and had lately flirted with her husband's unsuccessful rival. Took no interest in husband's hobbies—a point of contention between them—and seemed to have drawn away from him. Tried to push him on, but not successfully it would seem. Further point of contention: husband's outlay on his hobby. Considered own and husband's savings as insufficient for their social position. Certainly did not hate husband, and apparently estrangement had not even reached stage of mild dislike.

RICHARD DEXTER: cousin of deceased. Financially stable, and consequently no motive there. Seems to have weakness for women, but strong instinct for self-preservation would seem to be main obstacle when considering his capability of murdering Bob to get Lesley. Suspected of having first-rate mind, even if he did not make best use of it—normal human weakness, this! Provided alibi, with or without intention or knowledge, for Dennis Rawley. Note: Put the screw on him.

DENNIS RAWLEY: neighbour of deceased, and friend—possibly. Considering his type, the avenging-honour motive doesn't seem strong enough in his case to push him into murder. No other apparent motive for killing Dexter, and yet deliberately lied to wife as to whereabouts on night of murder. Suppose that wife played Lady Macbeth, inciting him until he cracked under the pressure? Then, as he turned weak and tried to regain entrance to own house, she urged him on, and used his call to provide melodramatic alibi? Sounds feasible.

MARGOT RAWLEY: wife of the above. Queer streak of masculinity in her mental make-up. Don't trust her. Sticks too closely to her story, as if carefully rehearsed. Most unwitness-like—

Knollis wrote "Oh damn!" under the list, and sat back to regard his notes. It looked all too complicated, and yet he knew very well that once he got a lead it would come out as smoothly as wool from a wool-box. It was merely a matter of finding the lead, the one loose end which, when pulled, would release the rest in the right order. And there were loose ends sticking out at all angles!

One thing he must not do was alarm Rawley. How then, to get at him? Where was Rawley last seen before the murder? The answer was on the table before him, in his notebook: outside the Angel at Little Watney. And that gave another hint—and, by jove, it was an important one. Why had he overlooked it? *It was Dexter the Second who had given away Rawley!*

Knollis plaited his fingers and thought that one out. *Was* Rawley in Little Watney? Apparently he was. He had been recognized, and that without any chance of a mistake. But where did he go after that? He had not been seen again until he showed up at the Granby at half-past ten on the Friday morning! There was a period of twenty and a half hours to be accounted for.

And, Knollis asked himself, why had Dexter given him away, for it was becoming more obvious every minute that they were partners in a conspiracy?

He stalked round the room with his hands plunged deep into his trouser pockets. There was a similar patch in all these cases. It was like the darkest hour before the dawn, when everything seemed abysmally hopeless, and the end of the world seemed to be in sight. There was always that same danger, too, of mistaking the greyish light of the false dawn for the real dawn . . .

He went down to the dining-room, to find Ellis at the breakfast-table, and struggling with an austerity fish-cake.

"You get no bread with one fish-ball," misquoted Ellis. "Good morning, sir!"

"'Morning, Ellis. Wrestling with Satan?"

"Satan? I bet this fish pulled the bloke out of the boat—if it is fish. You're late this morning. Had a bad night?"

"No, just a very early morning," replied Knollis. "I've been trying to see my way through the case, and I've come to the conclusion that I'm either going stale or something else equally absurd—dull, because I'm hanged if I can see anything but a most inglorious jumble. What do you make of it, Watson?"

"Not much," replied Ellis, "but if I leave it I get nothing else to eat."

"I'm talking about the case, you ass, not the fish!"

Ellis looked up with mock surprise in his eyes.

"What can you expect me to do with it when the master mind is baffled! You know, Holmes, you are a most disappointing fellow. You haven't collected one cigarette-butt on this job!"

"So short of smokes?" chuckled Knollis. Then the smile faded, Knollis-like.

"I've got a rotten job for you, old man!"

"I know! I know!" said Ellis, assuming a sorrowful mien. "You don't have to tell me. You want me to go to Little Watney and attempt to trail Brother Rawley through the day and all through the night."

"How the deuce do you know that?"

"I'm turning psychic," said Ellis. "Seriously though, isn't that the obvious move?"

Knollis raised respectful eyebrows. "Any other *obvious* moves you can suggest?"

"Well, ye-es—if you don't mind them coming from me."

"Go on," Knollis said shortly.

"Give Goldilocks a dose of third degree—as far as British law allows that sort of thing."

Knollis stared across at him. "What on earth for?"

"Well," said Ellis, "she's a bad girl, isn't she? Judging, that is, by all normal standards. She may not be a common prostitute, but she's certainly Dexter's mistress."

"Yes, true enough," said Knollis, as if the idea had only just occurred to him.

"And you treated her as if she was a poor little fallen angel. She almost wrung your withers as well as your heart."

"Ellis!" protested Knollis.

"Well, it's true enough, sir. She said, didn't she, that she would willingly come to Burnham if it was necessary to keep Rawley's name as pure as the driven snow—or words to that effect?"

Knollis considered the ceiling. "I wonder if she really is bad— in the loose sense, I mean."

"All I know about it," said Ellis, "is that when I was taking her to the station last night she made a broad suggestion re spending the night in town with me! No, sir, she's a wrong 'un. She came to clear Rawley's name, and she did it—but not in the way you expected! There's depth in that there girl!"

"She proved that he was not in Birmingham," replied Knollis. "She proved that his alibi was faked, and that without her knowing it!"

"But she proved that *Richard Dexter* was not in Burnham," protested Ellis. "She doesn't know a thing about Dennis Rawley, the real Dennis Rawley."

"If she does, then it means that last night's interview was a put-up job—deliberately designed to let down Rawley," Knollis murmured in an intense tone.

"Then what is the plan of action?"

"I'll take your advice," said Knollis. "I'll turn Russett loose on her. Perhaps his brusque manner can break her down where my winkling methods have failed. We'll have her flat searched as well—while she is at the station. I'll follow up Richard Dexter, and you borrow some men from Russett and start trailing Rawley's peregrinations."

"We really are moving now," Ellis said happily.

"Where is my breakfast?" demanded Knollis. "Ah, here it comes."

"Before we drop the subject for half an hour," said Ellis, "to which of them is the trail going to lead?"

"My guess is Dennis Rawley and Richard Dexter, or those two plus Margot as accessory."

On arrival at the Central Police Station an hour later, they found Russett poring over a sheet of paper.

"Hello!" he greeted them. "I've been to work this morning. Had an idea in the night, and as soon as the bank staff arrived I went down and asked to see Rawley's account. Had the usual trouble, because I'd no written authority, but I was eventually allowed to examine it. I was wondering if any money had passed between Richard Dexter and Rawley—"

"But Ellis and myself went into that yesterday with Dayton," Knollis interrupted.

"Well," continued Russett, unabashed, "I bet you didn't find this! A month ago, Rawley drew out fifty quid in one-pound notes. Now what would you suppose that was for?"

"Household expenses," suggested Knollis.

"That won't work, Knollis," said Russett proudly. "He pays all household bills monthly, and by cheque, and that includes the butcher, the baker, and the candlestick-maker. He makes eight-ten a week, and banks five of it as regularly as clockwork. Now why would Rawley want fifty pounds in cash?"

Knollis smiled. "Good for you, Russett! It's more interesting than appears at first sight. We'll find out. Meanwhile, I've mapped out a plan of campaign. Ellis insists that Goldilocks fooled me—worked a neat double-cross. Are you prepared to go to Birmingham and grill her?"

Russett gave a grin, and brushed his moustache in his clear-the-decks-for-action manner. "Let me get at her! What do you expect me to learn?"

Knollis laid his notes on the table, and quickly explained the conclusions that he and Ellis had reached.

"Nasty little conspiracy, eh?" murmured Russett, "Yes, I'll catch the first train. Rogers can go with Ellis if you like, and there are five other men I can spare for the Little Watney expedition—better rope in the Watney constable as well; his knowledge of local conditions will be handy. You will see Dexter? Then you'll want a man with you! Try my other sergeant, Dale. He's on a breaking and entering job at present, but it won't go cold through being left for one day—we know who did it, anyway! Yes, I'll go to Brum, and take a pocketful of pictures with me, *and* I'll come back knowing which of them she really slept with."

He sucked the end of his thumb.

"Wish I could get on to that fifty quid! Intrigues me, it does. Doesn't seem natural somehow!"

"There is another point that occurs to me, Russett. Assuming that Rawley was in Burnham on Thursday night, then how did he get to Birmingham—or, to put it better, why didn't he get to Birmingham before ten-thirty? I mean, which route did he take, and how did he travel? Yes, and where did he spend the night?"

"Quite a handful of points!" said Russett. "If he went by train he would take the L.M.S. line—local to Derby, and pick up the Newcastle-Bristol express."

"And that," groaned Knollis, "means a check on all the stations. How in the name of Heaven are we going to pull everything in!"

"Look," said Ellis; "assuming that he did the job, he would surely want to get out of Burnham as quickly as possible, and I can't imagine him taking the train. There aren't many passengers at that time of the night, and he would run a very great risk of being noticed."

"You have something there," said Russett.

Ellis suddenly thumped a fist into the palm of his other hand. "I've got an idea. Now I see where Little Watney comes in. Let me have my men, sir, and I'll be off. The brain is working at full strength."

"Come clean, Ellis!" pleaded Knollis.

"Give me a chance! If I'm right I'll be back by mid-afternoon with really vital evidence."

Knollis sighed. "Very well, Watson. Meanwhile, I'll take Dale, and visit Dexter."

They went on their respective errands, and twenty minutes later Knollis was ringing the bell in Hawthorn Grove, with Sergeant Dale at his side.

There was a certain wariness in Richard Dexter's eyes as he awaited them in the room in which the previous interview had been conducted, but there was still more wariness in the narrow eyes of Knollis.

"I'm surprised to see you again," said Dexter. "I thought I had seen the last of you."

"We are nuisances, aren't we?" Knollis replied blandly. "There are a few more points regarding your cousin's affairs which we would like to get straightened up."

"You said that last time," said Dexter.

"Yes, it's almost a standard opening, isn't it? King's pawn to King's fourth—or to the third, depending on how far you want to go."

Dexter smiled a superior smile that was almost a smirk.

"So you have not yet found my cousin's murderer!"

"Haven't we?" said Knollis, smiling back.

"Ah, then you have hopes!"

"Very definite hopes, Mr. Dexter. Now I should warn you that you are not bound to answer this question, but—where were you on the night of your cousin's death?"

Richard Dexter stared at him, and then walked over to the window. Over his shoulder he said: "Didn't I tell you on the occasion of your last visit?"

"You said that you were in this house. You also said that you had no proof of the statement!" Knollis reminded him.

"And that statement is not good enough for you, Inspector?"

"I'm afraid it is not—in the light of new evidence which has become available."

"Oh!"

Dexter turned suddenly, but he did not move from the window, so that his face remained in the shadows of the curtains.

"How am I going to prove that I was in the house when I was the sole occupant? Answer that for me, Inspector Knollis."

It was a challenge, and Knollis recognized it as such.

"At what time did you retire?" he asked.

"Oh, elevenish."

"You sleep at the front of the house?"

"Yes, as a matter of fact I do. Why that?"

"And what were you doing until then?" asked Knollis, carefully ignoring Dexter's own question.

"Reading, and listening to the radio."

"What programme, Mr. Dexter?"

Dexter laughed uneasily. "Hanged if I know. I switched it on, turned down the volume, and was reading a novel with the music as background."

"Alone!" said Knollis.

"Damn it, yes! I've told you that I was alone," Dexter retorted irritably. "Why are you so persistent in suggesting that I was not alone?"

"I am not suggesting that you were not alone, Dexter. I am suggesting that you were not in the house!"

Dexter strode forward, his fists clenched by his side.

"You—you are surely not insinuating that I had anything to do with my cousin's death?"

"At the moment," Knollis replied stubbornly, "I am merely suggesting that you were not in this house at the time your cousin died."

Dexter brushed a hand across his forehead. "But I was!"

"Then you will be prepared to face a witness who swears that your double or yourself was in Birmingham on Thursday night—at the Fir Tree Hotel, to be exact?"

Dexter started back. "Good Lord!"

"Well?" asked Knollis. "Do you deny it?"

"What's the use?" Dexter said wearily. "But how can anyone swear it was me?"

"Photographs," Knollis replied.

Dexter smiled wryly. "So that's how you worked it!"

"The queer point is," went on Knollis, "that Dennis Rawley also insists that he was at the Fir Tree on the same night."

"Well, he may have been for all I know, but I certainly never saw him."

"No, I can hardly expect that," said Knollis. "He was with a girl—a girl named Locke."

A mere flicker appeared in Dexter's eyes, but outwardly he was calm again.

"In which case he would most likely keep clear of the public rooms," he said. "That would explain why I never saw him."

"We got Miss Locke to come to Burnham last night," Knollis went on in a level voice. "She had offered to come over if it was necessary to prove that Rawley spent the night with her, and consequently was not in Burnham."

Dexter spread his hands, and stared fixedly at Knollis.

"All very, very interesting, I dare say, Inspector, but how does it concern me?"

"You can probably explain that better than I can," retorted Knollis. "I have, as a matter of fact, come for an explanation. For some peculiar reason, when we gave her a handful of photographs to examine, she chose yours and said that she knew you as Dennis Rawley."

Knollis's tone quickly changed, as it could on occasion. "Do you care to talk here, or must I invite you down to the station?"

Dexter strode to the window, then came back, and halted facing Knollis. "There must be a mistake somewhere!"

"There is," said Knollis, "and you are making it! If you think you are dealing with children, Dexter, then you should change your mind. I don't doubt your knowledge of antique furniture, and your ability to pick the false from the true; don't you under-estimate the efficiency of the police when engaged on a murder investigation! You are not dealing with one man, but with a trained team. I *know* that there have been dealings between you and Rawley, and I want the truth from you. I would point out that if nothing criminal has eventuated, then you have nothing to fear from us, but if I do not get the truth I shall arrest you on a charge of being concerned in the death of your cousin—and you can imagine the result of the publicity for yourself. I can afford to take no chances!"

Dexter's flamboyancy suddenly left him. He flopped into a chair and stared hopelessly at the two men.

"You damn' well never know where your roads are going to take you, do you?" he murmured. "I'd no idea that Rawley was intending to kill Bob."

"And was he? Did he kill him?" Knollis demanded.

"I wish I did know," Dexter replied wearily. "You see, I know him fairly well, and he confided in me about my cousin's lamen-table behaviour towards Margot—Rawley's wife . . ."

"I'm listening," Knollis said briefly.

"It seems that Bob, the damned fool, made overtures to Margot Rawley, and—naturally enough—she resented them. Further to the point, she told Dennis. He's a fairly quiet chap, even-tempered normally, but he was badly roused and wanted to go round and beat up Bob. I told him, as his wife had done, not to be an ass. Such things aren't done these days. Anyway, all this was six or seven weeks ago. You know how a fellow's mind can get into a vicious circle, don't you? He looked at Bob, and he looked at Margot, and he got the stupid idea into his still more stupid head that they were in love with each other and carrying on behind his back. As he was at work with Bob all day, and either at home with Margot or at the pub with Bob each evening, I don't know how he thought they were managing to do this 'carrying on.' I got sick of the whole subject, because he would corner me every time he went in the Key and Clock and talk, and wonder, and insinuate, until at times I was almost ready to fell him. And as Bob was my cousin, Dennis seemed to think I should do something about it—kind of retrieve the family honour and all that."

"I take it that you were not interested?" said Knollis.

"Well no," Dexter said reluctantly; "not, that is, as far as Rawley was concerned. Although I did go out of my way to meet

Lesley, and I pumped her steadily over a period of weeks, and all I could find from her was that Bob had told her that *Margot* had made improper suggestions to *him*, and that for two pins he would mention it to Dennis Rawley. It was on learning this that I decided to keep clear of the whole unsavoury business."

"And in keeping with that decision you decided to provide an alibi for him at the Fir Tree!" Knollis said caustically.

Dexter lit a cigarette, and ignored Knollis's tone, although not the question.

"Like an ass, I did. The idiot wanted to spy on his wife, and I thought it would do him good to find out that nothing was happening. He booked a room at the Granby, and went there next morning to take over the room for Friday. That was mainly so that he had an hotel bill for his wife to find lying about at home."

Knollis considered Dexter thoughtfully, and then asked: "Then why the complication at the Fir Tree? Surely that was both unnecessary and melodramatic?"

"Oh, blame Rawley for that!" Dexter replied. "He rang up after Bob's death and asked me if I could fix it for him, and, of course, I did so."

"By telling Nancy Locke nearly six weeks ago that your name was Dennis Rawley? You must be clairvoyant, Dexter. Come now; you can't expect me to believe that! I'm afraid I shall have to ask you to come with me to the station. You are a pretty bad liar, aren't you? You have been associating with Nancy Locke for a year. She thought your name was Ralph Denham until a few weeks ago, and then you suddenly decide that you are Dennis Rawley. Neat, clever, but not convincing. Your plans for the night of your cousin's death were made weeks in advance."

Knollis tapped the table with his forefinger. "I am not prepared to stay here all day listening to your literary inventions. I advise you to tell the truth. We know more than you imagine, and at this moment Nancy Locke is in the police station, and her flat is being searched."

He felt no remorse for his exaggeration of the truth, especially as he saw that Dexter's manner was altering. He was going down like a punctured tyre.

"All right," said Dexter; "here it comes. Rawley made the plan several weeks ago. I told Goldie that my name was Rawley, and knew that if she was questioned she would answer in all good faith."

"But Rawley already had an alibi at the Granby!"

"He hadn't," replied Dexter; "because he never used the room that night, as you know. That was only for his wife's benefit. Goldie was dragged in just in case you fellows came on the scene."

"So that Rawley did intend mischief?" snapped Knollis.

"What do you mean?"

"As far as I know," replied Knollis, "there is no law that prevents a man spying on his wife if he feels inclined that way, and I can't see how the police were expected to be interested if, as you say, no mischief was intended."

Knollis paused, and regarded Dexter steadily. Then he pointed an accusing finger at him.

"Shall I tell you what was in your mind when you conceived the idea—or shall I say put into Rawley's mind for him to suggest to you?"

Dexter sat, and waited.

"Candidly," went on Knollis, "I think you are about the dirtiest twister I've come across. You provided him with a so-called alibi for his wife's benefit, and then provided circumstantial evidence which you intended should get into his wife's possession so that she would turn against him as well. You were trying your best—or worst—to set those three people at each other's throats! Unfortunately, I can't do anything about you just yet, but I rather fancy that I will be picking you up during the next few days. And I do advise you not to attempt to slip away."

Dexter sprang to his feet. "Look here, Inspector; you've said too much, and I'm not sure that it isn't actionable. Why would I want to set them at each other's throats as you suggest? What would I—what could I get out of it?"

"Well," said Knollis with complete frankness, "I haven't quite sorted out the ramifications of your plot, but I do know what you *hoped* to get out of it!"

"And what would that be?"

"Lesley Dexter," answered Knollis. "You have always wanted her, haven't you?"

"Damn you," said Dexter. "Leave Lesley out of this!"

"You didn't!" Knollis pointed out.

"I'll see a solicitor to-day," stormed Dexter. "I consider that I have perfect grounds for an action!"

"I am more certain every minute that I have," said Knollis. "You are a clever man, Dexter, but not quite clever enough."

"I don't know what you are talking about, and I've had too much of this. Get out, damn you! Get out of my house!"

"Yes," Knollis said sorrowfully, "I think we should leave you now, but before we go I take it for granted that you admit being the one who spent the night with Nancy Locke at the Fir Tree?"

"Yes, damn you! I admit that!"

"And that Rawley never knew her?" persisted Knollis. Dexter hesitated, and then replied: "He—he met her once. He ran into us in Birmingham, but to the best of my knowledge and belief he's never seen her since."

Knollis bent the brim of his hat and flicked it lightly with his finger, so that it sprang into shape again.

"I take it that you were about to ditch Nancy?"

"Ditch her? What the devil do you mean?" demanded Dexter.

"Well, weren't you?"

"Yes! Yes, I was," Dexter admitted reluctantly, "but how the hell you guessed that is beyond me."

"Quite simple, if you think it out," murmured Knollis. "Lesley is free again now, and can be regarded—shortly—as an eligible widow. You have waited, and your chance has arrived, and you will want to appear as the knight without reproach. Consequently, you must not have an unexplainable trip to Birmingham or anywhere else—until you are married to Lesley. You know, Dexter, Nancy is not going to like that—and I don't think she is the type you can buy off or pension."

"Nancy can go to the devil!" shouted Dexter.

"She'll probably come to you, as you suggest," Knollis replied smoothly. "By the way, Dexter, where *did* Rawley spend the night?"

"How the deuce do I know? You are supposed to be the sleuth," sneered Dexter. "Work it out for yourself. I'm heartily sick of you, and Rawley, and Bob as well."

"Who killed your cousin, Dexter?" Knollis asked quietly.

Dexter relaxed. His arms fell by his side, and he looked Knollis straight in the eye for perhaps the first time during the long and stormy interview.

"I don't know," he said simply. "I wish I did. But I'm certain in my own mind that Dennis Rawley didn't. He's the wrong type. Oh, he gets hot-headed, and hot-blooded, but he cools off too soon. Unless he had someone behind him right to the last minute, someone who could keep him at fever heat, why, he couldn't bring himself to knife even his worst enemy, or a suffering dog. No, Inspector Knollis, if you are suspecting Dennis Rawley you are barking up the wrong tree."

He gave a harsh laugh. "Why, I'm a more likely suspect than Rawley!"

"But you couldn't have done it," murmured Knollis. "You have such an excellent alibi!"

"I did not do it—and I certainly have an excellent alibi!"

"Then you have no suspicions which you care to offer?"

"After this interview, I'd keep them to myself if I had," Dexter said bitterly. "I don't like your methods, Inspector Knollis. You came here thinking that you were going to scare me into an admission, and I have nothing to admit."

"Has Rawley ever paid you any money?" asked Knollis. Dexter stared. "What on earth for? Why should he?"

"I merely asked a question," said Knollis.

"And I've answered it, Inspector!"

Knollis stared silently at him for a moment, and Dexter wriggled uneasily under his gaze.

"Well?" he demanded. "What is it this time?"

"When did you last see Margot Rawley?"

"Oh, the morning before—before Bob's death. She was in Hawton's Café—the bloody woman almost lives there! She would so like to be a socialite!"

"Are you on friendly terms with her?"

"I'm on speaking terms with her, if that answers your question. She and Lesley usually go to Hawton's together, and that is how I came to know her."

Knollis wagged a finger at Dexter, a warning finger.

"Now I want a straight answer to this question. Did Margot Rawley, at any time, mention your cousin's alleged improper behaviour?"

"Yes, she did," Dexter said surlily. "Hanged if I know why. Damn it! I'm not my cousin's keeper!"

"So that we can assume that there was a definite anti-Dexter feeling in the Rawley household?"

"You can—if you mean with regard to Bob. They were both highly heated on the subject."

"And what is your own private opinion about the situation? You won't mind telling me that?"

Dexter sniffed, and lit yet another cigarette before he replied: "My opinion? I'm more inclined to believe Bob's version of it, as related to Lesley, and as related by her to me. Margot made the approaches, and Bob turned her down in no uncertain manner. Bob was completely lacking in tact, and he was something of a Puritan. I can imagine the nature of his response to her suggestion. He would first recoil, and then come back to dress her down well and truly."

"And then?"

"Well, Inspector," Dexter said smoothly, "I fancy that I know a little about human nature, and I think that Margot, incensed at the rejection of her scheme, would try to cover herself, and she spun the yarn to her husband in case Bob himself kicked up a row—on the principle of getting her blow in first. Doesn't that sound logical to you?"

"Quite logical," agreed Knollis.

He then left with Dale, and sat staring through the windscreen for some minutes before he eventually pressed the starter-button.

Chapter XII

THE FOLLOW-UP

On reaching the station, Knollis asked if there was anything new, and the sergeant handed him a slip of paper.

"Message telephoned through by Sergeant Ellis about half an hour ago, sir."

Knollis read aloud: *"Need details of Ostrer motor-bike, VXO 4756. As anticipated by me, Rawley bought same."*

The sergeant coughed. "I found it, sir. Thought the number was familiar. It came through in Saturday morning's *Supplement*. The cycle was found, apparently abandoned, in the Greet district of Birmingham."

"Roughly a mile from the Fir Tree," commented Knollis. "I think I'll slip along to Watney and find Ellis. Good work, Sergeant!"

Ellis was in a highly satisfied state of mind when Knollis eventually ran him to earth in the next village to Watney.

"Doing pretty well, sir!" he smiled. "Any joy with the mo'-bike yet?"

Knollis passed on the station sergeant's news, and Ellis's smile broadened.

"That more or less clears up the fifty pounds that Rawley withdrew. He bought the thing from the blacksmith-cum-engineer at Watney for thirty-five quid. He also bought a helmet, four-ply weather coat, and leggings; all for seven quid."

"When?" Knollis asked eagerly.

"A month ago. He garaged it with the blacksmith until he could call for it, and paid a month's garage rent in advance—a further fact that seems to indicate a fixed plan for last Thursday night."

"What about the licence?"

"He doesn't seem to have bothered about the legal end of the bargain. Neither has the blacksmith—and he's sweating on the top line now because the bike is still in his name. And so they picked it up in Brum! Very interesting."

"I suppose," asked Knollis, "that he fetched it away on the Thursday afternoon?"

"No," replied Ellis. "I had the same idea, but I was wrong. A friend fetched it on the Wednesday evening, with a car."

"Then I suppose they parked it somewhere handy," Knollis commented thoughtfully.

"Well, that is the angle I'm working on now, but it seems to me that it would be parked somewhere near River Close, probably on or near the towpath, all ready for a speedy getaway."

"How did Rawley's friend take it, Ellis?"

"Strapped and tied to the luggage grid."

Knollis tapped his toe on the ground. "I may be wrong, but it appears to me that Richard Dexter and Margot Rawley were determined that Dennis should kill Bob Dexter. They were pushing him every inch of the way—and I wouldn't be surprised to hear that they pushed the knife into his hand."

"You've interviewed Dexter again this morning, sir?"

"M'm!" said Knollis. "A most interesting interview it was, too. I didn't get a great deal from him directly, but his evasions told me more than he realized. I don't think there is any doubt now that a conspiracy existed between he and Margot Rawley to dispose of Bob Dexter. Richard, as you surmised, is a dirty piece of work."

"Motive?" murmured Ellis.

"Margot to get rid of Dexter and protect her good name, save the mark! Richard to get Lesley."

"And what happens about Rawley?"

"Richard Dexter left holes in the alibi so that he would be certain to pick up Rawley. From the Richard-Margot angle, there was a clear case, and no suspicion could rest on them. Margot, if questioned, would admit, oh yes, that she had complained to her husband about Bob Dexter's attitude towards her, but she never thought for one single moment that he would ever consider the killing of him. As far as she knew, he was in Birmingham—and there was the Granby Hotel bill to prove it. Then we, poor dumb animals, discover that Rawley did not use his room, and pound him into an admission that he spent the night at the Fir Tree with Goldilocks. Splendid! That sets up Margot's back. She thinks he skipped off to Birmingham ostensibly to forge an alibi, and then played false to her by spending the remainder of the night with another woman. Margot, scorned once more, and this time by her own husband, begins to let slip a few more details to us—well, yes, her husband *had* said that he would do for Bob Dexter, but again she never thought for a moment that it was anything but a worthless threat."

Knollis grated his teeth, to Ellis's annoyance, and added:

"I don't like Richard Dexter!"

"He does seem to be an unsavoury type, doesn't he?" Ellis agreed. "Now look, sir; over this motor-bike; think an appeal in the Midland papers might help? Ask for anyone who may have seen it to call in on us?"

Knollis shrugged. "We can do that, but I'm not optimistic over the results."

"I wonder what Inspector Russett will get from Goldilocks?"

"I can't even guess," replied Knollis. "I think I'll get back to town and try to trace your motor-cycle from that end."

An hour later he and Dale were standing on the towpath below River Close, and the sergeant in charge of the dragging operations was by their sides.

"You are a river man," said Knollis. "What kind of a job would it be getting a motor-cycle into a skiff from this bank and getting it out again in that backwater?"

The sergeant gave a grim laugh. "I wouldn't like to do it by myself, sir. I don't think I could do it without overturning the whole show."

"Thanks," said Knollis. "Call the launch in, please. I'd like to go across to the backwater."

On the farther bank, Knollis walked beyond the screening willows and a hawthorn hedge, and found himself in a narrow lane. He examined the ground inside the five-barred gate, and muttered softly to himself.

"Where does this lane lead?" he asked the sergeant.

"Three-Tree Farm, sir. There is no through road."

"See the motor-cycle tracks?" said Knollis. "And the deep indentations where it has stood?"

"Yes, sir. Good, clean tracks, aren't they?"

"So good," said Knollis dryly, "that I want you to put a man on to watch them. As soon as I get back I'll send the photographer along, together with someone to take casts of them. Yes, I think we are moving!"

He considered the countryside carefully, and then asked: "This lane joins the main road?"

"Yes, sir, on the south side of the bridge."

Knollis returned to the station, and there consulted the station sergeant.

"Who was on duty in the neighbourhood of the bridge at Westford on Thursday night, at midnight?"

The sergeant consulted his book.

"See, Thursday . . . Edwards, sir; relieved at midnight by Jackson. Both men are off duty at present."

"Then give me their home addresses, please."

A few minutes later he was in the car again, with Dale driving.

P.C. Edwards sought his notebook as Knollis asked his first question.

"A man coming up from the towpath to the main road shortly after midnight, sir?"

"And probably hurrying," said Knollis.

"No, sir, I saw nothing of anybody coming up from the towpath, but there was a man leaning over the parapet of the bridge, having a smoke. Light mack and trilby he was wearing."

"You did not speak to him?"

"I said good night, sir, and he replied good night and said he'd better get home before his wife began to wonder where he was. He walked off down the Loughborough Road."

Knollis pushed his hat back. "Why the dickens didn't you report this? Anyway, there is another question! Did you see a motor-cycle going south shortly after that?"

"A motor cycle? Well, after Jackson relieved me I went off towards town, and a military convoy passed me. It had a dispatch-rider at the head, and one at the tail, both in the usual dress—leather coat and crash-helmet."

"At what time would that be, Edwards?"

"Ten to fifteen minutes after midnight, sir."

"Thanks," said Knollis. "Round to see Jackson, Dale!"

P.C. Jackson's eyes brightened as motor-cycles were mentioned.

"Yes, sir! Three of them. Two army cycles conducting a convoy, and a civilian who was passing the head of the convoy as I turned to set off on my beat. The civvy was in a hurry, too.

He went down the Loughborough Road as if the squad was on his heels."

"And the time, Jackson?"

"Quarter past twelve, sir."

"Any idea as to its make?"

"No, sir, but I should say it was a medium twin—judging by the noise and the speed."

"Now," said Knollis, "I want you to think very carefully, Jackson. When you first heard or saw him, was he travelling at a regular speed, as if he had been in top gear for some time?"

Jackson wrinkled his brows for a moment. Then they cleared, as he said: "No, sir. It struck me at the time that he had just revved up and changed into top."

"You know the lane that runs behind the water meadows?"

"The one down to Three-Tree Farm, sir?"

"Yes, that is the one."

"Yes, I go down there on my patrol, sir."

"How far from the entrance of the lane were you when you first heard the cycle?"

"About three hundred yards south, sir, and round the bend in the road."

"So that he could have come from the lane?"

Jackson looked surprised. "Why yes, he could, although it never struck me that way at the time. Yes, that would be the most logical explanation for his gear-change, because the road behind him was good and straight, right over the bridge and back to the city. I mean, sir, the bend is a long one, and not sharp enough to warrant any changing down."

"The convoy was travelling at the uniform pace usual with military convoys?"

"Yes, sir."

"No obstructions or delays between the head and tail of the convoy? No obstructions on the road, such as repair work, trenches, diversions?"

"No, sir. I had just walked along from the bridge after relieving Edwards, as he will corroborate, and the road was perfectly clear."

Knollis nodded thoughtfully.

"Take any notes on the convoy?"

"I noticed the divisional signs, sir, and made a note of the army registration number of the last vehicle."

"Good man!" said Knollis. "Let me have them, please." He left a few minutes later.

"Toughish job for you, Dale," he said as he dropped him at the station. "Trace that convoy to its destination; then get the nearest C.I.D. to ferret for information about the cycle. We may not be lucky, but it's worth trying."

He went to Sir Wilfrid's office, and spent the next two hours poring over a large-scale map of the Westford area, after which he made a rough sketch-map of River Close and the adjacent reach of the river, and studied it closely. He had lunch brought in from a nearby café, and continued to work as he ate.

Ellis returned during the early afternoon, and threw his hat across to the pegs.

"Any luck?" asked Knollis.

Ellis shook his head.

"Trail faded out completely after Little Watney. Not a breath nor a whistle of Rawley after he walked out of the village street. And nothing of Dexter the Second after he drove away with the motor-bike on his luggage grid."

"Grim," murmured Knollis, and related his own experiences of the morning.

"Pity we can't fill the gap between Little Watney and the bridge," he added. "We may be satisfied in our own minds as to the route, but the public prosecutor will jib at what he may consider to be circumstantial evidence. You have left the others working on it?"

"Yes," answered Ellis. "I thought it wiser to return in case there was anything more important to be working on."

"Well," said Knollis, pulling on his ear; "to be quite candid, I don't know what to do for the next move. A lot depends on Russett's luck with Goldilocks. You see, Ellis, I want to know where Rawley spent the night after he left Burnham. *And* I'd like to know what happened to the knife. I'm afraid you'll have to supervise the searching of the drains and the digging of the garden. It should have been done before this, but I had faith in the river, and it let me down."

"You're quite satisfied that it is Rawley?" asked Ellis.

"Ye-es," Knollis replied slowly. "I had quite a different idea until yesterday, but the evidence is becoming conclusive."

"And when are we going to pull him in?"

"Any time now, Ellis. I'm hoping to get a few more of the gaps filled, and then we'll execute a warrant and grab him. The point I'm worried about is whether Margot was a party to the affair or not, and I really would like to get that tied up before I take him."

"How do we find out?" Ellis asked.

"Shock tactics, I presume. Anyway, organize the digging, will you? I'm spending the rest of the afternoon working out a further plan of campaign."

By five o'clock Ellis reported that he and four sturdy constables had made the garden of Himalaya Villa look like a bombed site, but that there was no trace of a knife.

"Mrs. Rawley was very interested," he said with a grim smile. "She leaned on the hedge and made useful suggestions. At half-past three she passed over two large jugs of tea. We accepted them readily enough, but I was amused. She said, truthfully enough, that she didn't think the killer would have had time to bury the knife, because not more than a minute or so elapsed between the knifing of Dexter and her arrival at the door."

"What did you say to that?" asked the amused Knollis.

"I said that I still couldn't understand why she hadn't seen him, because a man can't get far in one minute. She replied that it really was astounding, and the more she thought about it, the more astounding it seemed. There was something mildly mocking in her tone, and so I decided to play the same game. I asked what she would have done with the knife supposing she had killed Dexter, and she replied that the obvious thing was to take it back into the house and wash it.

"I suggested that perhaps she hadn't a carving-knife, and she said that she had. She went into the house, and came back with one—usual bone-handled thing with a sharp edge, a good point, and a damaged backbone."

Knollis looked up sharply. "Damaged backbone?"

"Yes, the unsharpened edge. Looked as if she had whacked it with a hammer. The back edge was slightly turned over."

Knollis jumped to the files of the case. "I want Whitelaw's report. Here we are. Listen to this, Ellis: *I am of the opinion from my examination that a household carving-knife, or some similar knife, was used. The sharpened edge was the lower one as it entered the body, the lower edge of the wound being a clean incision, while the upper part of the wound was jagged, indicating a single-edged blade. On removing the sternum I discovered a splintered ridge which seems to qualify my opinion that a single-edged knife was used. . . ."*

Knollis raised his eyes, and smiled wryly at Ellis.

"I hope Margot Rawley doesn't use the knife for steaking or filleting fish!"

"What on earth do you mean?" Ellis exclaimed.

"Never watched housewives making cod into steaks? They usually use the best knife in the house, and having cut down to the bone they then imitate the fishmonger, but not having a wooden mallet they take the kitchen poker and bring it down on the back of the blade. It severs the bone, but does not improve the back of the knife!"

"M'm!" Ellis commented. "Another good idea gone west!"

"Almost, Ellis! Almost—but not quite."

The door was pushed open, and Inspector Russett appeared, one hand clutching the arm of Nancy Locke.

"Evening, Knollis! I decided to bring Nancy back for another little chat. Hurried, too! You should see my radiator! Looks like Etna in eruption. We've travelled far and fast, haven't we, my dear?"

"Take your hand off my arm," Nancy Locke said sulkily.

"Why certainly," said Russett. "I don't think you will walk out on us, because we are your best friends, aren't we? Here, take a chair! Now tell the nice gentleman everything you can remember of Thursday night—and don't forget anything this time!"

Knollis and Ellis glanced at each other, and shook their heads sadly.

Russett grinned at them. "I got the truth out of her, and she's going to replay the record—aren't you, love?"

Nancy Locke sulked, and made no effort to speak. Russett dropped a hand on her fur-coated shoulder. "You wouldn't like to spend a few months in quod, would you?"

He turned to Knollis. "Complete little liar, Knollis; that's what she is. Knows the whole story from A to Z. Rawley joined her and Richard Dexter at two o'clock in the morning, and slept on the floor wrapped in an eiderdown. Entered by the service door, and left later the same morning. She knew Richard Dexter *as* Richard Dexter, and not as Ralph Denham. She was told that Bob Dexter had possession of a valuable manuscript which belonged to Richard, and that Rawley was to get it back for him. She was to help provide the alibi—for fifty quid.

"She engaged a room at the Fir Tree in the names of Mr. and Mrs. Dennis Rawley. She and Dexter took possession of the room, and when Rawley arrived, Dexter left in his car, which was parked in an all-night garage on the Coventry Road. At that, Rawley spent a virtuous night on the floor, and at seven the next morning he left Goldilocks with the money to pay the bill, and walked out. I don't know where he was between then and showing up at the Granby, and I don't know where Richard

Dexter went, but that is the whole of the story chiselled from our little friend, and she is prepared to sign a statement, aren't you, beautiful?"

"I know when I'm beaten," she muttered surlily.

"You didn't know, of course," said Knollis, "that your gentlemen friends were arranging a murder, did you?"

"No, I didn't!" she replied. "That's the only reason why I'm going to talk. I'm not going to be mixed up in a murder trial and have my photo in all the papers."

"Pity you think that," Knollis murmured under his breath.

Aloud he said: "What are we going to do with her, Russett? We can't let her go, and we can't keep her—or can we?"

"Accessory before and after the fact, surely!" protested Russett.

"And warn Dexter and Rawley before we can pull them in? I still lack conclusive evidence on Rawley's killing of Dexter. We're in a fix."

Russett put his hand in his inner breast pocket and produced a form. "Use this. She slipped away from the Fir Tree without paying the bill, and the manager was persuaded to swear a summons against her. We can have her taken back to Brum, where she'll be charged in the morning, and we'll arrange for her to be remanded while further inquiries are made. That should satisfy Dexter and Company."

"Good enough," commented Knollis.

"Nice set of twisters, aren't you!" exclaimed Nancy Locke.

"Do you trust your gentlemen friends?" said Knollis.

"Well, no—not now!"

"And you wouldn't like to finish up in the river, or with a knife between your shoulder-blades? You should regard this twisting, as you call it, as protective custody!"

"Oh well," she said shortly. "It'll be a nice change!"

"And you are willing to make this statement, and sign it?" asked Knollis.

"I suppose so."

"You are not bound to do so!" Knollis warned her.

"Not much!" she replied. "Anyway, I didn't know they were doing any killing, and I'm not helping in a game of that sort! It was all on the up and up by the way they told me, and they made out this cousin of Dick's was a proper no-good type. Yes, I'll talk."

And so Ellis took his fountain-pen, and Nancy Locke made a full statement, and when Ellis had typed it from his shorthand notes it was read back to her, and she agreed that it was a correct copy of her verbal statement, and then signed it. She was then returned to Birmingham in the care of a large and capable policeman.

"Well, thanks for that!" Knollis said fervently. "You've helped matters considerably. I can't tell you how grateful I am."

"I was a bit slow starting," said Russett with a smile, "and to be quite frank I've appreciated the chance of pulling in the slack."

"Major crime is a fairly rare event," said Knollis, "and you have to get warmed up before you can get beyond cruising speed. I was in a similar state when old Lomas passed out. We fellows at the Yard are more or less warmed up all the time, and it certainly does make a difference. Anyway, what are we going to do now?"

"I take it that you have already decided that?" grinned Russett amiably.

"I'm going to call on Dexter's housekeeper after tea," said Knollis. "I prefer to do it when he isn't at home."

"I can put a man on to watch the house, and 'phone us if and when he goes out."

"Yes, that's an idea. Will you do that, please? While I interview her, I suggest that you tackle the houses opposite and find out if they saw him between, say, four in the morning and breakfast-time. I fancy that you will learn that they did! Dexter would see to that."

The message came through at half-past six, and the scheme was put into operation, Knollis inviting himself into Richard Dexter's home.

He glanced at a slim and frightened girl who was trying to hide behind the housekeeper's bulk.

"Are you the day-girl here?"

"Ye-es, sir. I was just going."

"There's nothing to be afraid of. Tell me, at what time do you start work in a morning?"

"Half-past seven, sir."

"And can you remember as far back as last Friday?"

"Yes, sir."

"Good!" said Knollis. "You came at the usual time?"

"Yes, sir."

"And your master was at home?"

"Oh yes, sir! I heard him singing in the bathroom, and he came down to breakfast at eight o'clock."

"Right! Then you can skip off home if you have finished work. That will be all right—" He glanced at the housekeeper. "I don't think I caught your name?"

"Amelia James—Missus!"

"Then you can spare your help, Mrs. James?"

"Yes, she can go."

"Now, Mrs. James," began Knollis; "were you in the house all day last Thursday?"

"I live in, sir, but it was my day off. Mr. Dexter had been promising me a full day and night off for a month, and the day before, which was Wednesday, he said I could go for the whole of Thursday, providing I was back in time to get his breakfast on Friday morning. I left my daughter's home—where I'd been—at six o'clock, by a workman's bus, and got in at seven. Is that what you wanted to know?"

"Almost everything," said Knollis. "One more question. Mr. Dexter was then at home?"

"He certainly was, sir. He called down to ask if it was me letting myself in."

"Thank you, Mrs. James. There will be no need to tell Mr. Dexter that we called. We are merely checking on a statement he made to us. He assured us that he was at home all night."

"Then he would be, Inspector!"

Knollis and Ellis waited in the car until Russett appeared, and when he did appear he was grinning.

"Dexter certainly made sure of advertising his presence!" he reported. "Disturbed the people opposite, and quite a few others, by knocking a window box off the bedroom sill at half-past four in the morning. When they stuck out their heads to see what had happened he apologized, and said he had been trying to drive away two courting cats—which nobody else had heard."

"Good enough," said Knollis. "We can now go back."

CHAPTER XIII
THE STORY OF THE RECTOR

KNOLLIS AWOKE on the following morning with the feeling that something was going to happen. He had no idea what it was, or from which direction it would come. It was a stirring at the back of his mind, a feeling of movement which reminded him of a chick in an egg making its first attempt to reach the outer world.

The *something* which had been puzzling him for some days was about to make its debut. He knew, as he had known all along, that it could not be forced. "There was a time for all things, and all things appeared in their due season." He went down to breakfast, bade Ellis a good morning in an absent manner, and since Ellis understood his chief he did not attempt to make conversation. Knollis stared at his plates throughout the meal, and was scarcely aware of what he was eating. The meal over, he lit a cigarette, and watched the smoke as it spiralled and wreathed towards the large open fireplace, to which it was carried by the draught from the door.

In his mind he created a phantasm, a mere silhouette of a man in a long black coat and a black velour hat. He then made a similar silhouette of each of the people who had figured in the case, and fitted each in turn over that of the unknown, which he used as a template. Robert Dexter, Richard Dexter, Lesley Dexter, Dennis Rawley, Margot Rawley, Courtney-Harborough, Newnham, Mrs. Hendrick Stanley—

He jumped to his feet, knocking over the remains of his cup of tea.

"Good heavens above!"

Ellis looked up, and blinked. "What the deuce—?"

"Get your coat and hat," snapped Knollis. "Get the car round at once. The thing has clicked in my mind at last—and why was I so dense?"

He looked down at Ellis.

"Come on, man!" he said irascibly. "Leave your breakfast!"

Ellis cast a regretful glance at the toast-rack and the marmalade jar. He shrugged, rose from the table, and followed Knollis from the room, although at a much slower pace, for Knollis was racing upstairs two steps at a time. And when Ellis had collected his outdoor clothes, and had driven the car to the main entrance he found Knollis pacing up and down, keen-eyed and intense.

Knollis almost threw himself into the car. He slammed the door. "Well, get going!"

"Quite so," murmured Ellis patiently, "but where? Round and round the Council House Square? Out to Little Watney? River Close? Where? That is all I want to know!"

"Windlow Rectory!"

Ellis's jaw dropped.

"The man in the long black coat and the black velour . . ."

Ellis got going.

"You know, Ellis," said Knollis as they bowled along towards Derbyshire, "the human intellect is queer! Do you remember that story by Chesterton—one of the Father Brown stories it is—where men keeping observation on a block of flats report that no one has entered or left the building? And Brown proves that someone had done both, and had not been noticed because people were so used to seeing him? It was, of course, the postman."

He gave a deep dissatisfied sigh.

"We have done the same thing here—disregarded the obvious. We have looked for, and eventually disbelieved in, a theatrical figure tricked out in a disguise. And for why? Because the generality of men do not wear long black coats and black velour hats! The average man would be too conspicuous in such a garb. And who, other than the average man, could wear a long black coat and a black velour and not be noticed? You know the answer now. A parson!"

Ellis grunted.

"And who had so good and so deep a motive? A man in financial difficulties. A nervy man bordering on neurasthenia. Bob Dexter stood between him and financial security; between him and peace of mind. He couldn't get the manuscript which would mean relief from penury, and he grew to hate him. The hate grew into an obsession . . ."

Vocal silence fell over the car, and was unbroken until Knollis descended from it at the rectory gates.

"This is where we learn something, Ellis!"

He rang the bell, and the door was opened by a good-looking young woman of twenty-five. She had fine hands unspoiled by housework, and was wearing a wedding-ring.

"I am Inspector Knollis, of New Scotland Yard. I would like to speak to Mr. Saunders if it is convenient."

She hesitated, and then said: "Come in, please."

She led them into the dining-room, and closed the door. "Is it essential for you to see him, Inspector?"

"I'm afraid it is, ma'am," replied Knollis.

She bit her lower lip and appeared to consider.

"He is ill, Inspector—mentally ill. The housekeeper sent for me. I should explain that I am his youngest daughter, Mrs. Bradwell. The housekeeper did not like the look of my father. I learned on arriving that he has been wandering on the moors, and has twice been brought home by villagers. The doctor is with him now. Wait a moment, please! I think he is coming downstairs."

She opened the door, and a stout man stepped into the doorway. "Well, Mrs. Bradwell—oh, I beg your pardon! I wasn't aware that you had visitors."

"I think you should meet them," said Mrs. Bradwell. "This is Inspector Knollis, of Scotland Yard. Dr. Hellick, Inspector. Now, Dr. Hellick, the inspector wishes to see my father. Perhaps you will explain how impossible that is."

The doctor put down his hat and bag on a chair, and fingered his chin. "I am not so sure, Mrs. Bradwell!"

"You mean . . . ?" she asked.

"Your father needs a mental purgative. He has something on his mind, something connected with a police case. I am almost inclined to think that it might help him if he did talk to the inspector."

He looked questioningly at Knollis.

"I fancy that Mr. Saunders has valuable evidence connected with the Dexter murder case in Burnham," said Knollis.

The doctor pondered a moment. "Look, Inspector, if I allow you to see him, will you allow me to be present at the interview?"

"Frankly, I would prefer it that way," answered Knollis.

"You are sure it will be the best thing for my father?" Mrs. Bradwell asked the doctor.

"By what little your father has said to me, Mrs. Bradwell, I think he is in sad need of a father confessor, and the Inspector seems to suit the role in this instance."

"In that case . . ." said Mrs. Bradwell, and spread her hands in a gesture of acceptance.

The doctor turned to Knollis.

"You are prepared to terminate the interview if I consider that its continuation will be detrimental to my patient, Inspector?"

"I am in your hands," said Knollis.

To Ellis he muttered: "Verbatim report."

The doctor led the way upstairs. The Reverend William Saunders was in his bed, propped up on pillows. Knollis glanced at him sharply and could not decide whether the expression that flashed over his sallow features was anxiety, relief, or a mixture of both.

"Good morning, Mr. Saunders. You do remember me?"

"I remember you, Inspector," the old man said wanly. "I am pleased to see you."

"Then you have guessed why I am here?"

The rector smiled. "You have discovered that I was in that street of death, Inspector?"

"Not discovered," corrected Knollis. "I have only guessed it. I would like to hear you say so yourself."

Knollis fought a mental battle with himself. He wanted to question and cross-question the old man, but could not bring himself to do it. Further to the point, he realized that he would probably get a more complete story by letting him carry on his own way, rambling though that way might be.

"I was in the street, Inspector," said the rector.

"Tell me the whole story, exactly as it happened," said Knollis. Then, remembering the regulations, he added: "If you care to do so, that is."

The rector took hold of the hem of the sheet and began to pleat it with his thin, bony fingers.

"It was last Thursday morning when the letter came. It was from the gentleman from whom I had borrowed the money. He was very pressing, and said that he would have to take legal proceedings unless I paid the interest which was now very much overdue. I did tell you that I had borrowed the money, did I not, Inspector?"

Knollis bent his head.

"I don't quite know what came over me then," went on the rector. "Now that I am in bed, and resting, I see things in a very much different light, but last Thursday morning it seemed to me that the whole world was crashing down on me. Legal proceedings would mean exposure of my foolishness, and disgrace would follow, and then there was the Bishop's attitude to consider. I went for a walk on the moor to try and think clearly. It seemed to me that if only I could persuade Mr. Dexter to let me have the manuscript, then the hundred pounds which Mr. Richard Dexter said it was worth would free me of my troubles temporarily, and I could seek for some way of clearing the rest.

"I returned to church, conducted the morning service, and set out by bus for Burnham. It was turned noon when I arrived, and I went to a café for a cup of tea. I could not eat. I had no appetite. After resting for a while, I asked the way to River Close, for, as I have already told you, I found Robert Dexter's address in the telephone directory. But there was no one at home when I got there, and a lady whom I saw leaving a house higher up the street told me that there was not likely to be anyone at home until the evening.

"I walked back to the city, and rested on a seat in the park. I was feeling ill, and I realize now that it was probably due to hunger, for I had eaten neither breakfast nor lunch. I fainted, and was taken to a nearby house, where the good lady who lived there looked after me. She insisted on giving me a meal, and I admit that I felt much better after it. I stayed there until her husband came home at half-past five, and after another cup of tea he accompanied me to the bus station, and put me on a bus for home.

"It was while sitting in the bus that I realized that I had done nothing about my errand. I saw myself going back to my home, and with nothing awaiting me there but the letter from the—the man who had lent me the money. A sense of dread overwhelmed me, and I rang the bell and got out at the next stop. I was back in River Close by half-past six, but although I walked past the house several times I could not bring myself to ring the bell, because, you see, in order to convince the man that I must have the manuscript I would have to expose my straitened circumstances, and I dreaded to do that.

"I walked to the end of the street, and saw that there was a gate in the fence, and it was open. I went down the embankment to the towpath, and walked along by the river—"

"Did you meet anyone?" asked Knollis, interrupting for the first time.

"Meet anyone?" repeated the rector. "Did I meet anyone? Only the woman, and she did me a very good turn. I ran into her in the darkness, you see, and she saved me from a nasty accident. She said that someone—I think she said it was a fool—had left a rope stretched across the towpath, and she did not want me to fall over it. I thanked her, and went on, leaving her to do something or other with it . . ."

Knollis made a peculiar noise in his throat, and then gestured the rector to continue.

"All that is beside the point," said the old man. "I walked on, and I must have walked for hours, for when I next looked at my watch it was nine o'clock. I shook myself and realized that I must hurry if I was to call at Robert Dexter's house and then catch the last bus home—for by now I had made up my mind that I would, really would, call. And so I turned and began to walk back, and it was then, and only then, that I realized how far I had walked. My legs ached, and my back ached, and my shoulders ached. You must realize, Inspector, that I was not by any means in my normal state of mind. I was worried by the thoughts of my troubles, and excited by the possibility of getting my affairs straight once more. You do realize that?" he asked anxiously.

"I fully appreciate the position, Mr. Saunders," Knollis said gravely.

"I pressed on, Inspector, hurrying to get to River Close before Mr. Dexter retired for the night, but I lost a lot of time, unfortunately. I ran into a drunken man. He pulled me up and wanted to discuss his chances of salvation. Quite insulting he became, too! I tried to get away from him, but he clutched my arm and insisted on being told—before he would release me!—that he was safe from hell-fire. I am somewhat ashamed of my behaviour there, so anxious was I to get away. I told him that he was safe from hell-fire—may God forgive me for the lie—and muttered beneath my breath as I hurried away that it was conditional on his repentance.

"I slowed my pace, I remember, as I drew near River Close, for although I had not paid much attention to the woman earlier in the evening, I now recalled quite vividly her remarks on the rope, and I had no wish to precipitate myself into the river by falling over it. I went forward very cautiously, a step at a time. However, it must have been moved, for I did not encounter it. I climbed the embankment, opened the gate, and once more found myself in the street."

"The gate, Mr. Saunders? It was fastened?"

"Oh yes, Inspector. There was a loop of wire round it, and I had quite a task in undoing it in the darkness."

"And you fastened it again?"

"Oh yes! I was brought up in the country, you know, and one always fastens gates, to prevent cattle straying."

"Thank you," said Knollis. "Please continue."

"I was in a dilemma," the rector went on, "for I could not now remember whether it was the second or the third house from the bottom of the street. I walked to the opposite side, and tried to decide which it really was."

He smiled sheepishly. "So silly of me, was it not?"

Knollis did not answer.

"As I stood there, a light came on in the front bedroom of the second house, and a lady came to the window and drew the curtains."

"Have you any idea what time that was?" asked Knollis.

"I remember distinctly, Inspector, because I looked at my watch. It was five minutes to twelve. I decided then that it really was too late to call, and I wondered where I should go for the night, the last bus having left for Windlow at half-past eleven.

"I was about to move away when a light appeared in the hall of the third house. Through the glass panels of the door I could see two people. One was in a very light-coloured attire, and the other in much darker. The one in light seemed to push the other towards the door. The light then went out, and I heard the front door being opened. A man emerged, and went up the street—"

"Up the street? Not down to the river?" Knollis asked excitedly.

"Up the street, Inspector. I watched him go. He turned right at the top of the street."

"That way, Wisden Avenue, leads to the bridge," Knollis said softly to himself.

The rector caught the remark. "Exactly, Inspector. I decided, as someone was up, to go across and inquire if that might be Mr. Dexter's house, for I thought they might have been saying good-night to a departing guest. I was some minutes making up my mind, and the striking of midnight by Old John brought me back from my thoughts. I went across the street, and knocked at the door. The light went on, and a lady opened the door, a lady in very filmy night attire . . ."

The rector gave a deep sigh.

"My heart failed me," he said sadly. "I lamely asked where a Mr. Smith lived. Having brought myself right to the point, I failed! The lady said there was no Smith in the street. I fumbled mentally for a reply, and said something about that being very queer, and that there must be a mistake. She looked at me rather queerly, I thought, and then told me that the Sampsons—I think that was the name, for the biblical similarity interested me—the Sampsons lived on one side, and the Dexters on the other. I thanked her, apologized for troubling her, and walked back up the path to the street."

"Go on," said Knollis, as the old man lay back on his pillows and stared at the ceiling.

"There is little more to tell, Inspector. Once more I plucked up my courage, and decided to go back and ask her on which side was the Dexters' house. As I got to her door, I heard it being opened. I was suddenly afraid, and I hurried down the path beside the house, on tiptoe. I reached the rear gate, found it open, and went through into the service lane. There was a light at the far end of it, a street lamp, and a policeman was just turning into the avenue. I hurried along, turned to the left, and began to walk home. I had good fortune almost before leaving the city, for a long-distance transport driver pulled up and asked me if I would like a ride. He took me as far as the crossroads at Tideswell, and I walked from there. I arrived here about four o'clock in the morning, just as my housekeeper was about to ring up the police."

"And that is the whole story?" said Knollis.

"Yes," said the rector, smiling, "and I feel better for telling you. I have done nothing wrong, have I? I have really done nothing wrong?"

Knollis looked across at the doctor. "May I ask a few questions now?"

Dr. Hellick nodded.

"Tell me, Mr. Saunders; did you see anyone enter the street after you went to the house on the first occasion, when you asked for the Smith house?"

The rector shook his head. "I never heard anyone, and I never saw anyone, except a baby crying in a nearby house," he added with a faint smile.

"And you did not go to the Dexter house?"

"I did not go to the Dexter house," the rector said wearily. "You see, Inspector, I was not sure which it was!"

"Can you describe the woman who answered the door to you?" asked Knollis.

"With difficulty, Inspector. I was tired, and troubled, you must remember, and not concerned with noting appearances, but I seem to remember her as a—a full-figured woman with a commanding manner. That is really all I remember of her! Indeed it is!"

"And the man who left the house? Can you give me any description of him? Can you say what he was wearing?"

The rector shook his head. "I cannot describe him, but I have an impression of him wearing a light raincoat."

"And what were you wearing, Mr. Saunders?"

A wry smile crossed the rector's lips.

"There was little choice, Inspector, because I have only the one coat and hat—my clerical ones."

"Black coat and hat?"

"Those are all I have."

"Your coat collar was turned up?"

"Yes. Yes, it would be, because I had left home without a scarf."

"Then your dog—your clerical collar would not be visible, Mr. Saunders?"

"No, it would not be seen, Inspector."

Knollis crossed one knee over the other, and leaned forward. "Now try to remember something else, Mr. Saunders. After you went back to the street, can you say whether the bedroom light was still on in the next house?"

"I think it was, Inspector. I seem also to remember voices coming from the room, although I am not sure. I was in a terrible mental state that night. I can still hardly believe that I allowed myself to act in the manner I did!"

"Can you by any chance remember the name of the owner of the lorry which brought you home?"

"Not the name, Inspector, but I can remember that it belonged to a potato merchant in Buxton. The driver was an employee, taking potatoes from Lincolnshire to Buxton. The man was very loquacious about himself and his affairs, but I was not listening, you see, being so overwhelmed by my own failure to achieve my object."

"Whereabouts did you chance upon the drunken man?"

"It would be at least two miles away from River Close, Inspector, and north of the town."

"And the woman you ran into on the towpath? Can you describe her? I am aware that it was a dark night, but you should be able to say whether she was slight or heavily built, and whether she was young or old."

The rector shook his head. "She loomed up at me like a massive piece of rock, Inspector. I can remember nothing more of her than that."

"Did she," said Knollis quietly, "resemble in any way the woman you spoke to at midnight?"

The rector stared at Knollis for a moment. "They were somewhat similar in build, Inspector, and there may have been a similarity in the voices, but I could not say that it was the same woman. It was a very dark night!"

He continued to stare, and added: "It could have been!"

"Can you describe the woman you talked with in River Close during the afternoon, Mr. Saunders?"

"She was wearing a red hat and red shoes. It was those that drew my attention to her. I can remember no more, I am afraid."

"One more question," said the insatiable Knollis. "This one is with regard to the man who left the house at midnight and went up to Wisden Avenue. Did he walk, hurry, or run?"

"He walked slowly, as if in deep thought, Inspector."

"Well, thank you very much, Mr. Saunders," said Knollis. "My sergeant has made notes of all you have told us. Will you be prepared, when it is typed out, to sign it as an accurate record of your movements on Thursday?"

"As far as I remember them, yes. I don't think that I have missed anything out, Inspector. I feel better for it. When your friend buys my manuscript, and I have cleared my debts, then my conscience will be easy again—although I dare not think what the Bishop will say! I should have trusted in God, and not tried to force my affairs to sort themselves out. It has been a bitter experience, but a valuable one. I thought I was capable of shaping my own life. *Vanity of vanities! All is vanity!*"

Quite casually, Knollis said: "You never felt impelled to take the life of Robert Dexter?"

The rector's jaw dropped.

"To take life! May God preserve me from such depths, Inspector! It could never have entered my mind."

As an afterthought he said: "It could not have benefited me!"

"Quite true," said Knollis; "it couldn't!"

Dr. Hellick rose.

"Well, Inspector, I think I must call a halt there. My patient is looking very weary. It is time he rested."

"Yes, I agree," said Knollis. "I am grateful to you for allowing me to bother him in this way. Incidentally, Mr. Saunders, did Mr. Friend call to see you?"

"He is coming over this afternoon, Inspector—and thank you! He telephoned me this morning, early. I do thank you for the introduction. Indeed I do!"

"You've paid for it," Knollis said grimly. "Good day, Mr. Saunders. I wish you a speedy recovery."

Mrs. Bradwell was waiting at the foot of the stairs. "Everything all right, Inspector Knollis?"

"As right as rain, as the saying goes," replied Knollis. "I think your father will soon be fit and well again—and I'm not a doctor!"

On the way home, Ellis shook his head sadly.

"I'm damned if I see it yet!"

Knollis clapped him on the back.

"I thought I'd got something when we came out this morning. I didn't get what I expected, but I have got a lot more. I can see the whole thing as clear as daylight now. Think about Rawley's peculiar conduct, and then about what Bob Dexter said when he opened the door, and you have the solution to the problem. We'll have the killer in one of our little grey cells by this time to-morrow—and that, my dear Watson, is a promise."

Knollis hummed a lullaby as the car sped along the wild Derbyshire moorland roads towards the Nottinghamshire border and Burnham.

CHAPTER XIV
THE STORY OF RAWLEY

KNOLLIS RANG THROUGH to Groots on reaching the station, and in a voice calculated to lull any suspicion, asked Dennis Rawley if he could make it convenient to come down to the station within the next hour, where he wished him to clear up a minor point that had arisen. He regretted that he was unable to get to the works, but he could not spare the time. Rawley replied that he would oblige.

Knollis then turned to Ellis.

"Get Dale and Rogers to read Saunders's statement as soon as it is typed. One of them is to organize a search for the red-hatted woman, and the other to find the driver of the potato lorry. Then I want the woman who acted as Good Samaritan to the old boy during the afternoon, and the driver and conductor of the bus which he boarded and then left. They have twenty-four hours!"

"As good as done," said Ellis.

"How good is your shorthand?" asked Knollis. "Can it be read by anybody, or is it unintelligible to anyone but yourself?"

"I'll have you know," replied Ellis with mock gravity, "that I am considered to be a writer of shorthand which can be read by the newest beginner."

"Then turf your notebook into the outer office and let someone else transcribe the notes. I want you here to make new ones when Rawley arrives."

Ellis sucked a tooth, and looked at Knollis from the corners of his eyes. "We haven't got a warrant."

"I'm not going to arrest him, you chump!"

"But dammitall!" protested Ellis.

"You think over the Reverend Mr. Saunders's story a wee bit more," replied Knollis. "A great light will then dawn upon your mental darkness. The warrant-swearing comes to-morrow. In the meantime I need a few more facts."

Dennis Rawley was shown in an hour later. He stood in the doorway, twiddling the brim of his hat. "You—you wanted to see me!" he stammered. "I've told you all I know about Bob Dexter. I've been thinking about it ever since it happened, and I'm certain I've told you all I know."

"Oh, this has nothing to do with the murder," Knollis said almost jovially. "Come in, close the door, and take a seat."

Rawley looked round suspiciously, and continued to eye Knollis warily as he settled himself into a chair. He seemed particularly uncomfortable as he noticed Ellis's pencil poised over his pad.

"I don't understand," he murmured.

"Now we are all comfortable, I'll tell you," smiled Knollis. "You bought a motor-cycle a few weeks ago, from a gentleman at Little Watney; an Ostrer."

Rawley hesitated for a second. "Yes," he said shortly.

"It would seem," said Knollis, "that you neglected to observe certain formalities in transferring ownership of the cycle."

"The deal was not completed," protested Rawley. "I handed over the purchase money, but I hadn't taken over the cycle."

"Now come, Mr. Rawley," said Knollis. "The cycle must have been yours if you had paid for it!"

"Well, yes," Rawley admitted reluctantly; "in that sense I suppose it was, but it hasn't been taken on the road. I can see about completing the formalities today."

Then he looked questioningly at Knollis.

"I don't get this, Inspector! Since when have Scotland Yard taken over local police duties?"

"Oh, we share and share alike," Knollis said casually. "The local police are very busy just now."

"My cycle isn't connected with Bob Dexter's death. I don't believe you! There is a trick in this!"

"Where is the cycle now?" Knollis asked quietly.

"Little Watney, of course. I left it with the blacksmith, in his garage."

Knollis wagged his head. "Really! Then you will be surprised to hear that it is in the police garage at the rear of these premises?"

Rawley gulped. Knollis found it impossible to interpret his expression.

"My—my motor-cycle?"

"Your motor-cycle!"

Rawley licked his lips and glanced desperately round the room. "How could it get there?"

The question was forced from his lips.

"I'll tell you," said Knollis. He leaned forward, clasping his hands.

"It was found in a side street in Greet, which, in case you don't know, is a district of Birmingham."

"Birmingham!" Rawley exclaimed in an unconvincing tone.

"Birmingham," repeated Knollis stolidly.

"Do—do you mind if I smoke?"

"Not at all. Carry on!"

Rawley found a cigarette with trembling fingers, and lit it, although he could hardly keep the burning match and the end of the cigarette together.

Knollis glanced across at Ellis and winked solemnly. Rawley took several deep puffs at his cigarette, and then blurted out: "How did my bike get to Greet?"

"I was hoping that you could tell me that," said Knollis.

"The whole thing is—is a mystery to me, Inspector. The last time I saw it was in the garage at Watney. Someone must have stolen it!"

"No, it wasn't stolen," replied Knollis. "I know something of its adventures. It was collected from Little Watney last Wednesday afternoon by Richard Dexter, who strapped it to the luggage grid of his car, and drove away. Shortly after midday on Thursday afternoon you collected it from behind a five-barred gate in Three-Tree Farm Lane, and rode it to Birmingham. It was found in Greet, as I have informed you. You arrived, on foot, at the Fir Tree Hotel, at two o'clock in the morning, and stayed until daylight."

Rawley sagged visibly as Knollis's story progressed, and his eyes played with the pattern in the carpet.

"Now," continued Knollis, "you will notice that there are obvious gaps in the narrative. Do you care to fill them for us?"

"I—I don't know what you are talking about! It's all a concoction—and you are trying to mix me up with Bob Dexter's death! I know nothing about it, I tell you! I know *nothing* about it!"

"But you do admit taking on to the road a cycle that was neither licensed nor insured!"

"There's nothing criminal in that," Rawley said defiantly. "Issue a summons if you want to do so. Get on with it! I admit taking the cycle on the road, but I still can't see why Scotland

Yard should concern themselves with it. It's a matter for the Burnham police."

Knollis smiled.

"I am not accusing you of anything—yet. I am fishing for evidence that you may be able to give. And I'm sure that you do wish to help us, don't you?"

Rawley pouted like a sulky child.

"What do you want to know?"

"You were in the Close shortly before midnight on Thursday, weren't you, Rawley?"

The answer came reluctantly. "Well, yes. I was, if you want to know—and there's nothing wrong in that!"

"And walked up the Close to Wisden Avenue, where you turned right, in the direction of the bridge?"

"You seem to know everything!" Rawley grunted.

"But that is a fact?" persisted Knollis.

"As a matter of fact, it is," Rawley admitted. "I must have left the house shortly before midnight."

"Good!" said Knollis. "We are getting somewhere at last! Now please think carefully! Did you see anybody in the street, either man, woman, or child?"

Rawley nodded. "There was someone standing on the pavement across the street. It was dark, there being no lamp in the street, but there was a faint glow from a bedroom window— Dexters', I think—and I saw someone standing about against Courtney-Harborough's gate. I was thinking about something else, and didn't pay particular attention, but it flashed across my mind that it would be Courtney-Harborough going home, because he's a bit of a night-owl. I didn't speak, and so I don't know whether it was him or not."

"And you forgot to tell us this!" Knollis said in a tone of reproach. "Surely you immediately thought about this man when your wife told you of her experience with the late caller? Didn't it recall his presence in the Close?"

"I'm afraid it did not, Inspector," replied Rawley. "The news of Bob's death upset me so much that I just couldn't collect my thoughts."

Knollis picked up his pen and beat a gentle tattoo on the table, meanwhile looking reflectively at Rawley.

"There is one other thing you can do for us. I will explain, and then you can go—and I may be able to persuade Sir Wilfrid Burrows to drop the matter of the cycle. When you leave here, I want you to think over certain facts which I am going to place in your possession—confidentially. Consideration of these facts may bring into your mind some other factor, some small item of evidence which you have temporarily forgotten, or ignored. You see, Mr. Rawley, we have reduced the time-factor in the case to a very few minutes, the five minutes following your departure from the house. We know everything that happened outside those few minutes, and we think you may be able to help to decide what happened in that short space of time. By the way, I don't suppose you know who killed Bob Dexter, and how it was arranged?" Rawley jerked into attention, and blinked.

"You mean that—that you know?"

Knollis smiled. "Of course I know!"

Rawley waved his arms excitedly. "Then why don't you arrest him? A m-murderer at large—why, he may kill somebody else!"

Surprisingly to Rawley, Knollis smiled.

"Yes, he may! He killed Dexter because Dexter disappointed him, and if there is anybody else in whom he is disappointed— well, who knows?"

Rawley shifted uneasily.

"I want you to think it out for yourself," Knollis went on, "because once you have done so you will find to your intense surprise that, unwittingly, you have held the key to the mystery all the time."

"I have! You must be mad, Inspector!"

Rawley stared blankly, and added: "Good Lord—me!"

"Now listen carefully," said Knollis. "On Thursday night, after you left the Close, the man you saw standing across the street went to your house and asked for Smith, exactly as your wife stated. On being told that there was no Smith in the street, he walked back to the pavement. He then walked back to your door, and was about to knock on it again, when he heard it being opened, took fright, and hurried down the garden and into the service lane. He then walked to Wisden Avenue and left the city. That is Fact One."

"You know who this man was?" asked Rawley.

"Yes, and we have his evidence," replied Knollis. "Now I am not concerned with your motives, but you will admit that your cycle was in Three-Tree Farm Lane?"

"Well, yes, I admit that."

"That's all right," said Knollis. "That is Fact Two. Now I think you will be interested in these . . ."

He pulled a portfolio of photographs from a drawer and handed them to Rawley. Rawley looked through them with very puzzled eyes. "I don't understand, Inspector! What are these photographs?"

"The boat," said Knollis, "is Mr. Courtney-Harborough's. It is usually moored to the bank below River Close."

"Yes, that is right," Rawley agreed.

"On Thursday night it was not," said Knollis. "Look at the photograph in your left hand. You will see that it is a photograph of the towpath and the embankment, and that dotted lines have been superimposed by our photographic staff. Those lines represent a rope that was in a similar position on Thursday night. You will see that by untying the rope from the paling it was possible to release the boat without going down to the towpath—an important item in the programme of someone who was pressed for time. Now look through the series of photographs which are numbered in the top right-hand corners."

Rawley obeyed.

"You will see," explained Knollis, "that a rather unusual cross-current carries the boat to the backwater. Now here is a photograph taken from the backwater . . ."

Rawley took it from him.

"There is a screen of hawthorn bushes between the backwater and the lane. Directly in line with the point where the boat comes to rest is a five-barred gate—and against that gate you—or Richard Dexter—parked the motor-cycle. That is correct, Mr. Rawley?"

"Ye-es," Rawley replied in a puzzled voice.

"Of course," said Knollis, "at first we jumped to the conclusion that you had taken the cycle across the river, and had been helped by someone in the Close. Believe me when I say that the situation looked very unhealthy for you at one period of the case!"

Rawley made an undecipherable noise.

"And yet, on leaving the house to collect the cycle, you went along Wisden Avenue, and over the bridge?"

"I did," muttered Rawley.

"Pardon me for one moment," said Knollis. He scribbled on a sheet of paper and passed it to Ellis, who glanced at it and hurriedly left the office.

Knollis was silent until his return, and then he disturbed Rawley's thoughts by saying: "Tell me, Mr. Rawley; did you leave your cycle in that side street?"

Rawley slowly raised his eyes.

"No, Inspector, I did not! I garaged it at an all-night garage in Coventry Road. I don't understand how it got to Greet. I just don't understand anything. There is something screwy somewhere!"

Knollis smiled his agreement.

"I can give you another—er—screwy fact, Mr. Rawley, and this certainly does not make sense. On Thursday afternoon Mrs. Dexter cleaned out her handbag, and did it thoroughly, even to turning it inside out and applying the nozzle of the vacuum-cleaner to it, and yet, when we examined it the next day, what should we find in it but a note from your wife to Bob Dexter—oh, nothing compromising," he added quickly as he saw the fire spring into Rawley's eyes; "it was merely a note arranging to take him to the Amateur Dramatic meeting. The point is; how did it get there? Strange, isn't it? I mean, who had been upstairs?"

Rawley nodded silently.

"And the knife?" continued Knollis. "Where did it come from? To where did it go? Very enigmatic!"

Rawley suddenly shook his head as if he was appearing from under water. He looked closely at Knollis for a few moments, and then asked: "What is the object in telling me all these things, Inspector?"

Knollis's face was a picture of innocence as he answered the question.

"I'm glad you asked that," he said. "I have a theory. I believe that some small incident occurred in the Close either as you were going into Wisden Avenue, or shortly afterwards, some tiny incident which you did not notice consciously because you were thinking deeply, but which was probably absorbed unconsciously. Reflection on the points I have given you may bring it to the surface, and when you have got it, then my case is complete, and I can execute a warrant for the arrest of Bob Dexter's killer."

Rawley's eyes returned to the photographs. He examined them again, and the frown on his forehead deepened. "I don't get this business at all," he murmured.

"The rope came from the Westford Hall," Knollis explained casually. "The picket in the bank—any report on that yet, Sergeant Ellis?"

Ellis sorted the files. "The report says it is similar to those used by the Westford Tennis Club to hold the guys on the road-screens. One of theirs is missing."

Knollis rose.

"That seems to be about all, Mr. Rawley. I mustn't keep you any longer. I'll be grateful for your conclusions in due course."

Rawley walked slowly to the door. He had already turned the knob when he suddenly swung round and walked back.

"Inspector Knollis!"

"Yes, Mr. Rawley?" Knollis murmured softly.

"I—oh, look here! I've got to get it off my chest! I went back that night to kill Bob Dexter!"

Knollis seemed in no way surprised.

"But you didn't kill him, did you?"

"No, I didn't kill him, Inspector! I—well, I hadn't the guts when it came to the last act—and I'd planned everything so carefully, too."

"Had you, Mr. Rawley?"

Rawley took another step forward, his hands outstretched in desperate appeal. "Don't you want to know about what I planned to do?"

Knollis gave him a frank smile.

"I am only interested in the person who *did* kill Bob Dexter, Mr. Rawley. You must see that!"

Rawley flung himself into the chair he had just vacated.

"For six weeks I planned what I intended to do that night. I even lied to my wife and my friend."

"But your friend assisted you," Knollis pointed out. "He helped you with the cycle. It was Richard Dexter who parked the cycle in the lane, wasn't it?"

"Yes, it was Dick," Rawley said wearily. "I fooled him, you see. He had told me about the manuscript, and the poor old parson somewhere in the wilds who needed the money, and I offered to break into the house and get it back. He would not hear of it at first, but I told him that it appealed to my sense of adventure—oh, I fooled him all right. He arranged the alibi for me at the Granby, put me on to the cycle at Watney, and even went to the trouble to put it just where I wanted it."

Rawley nodded his head with satisfaction.

"It was a damned good plan if I'd had the guts to see it through. I was going to kill Bob Dexter, the swine, and take the manuscript with me so that it would be traced back to Dick. He couldn't have got out of it, because he'd arranged my alibi. That was a clever touch on my part!"

"Very clever indeed," murmured Knollis, as he sat and watched Rawley.

"I only told my wife part of the truth," Rawley continued. "How she hated Dexter—and no wonder! You know that he made suggestions to her? She wanted me to let the whole thing drop, for my own sake, but I had to square the account with him. As Dick said, what man with red blood in his veins could ignore such an insult to his wife?

"And then, well, it wasn't until I got to his door that I found I couldn't do it. I went in home and told Margot. I don't think she quite understood what I was saying at first, and then she said it was the best way out of it. She made me go on to Birmingham, because she said—and rightly—that it would look queer if I was seen at home, especially as Bob Dexter knew that I was supposed to be at the conference.

"I felt a hell of a coward as I walked back up the Close. My fingers went limp and useless—you see, I was going to strangle him. I had worked out every movement in my mind, right from the moment he opened the door. Margot didn't know that I was going to kill him; she thought I was just going to lay him out and steal that stupid manuscript!"

Rawley laughed wildly.

"All my planning to no purpose! It was all so unnecessary, too, because someone else had planned to kill him for me! I wonder who it was, Inspector? Why was he killed? Had somebody a stronger reason than myself? Dick didn't like his cousin— and Dick is a fool, too, because he actually suggested that there might be something between Dexter and my wife, as if my wife would have anything to do with him! Dick would hate him, of course! He always wanted Lesley. But Dick was already in Birmingham when I got there. Now I wonder . . . Did Goldie lie to me? I wonder if Dick had only been there a short time when I arrived? He could make it in his car, because he advised me to take the second-class roads, to make a detour . . . Suppose Dick was in the Close, watching me, and waiting? Suppose that I had only burgled the house, as I told him I would, and he followed me and killed Bob? It would look as if I had killed him, wouldn't it? And Dick could have done that and got to Birmingham first!"

Knollis took Rawley by the shoulder, and shook him.

"Come, Mr. Rawley, you must be going. We have a great deal of work to do, and the days are short ones."

"Aren't you going to arrest me?" Rawley asked as he hoisted himself from the chair.

Knollis laughed. "Go back to work, or go home."

Rawley blinked uncomprehendingly at him, and stumbled from the office.

Knollis's easy manner fell from him as the door closed.

"You acted on those instructions, Ellis?"

"Two blokes waiting outside to follow him. By now there will be two men in the Close, and two in the service lane. In addition to which the launch is stooging up and down that reach of the river. Richard Dexter's house is being watched front and back, and there are two men to tail him if he moves out."

"Good enough," said Knollis. "This is going to be the worst part of the game—waiting! I don't quite know what will happen, but there will be fur and feathers flying before morning. Keep our car ready for an instant take-off!"

"It's the first time I've seen you use those tactics," said Ellis. "My own nerves were beginning to suffer."

"In this part of the world it is known as setting the cat among the pigeons," Knollis replied grimly.

"He was determined to talk, wasn't he?"

"Yes," agreed Knollis. "He was determined to talk. Well, Watson, old man, we will carry on with the office work until the whistle blows the alarm."

The hours passed. They were joined by Sir Wilfrid Burrows and Inspector Russett. Both wanted to know what Knollis was waiting for, and he told them frankly that he did not know; it was just *something*.

It was ten minutes after midnight when the something happened. A sergeant flung open the door, and rushed in excitedly.

"Something wrong at River Close. Jackson has just 'phoned for an ambulance."

"River Close?" commented Knollis. "Then I was right all the time. Come on!"

CHAPTER XV

THE AFFAIR IN RIVER CLOSE

THE AMBULANCE was standing outside Alpine Villa, its engine gently ticking over. Behind it, at the gate, waited Dr. Patrick Whitelaw and Sergeant Rogers, both of whom stepped forward as Knollis's car pulled into the kerb. Knollis stepped out with a question on his lips: "Well?"

"I was waiting for you, Knollis," said the doctor. "I've got two patients in the blood-wagon—the Rawleys."

"What happened?"

"I can only give you the results," replied Dr. Whitelaw. "The male Rawley has a fractured skull and broken right arm, and his wife has apparently gone mental. Rogers knows the story as far as it is known, and so I'll get away with the victims. See you later!"

He walked to the ambulance, and Knollis turned to Rogers. "Now, Rogers! What happened?"

Rogers gave an uncertain laugh.

"I wish I could weigh it up, sir. Shall we go indoors? The lounge, please," he added as Knollis moved towards the front door. "I've got a few witnesses cooped in the dining-room."

They were followed in by Sir Wilfrid Burrows, Inspector Russett, and Ellis. Rogers carefully closed the lounge door before beginning his explanation.

"That's safer," he commented. "Now, sir, this was the way of it. I was at the Wisden Avenue end of the street when midnight struck, and I strolled along the avenue for a few yards. Edwards is with me, and I put him down on the tow-path with instructions not to move more than twenty yards from the street. I didn't know what was likely to happen, because you hadn't told me, but I was taking no chances."

"I didn't know myself," said Knollis; "but carry on!"

"Sergeant Dale and Jackson were in the service lane—and still are. I sent them back. Anyway, as I turned back towards the corner of the Close I noticed a woman leaning from her bedroom window on the opposite side of the street. There was no light in the bedroom, so I strolled across to investigate. She saw me, of course, because I had just passed the lighted kiosk. She beckoned to me, and as she was wearing a white nightie I saw her distinctly. She pointed down the Close to this house.

"Something was happening. Mrs. Rawley was leaning from *her* bedroom window, apparently engaged in a conversation with somebody down below, although I couldn't see anybody. She was waving as if she was saying 'Go away!' and I decided to freeze to the spot and see what happened. She turned back into the room and I heard her call out 'Don't go down, Dennis, you fool!' Not two seconds later the light went out, and she called 'It must be the fuses!' At the same time there was a rumbling noise. I didn't know what it was then, although I do now—it was Rawley going headfirst down the stairs!

"Well, sir, everything went very quiet, and I walked slowly down the Close and crossed the street to the gate of this house. There was a queer thumping sound, and I couldn't make out where it was coming from. And then I nearly jumped out of my skin, for the front door opened and Mrs. Rawley stood there in her *negligee*, yelling for help as loud as her lungs would let her.

"I chased down the path, with Mr. Courtney-Harborough from across the street hard on my heels. I asked her to switch on the lights, and she said that she couldn't because the lights had fused, and as an afterthought she said that her husband had fallen down the stairs. Mr. H. had a torch of his own, and he went to work on Rawley while I saw to the fuses. Incidentally, Mr. Newnham and a few others had arrived, but I ordered them to stay outside. Meanwhile, I went to work on the fuses, and these are what I found . . ."

He took his diary from his pocket and carefully parted the leaves. Between them lay four short lengths of fuse-wire. Knollis bent over them and gave vent to an exclamation.

"My God, they've been filed across!"

"Yes, sir; notched all the way along. Somebody meant them to blow, don't you think, when just one more light was switched on?"

"You're damned right, Rogers! Go on with the story!"

"Well, here is the peculiar thing, sir. I've told you that we four were guarding the Close and the service lane. All four of us will swear that no one entered the Close after half-past ten, and yet Mrs. Newnham has told me since that when she was first attracted by Mrs. Rawley's behaviour at the bedroom window, somebody was using the knocker on the door. She also insists that while this was happening, Rawley himself was standing behind his wife, trying to look outside!"

"Go on," said Knollis.

"We switched on the lights after I had fixed the fuses. Mr. H. was trying to render first-aid to Rawley, and Mrs. Rawley was bending over her husband. 'He's broken his neck!' she wailed. 'My Dennis has broken his neck. He's dead! He's dead!' Mr. H. told her to control herself and not to be a fool. Rawley hadn't broken his neck, and he'd live to tell the tale."

Rogers ran a finger round the inside of his collar.

"The next bit made my tummy turn over. She stared at Mr. H., and then slowly got to her feet. She stood with her arms hanging loosely by her sides, and her eyes sticking out like hat-pegs. 'He's not dead!' That's what she said, sir, and then she started to scream the place down. Mr. H. has he-man ideas, for before I could stop him he'd reared up and clipped her one on the jaw. 'Catch her, Sergeant,' he said. 'I can't work with him while she's making the night hideous!'

"I caught her, and laid her on the hall floor, and then helped Mr. H. with Rawley. The ambulance came, and Dr. Whitelaw was with it, and he took charge of that side of the business. I dived across the street and had a quick talk with Mrs. Newnham, and then came back and sent her husband over with instructions to dispatch his wife immediately, because I thought it would be better to have her on the spot when you arrived. And then your car turned into the Close."

"Good work," said Knollis. "Now who have you in the dining-room?"

"Mrs. Newnham and Mr. H. Courtney-Harborough."

Knollis pondered for a few minutes, and his companions waited for him to speak.

"Russett," he said at last; "how do you feel about rousing a magistrate from his slumbers?"

Russett grinned. "Nothing would please me better. Who is the warrant for?"

"Richard Dexter, for conspiring with two others to bring about the death of Robert Dexter."

"That's fair enough," commented Russett. "Who killed him, of the three?"

"I'll tell you that in about half an hour. Meanwhile, hop up to Hawthorn Grove and grab Dexter. He may try to skip if he hears about this affair."

Russett went.

Knollis followed him to the hall, and noticed a pair of camel-hair slippers lying against the wall.

"Those Rawley's?" he asked Rogers.

"Yes, sir. The left one was off when we found him, and I removed the other."

Knollis picked them up and examined them.

"Interesting! See the bare spot where the tufts have been plucked out?"

Sir Wilfrid looked over his shoulder. "What does that indicate, Knollis?"

"I'm not sure yet," Knollis replied. He sauntered about the hall, and then opened the front door and flashed his torch around the step.

"Ah-h!" he ejaculated, and bent down.

"What is it, Knollis?"

"About four inches of black thread. It has been a loop. See the knot? The break is opposite. Ellis! I want you and Rogers to come upstairs with me."

He led the way into the front bedroom.

"What are we looking for?" asked Ellis.

"A very long piece of string or thread."

Ellis went to work on the wardrobe, while Rogers turned out the contents of the dressing-table drawers. Knollis stripped the bed and looked beneath the mattress, although he shook his head doubtfully as he did so. "Men push things under mattresses; women push them in drawers."

"Would a fishing line interest you, sir?" asked Rogers, holding out a roughly coiled one.

"Where was it?" queried Knollis.

"Under a pair of lady's whatsits."

Knollis smiled at the description, and his smile increased as he examined the line.

"Good! Complete with half an inch of black thread. Just run downstairs, Rogers, and stand outside the front door."

He moved to the window as Rogers went downstairs. "Ready? I'm lowering one end. Can you see it?"

The light from Rogers's torch blinded him for a few seconds, and then Rogers called: "Got it, sir!"

"Right! Now close the door and tie your end round the knocker. Shout when!"

"When!" called Rogers.

Knollis wrapped his own end of the line round the palm of his hand, and waved Rogers away from the door. "Stand away there! Stand away! Do you hear me!"

The knocker sounded solemnly on the door.

"There's someone at the door!" Sir Wilfrid called up the stairs.

"By George!" came Rogers's voice from the darkness. "So that was it! Fairly gave me the willies for a minute, although I knew what you were going to do."

"Untie it, Rogers," said Knollis. "You needn't come back. We are coming down now."

The four men conferred in the hall.

"The knocker was the lure," murmured Knollis, "and the open window was the alibi . . ."

"The fuses blew when the staircase light was switched on," said Ellis.

"But how did he come to fall downstairs?" asked Rogers. "His wife was in the bedroom when he fell. Those tufts—do they tell you something, sir?"

"I may be able to tell that shortly," replied Knollis. "T think I'll see those two people you've corralled while my brain decides to wake up."

Mrs. Newnham's evidence coincided with that already given by Rogers, and it was only Courtney-Harborough who was able to supply any new facts.

"I'm glad Mrs. Newnham has gone," he said, "because what I have to say doesn't make pretty hearing. That Rawley woman is a fiend, Inspector!"

"I know that," replied Knollis, "but what do you know?"

Courtney-Harborough brushed his moustache.

"I'm not exactly a fool, you know, and when I saw men hanging round the Close to-day, and saw Rawley come home looking as black as thunder I told myself that something was afoot! So I took to the fashion, and spent the day behind the curtains in my wife's lounge. It isn't often I see the fool place!

"I'd put two and two together, you know, and while I probably made it five I had a notion of my own. I kept watch. Well, round about seven o'clock to-night there was a hell of a shindy across here. They were having a first-class row, and I'd have given two guineas for a ringside seat. It went on for half an hour, and Rawley was carrying on as if he had gone out of his mind. And then, as an anti-climax, it went as quiet as a midnight graveyard."

He broke off, and gave Knollis a knowing smile.

"The next bit is going to interest you no end! Just after ten o'clock she walked out and had a look up and down the street. She stood at her gate as if she was merely taking the air, but I knew she was seeing if the coast was clear! Me, I lay doggo! The next move got me worried, because I couldn't make out what she was doing. She walked to the wall of the house and was waving her arms about. Then she walked to the door and did something there. After that she went in and closed the door."

"Thanks for seeing that," said Knollis. "You'll be a star witness!"

"You know what she was on with?" asked Courtney-Harborough.

"I do, but I mustn't tell you at this stage. You do see my point?"

"You're the captain," said Courtney-Harborough. "The next move came a minute or so after midnight. You've heard what Mrs. Newnham saw? Well, I saw that, and heard more. After the light went out there was a continuous rumble—and that would be Rawley coming downstairs. There was about a minute's silence, and then a thumping noise. Look, Inspector! Have you ever chopped logs into firewood?"

"Very often," said Knollis. "Why?"

"Then you know what you do when the chopper locks itself in the log! You pick up the whole contrivance and bang it down on the ground, again and again. The noise coming from this house was like that! You can start guessing what that was while I tell you the rest of the story."

Knollis grimaced. "I've already guessed!"

"Well, when she ran out, your man was at the gate and he chased down the path. I was on his heels. He attended to the fuses while I took a look at Rawley. I could tell by his position that he had broken a wing—I've seen 'em like that in a rugger match! But what really horrified me was the finger-marks . . ."

"Finger-marks?" said Knollis.

"Finger-marks! On the side of his face that was uppermost, and on the side of his neck nearest the ground. I looked for the second set after seeing the first and realizing what the noise had been. I pointed them out to the doc as soon as he arrived. She's been—"

"Trying to beat his brains in," said Knollis grimly. His top lip almost disappeared from sight.

"Yes," said Courtney-Harborough with a deep sigh; "she'd been trying to beat his brains in on the hall floor. And all the time I was examining him she was shrieking that he was dead. I told her that he was a long way from dead, and would live to tell the tale. She took one look at me—sheer terror, it was—and then set up the worst banshee I've ever heard. Your sergeant has probably told you that I gave her one on the jaw to keep her quiet. And that is the whole of my story, Inspector."

Knollis suddenly jumped to his feet and disappeared from the room. He was back a moment later, to hand the slippers to Sir Wilfrid. "Have a good look at those, sir. I'll be back again shortly."

He bounced up the stairs until he came to the flat where the stairs turned to the right. There he got on his knees, and examined the skirting-boards. He gave a long sigh of satisfaction.

"Ellis! Rogers!"

Both appeared at the foot of the stairs.

"You know those expanding curtain rods—the spiral wire affairs? Turn the house inside out until you find a piece about two feet to two feet six inches long. And don't stretch it, because the missing tufts should be fast in the coils. Oh, and two screw-eyes as well. Her mind seems to work in a groove. My God, what a woman!"

He returned to the dining-room.

"The discovery of that wire will button up the whole case, Sir Wilfrid. There are two tiny screw-holes in the skirting-board on the staircase. She used two screw-eyes, and strung a curtain wire across. She talked to an imaginary caller through the window, and each time she waved her hand she was manipulating the knocker—"

"Ah, now I know what she was doing!" interrupted Courtney-Harborough. "Arranging the cord that worked it, eh?"

"Correct," said Knollis. "Now Rawley, with ideas about the man in black—despite the quarrel with his wife earlier in the evening, which I will explain; Rawley, I say, dashed downstairs. He switched on the light, and the fuses, previously arranged by Margot, blew out, putting the house in darkness. Rawley caught his foot in the wire and fell downstairs. Margot, with darkness for cover, removed the wire and the screw-eyes, and then went down and bashed his head on the hall floor. Satisfied that he was dead, she opened the door and yelled for help."

"A perfect explanation!" said Courtney-Harborough admiringly.

"And Robert Dexter's death?" asked Sir Wilfrid Burrows.

"Simple," said Knollis. "Margot was scared of Bob Dexter telling the truth—that *she* had made improper suggestions to *him*. She simply had to get rid of him. She knew that Richard Dexter wanted Lesley, and she went into partnership with him. Between them they cunningly incited Rawley to *rob* Dexter, but Margot cunningly worked on him until, apparently of his own accord, he decided to kill Dexter on the same night. Apparently of his own accord, but it was *their* plan all along."

"Then Rawley did kill him?" said Sir Wilfrid.

"He came to kill him, sir, and his courage failed him at the last moment. Enter Lady Macbeth! Old Mr. Saunders had just called at her door, and she, being a quick-minded woman, saw how to utilize the visit. She slipped out, went through the hedge, and killed Dexter with her domestic carving-knife—which we must send to the laboratory. Then she slipped back through the hedge, hid the knife, and waited until she heard Lesley calling to her husband from the stairs. Then she went back to discover, inquire, help, and sympathize. Her hate for Lesley is almost equal to her hate for Bob, and when she goes up for the blankets she slips the note to Bob from herself in Lesley's handbag, hoping to make Lesley believe that Bob was unfaithful to her—thus paving the way for Richard Dexter's eventual courtship, and at the same time rubbing acid in the wound."

"And the boat?" asked Courtney-Harborough.

"You realize the use it was put to?" asked Knollis.

Courtney-Harborough shrugged his shoulders. "I leaned over the fence and watched your photographer at work, and again I put two and two together and decided that some wangle had been arranged whereby it could be released and set drifting from the Close."

"It led straight to the spot where Rawley parked his motor-cycle," explained Knollis. "Margot slipped the rope earlier in the evening—another device intended to lead us to her husband."

"So that between them, Margot Rawley and Richard Dexter arranged for Rawley to do in Bob Dexter, and also arranged for him to swing for it!" murmured Courtney-Harborough. "Nice people! But look, Inspector—why did she try to do for Rawley to-night?"

"I can only assume the reason until Rawley is fit to talk, but I think you will find I am right in saying that Rawley, consequent on a talk with me to-day, realized the full ramifications of the plot. He also realized that it was Margot who committed the murder. He didn't know before. He really thought that the man in the black coat was responsible. The quarrel you heard was probably when the penny dropped, and Rawley accused her. She made up her mind then to get rid of him—and worked fast!"

Ellis entered the room, holding up a length of curtain wire. "This what you wanted, sir? Found it under the bath. There are threads of soft-camel hair entangled in the coils."

"Good man," said Knollis. "Look after it, and see that it goes to the laboratory—oh, and impound the carving-knife as well; Dr. Whitelaw will be interested in that."

"Look Knollis," said Sir Wilfrid Burrows, who had been gazing into the empty grate; "I can see that Margot Rawley had a sound motive for trying to kill her husband tonight, but why did she try to frame him over Dexter's death?"

A car drew up outside, and Inspector Russett came bounding into the house.

"Got him, Knollis! He came clean, too, with the whole story!"

"Then perhaps you will answer Sir Wilfrid's question for him, Russett? Why did Margot try to frame her husband over Bob Dexter's death?"

"Simple!" said Russett, with a magnificent wave of the hand. "Richard Dexter admits that he wangled that. He told Margot, and made her believe, that Rawley's conferences were mere excuses to spend odd nights with Goldilocks. Margot accepted the yarn, and swore to fix him."

"That answers your question, sir," said Knollis. "I suspected that to be the motive, but had no proof until now. That is the last thread in the case well and truly tied."

"There's one thing puzzling me," Russett said slowly.

"What is that?" asked Knollis.

"Right through the case you've been harping on the significance of Bob Dexter's last words. I still don't see any significance."

"Well," explained Knollis, "it was a hint rather than a clue. You see, Russett, if he had said 'Oh hell!' it would indicate that it was someone he didn't want to see, but if he had said, or started to say, 'Oh hello!' then it would indicate that it was someone he was *surprised* to see—and there is a lot of difference between the two. Lesley told me that he was a great swearer, but only when roused. See the point?"

"Ye-es," said Russett slowly. "Pretty smart thinking, Knollis, if I may say so. And that led you to suspect Margot right from the beginning?"

"It did," said Knollis.

"What do you do now?" asked Courtney-Harborough.

"Oh, the rest is mere routine," said Russett in as casual a manner as he could muster. "Magistrates' court, assizes, judge, jury, and hangman . . ."

"The hangman," murmured Knollis. "The sable messenger, whose errand knows no mercy!"

THE END

Lightning Source UK Ltd.
Milton Keynes UK
UKHW020637280419
341730UK00006B/163/P

9 781912 574292